ONE SWEET DAY IN LOVELY BAY

POLLY BABBINGTON

POLLYBABBINGTON.COM

Want more from Polly's world?

For sneak peeks into new settings, early chapters, downloadable Pretty Beach and Darling Island freebies and bits and bobs from Polly's writing days sign up for Babbington Letters.

© Copyright 2024 Polly Babbington

All rights reserved.

This book is a work of fiction. Names, characters, businesses, places, events, and incidents are either the products of the author's imagination or used in a fictitious manner. Any resemblance to actual persons, living or dead, or actual events is purely coincidental.

1

Cally de Pfeffer liked nothing better than revelling in her new life in Lovely Bay. It wasn't just the fact that Lovely was so pretty with its sweet winding streets, huge towering lighthouse, shell-shaped roof tiles, rows of gorgeous shops, and lines of pastel bunting. Oh no, there were many other aspects about living in the third smallest town in the country that she loved. She also liked things such as the riverboat and using it to get around. It was definitely one of the nicer modes of transport she'd used: it sure beat the dirty old bus she'd taken to school back in the day. Add on top of good transport and beautiful aesthetics, the friendly local community, Lovelies, as they were known, and setting up anew in the sweet little town by the sea had been one of her better moves in life.

Strolling along quickly with a bit of a hustle to her steps and her nose tilted up to the warm breeze, Cally smiled at the beautiful day as she made her way down towards the River Lovely. Lovely itself was oddly quiet all around her and she couldn't quite work out why. Maybe Lovelies had some knowledge she didn't yet know about that the ever-changeable Lovely weather was about to turn. On her way to meet Logan for a coffee, she kept her fingers crossed that that wasn't going to be the case. She'd much rather stick with sunshine and warm breezes, thank you very much.

A few minutes later, as she turned the corner, she slowed her pace as one of the River Lovely jetties came into her line of sight. She smiled to herself as she spied Colin, the skipper, standing by the little hut on the jetty, looking out in the direction of the bay. The riverboat bobbed and clanged around beside him and the sunshine glinted off the top of the water. By the looks of it, Colin and the boat were waiting for a train to come in from the nearby Lovely train station and for its passengers to make their way over to the boat.

Approaching the jetty with a wicker shopping basket in the crook of her arm, Cally pulled her phone out of her pocket in order to pay. She walked briskly across the old, weathered boards, and pointed her phone in the direction of the new little payment gadget slotted just next to the entrance to the hut adjacent to the gangplank.

Colin smiled as he came out of the hut. Cally raised her eyebrows and gave a little wave as she pointed to the payment machine. 'Hiya. How are you? The new machine is working well. How are you getting on with it?'

Colin laughed. 'I know. It's been good. Bit of a palaver to get it fitted but I got there in the end. They don't just call me a pretty face, you know, our Cally.'

Cally felt all the warm and fuzzies at being referred to the local way, whereby an 'our' was automatically put in front of her name. When she'd first heard Lovelies address each other as such, she'd thought it a bit odd, old-fashioned, and, to be frank, strange all around. Now, she clung onto it with a passion, so very happy to be considered and recognised as a Lovely. It was the little things about living in the town that made all the difference.

Cally bantered, 'Oh, I know you're more than just a pretty face. You got it working in the end. Was it too much of a faff?'

Colin rolled his eyes. 'Not too bad. It wasn't going to beat me.'

'Too funny,' Cally said as she walked onto the boat. 'Well, as long as you got there in the end.'

'I did, indeed.' Colin gestured with a nod of his head in the direction of the station. 'Just waiting for that lot and we'll get going.'

'Thanks.'

Once settled at the top, with her basket tucked up on the seat beside her, Cally sat waiting for the riverboat to depart. Lost in a world of her own for a bit, she stared over to the other side of the water, watching Lovelies doing their thing. A couple strolled along the river path hand in hand, two dog walkers chatted as they trailed behind their pups and a jogger looking very fit made Cally consider for a moment her intention to take up some exercise. The same intention she'd had for what felt like ever but had ultimately resulted in the fact that she'd never actually found the time. If truth be told, she'd never been that bothered and had little to no inclination.

As the boat finally pulled away, she settled in. The engine puttered, water swished against the bottom, and the river path began to slide slowly by. She heard Colin call out from the deck below. 'Next stop Lovely Harbour, then the bay. Stay on for the marshes and all other stops.'

Cally smiled, put her sunglasses on, squinted down in the direction of the bay, and marvelled at the weather. After working all the hours all week with early starts and late finishes, she was looking forward to meeting Logan, walking along by the harbour, getting a coffee, and doing not much with her day at all. Taking it easy was what she was going to do. No irritated retail customers, no cartons in the chemist, and no decluttering for people who didn't have the time, inclination, or effort to do it themselves. She was thoroughly looking forward to the gentle art of doing nothing. Bring that right on.

Edging closer to the stop for Lovely Bay, she took in the queue of people on the jetty waiting to get on and realised that, unlike the side of Lovely she'd come from, the beach area was busy. Picking up her basket, she slipped her phone in her pocket, held on tightly to the railing and made her way down the stairs to wait to get off. As Colin steered in the boat, she peered and shaded her eyes to see if she could spot Logan waiting for her. As she spied him, her stomach jumped, and her heart flipped. With a bag over his shoulder, sunglasses on his head, and a blue short-sleeved shirt, he was leaning on a railing watching the boat approach. When he saw Cally, he raised his hand and waved. As Cally waved back, she thanked her lucky stars that their two very different worlds had collided. It had been on the very boat she was standing on when the bottom of her bag had given way and spilt its contents all over the deck. Logan had been sitting on the back of the boat when her things had fallen all around him, a raw chicken breast landing at his feet. He'd been swift in his role as knight in shining armour. She'd liked that part a lot. He was her kind of knight, indeed.

Once the boat had docked and she'd made her way off, she walked up to him and kissed him on the cheek. As he put his arm around her shoulders and squeezed the top of her arm, she still couldn't quite believe that she and him were a thing. She'd take it for the team, though. She wasn't going to complain. Hottie patottie and then some.

Logan held up a brown paper bag. 'I have goodies from that bakery I was telling you about.'

'Excellent.' Cally mirrored his movement with her basket. 'I have goodies, too.'

'Ha. How was the boat?'

'Quiet the top end, busy down here.'

Logan nodded in agreement. 'I know. The sunshine brings out the beachgoers, right?'

'I thought the same as we made our way along the river.'

'Enjoy the trip?'

'I did. I sat and looked out at the world going by. I needed it after the week I've had.'

Logan pointed down the river. 'It never ceases to amaze me how nice the River Lovely is, and on a day like this, it doesn't disappoint. The colours are something else.'

'Agree.' Cally looked over her shoulder and took in the full view of the river. 'I've had worse places to commute to and from.'

'Tell me about it. How were the chatbot horrors this morning? Behaving themselves?'

'Oh, you know, the usual whining culprits. Someone was complaining that she was a technophobe and couldn't work out how to start a return - while she was speaking to me on the app via the wifi on a plane. But she's a technophobe. Course she is. You can't make it up.'

'Not that old technophobe thing. Makes me chuckle when people say that as they use an app to pretty much drive their car.'

Cally nodded. 'Trust me, I've heard it all in that job. My eyes are no longer able to roll far enough back in my head. How many times have I heard a parcel was lost in the post when I have the picture from the delivery driver of the parcel in situ?'

'You make me laugh.'

'A job, though, is a job, is it not?'

'You betcha.' Logan wiggled the brown bag. 'Remind you of anything?'

Cally put her head to the side and pretended to think. 'Hmm, let me think.'

'The day you threw a raw chicken breast at me just to get me to notice you. I mean, talk about desperate.'

'Yeah, nope, not quite, but I'll let you *think* that was what happened.'

Logan chuckled. 'If it hadn't been for that dodgy paper bag, we might never have crossed paths.'

'I suppose not. Though I might have met you at the manor.' Cally felt the ripple she felt, when Logan looked at her, zoom from her feet to her heart.

Logan smiled. 'If I hadn't been down here because my office was being renovated and I'd needed to keep an eye on the horses, we might not have ever met.'

Cally squinted and put her head to the side. 'You're right. I've never thought about it like that.'

'There were a few sliding door occasions. When we scrounged those speakeasy tickets that night, I thought you might be there and you were.'

Cally giggled. 'That's why when I came out of the bathroom, you were gone.'

'All part of a carefully strategised plan to get my wicked way.'

Cally punched Logan gently on the arm. 'It was not!'

Logan laughed, took Cally's basket, and hooked it over his arm. 'You made it easy for me. Chucking poultry at me and pulling shelves down on yourself.'

Cally shook her head as she remembered her first day working for Nina when a shelving unit had collapsed around her. 'Gosh. I thought I was going to have to pay for that unit.'

'But I saved the day.' Logan joked and smiled.

'You hero, you.'

'I think I made quite a good hero.'

'I guess you did.'

'You were quite the piece of work. I knew I had to up my game.'

'What? What are you on about? Up your game?'

'Hot air balloons, Royal boxes.' Logan gesticulated with the basket. 'Flipping picnics. I hope you know how lucky you are, Blackcurrant.'

'Right back at you, Henry-Hicks.' Cally laughed and bantered. 'You're the one who is lucky. It'd be good if you never, ever forget that.'

'Trust me. I won't.'

∽

Logan chuckled and smiled as they turned from the jetty. 'Well, let's hope we don't have any more calamities with bags. Right, let's get going. I need a coffee.'

After strolling along by the harbour and enjoying the sunshine, they stopped at a coffee kiosk and after Logan had queued up, they sat right by the water on a bench, and he handed her a cup. Cally sipped her coffee, looked up at the blue sky, and smiled. 'Well, this is the life. After a week of nothing but work, a nice coffee with this view is just what I needed.'

'You need a break, if you ask me. You're working like three jobs.'

'I didn't ask you. I'm fine.'

'Three jobs is quite a lot, you know,' Logan said with raised eyebrows. 'For normal people, at least.'

'Funny. I'm quite tired, but my little pot of savings is growing by the day, and that's all I'm interested in.' Cally rolled her eyes. 'Just a shame I have to work on that chatbot with women who spend more on a scarf than my laptop cost.'

'Is it still running really slowly?' Logan asked.

Cally rolled her eyes again. 'You could say that. I really need to get on with getting a new one. I've decided I'm just going to have to bite the bullet and get on with it. Eloise mentioned about getting a reconditioned one. She sent me a link. I'm going to have a look later. It's time for the old relic to go. I just need to suck it up and make it happen.'

Logan made a funny face. 'Well, you might not have to bother with that.'

Cally screwed her nose up. 'Yeah, I will. I've had that laptop for a long time. It's from the dark ages. It doesn't work properly with all the current technology and it's becoming an issue at work. I've had my money's worth.'

Logan pulled his bag around, put it beside him, and slid out a beautifully wrapped parcel. 'I was saving this until later, but seeing as it came up... it might help. I've just been to collect it. Great minds think alike, as it were.'

Cally looked at a box wrapped in pink paper with a huge white bow on the top. 'Sorry? What is this? It's not my birthday or anything.'

'Doesn't need to be your birthday for me to buy you something. I decided someone needed to do something about the state of your laptop and it wasn't going to be you any time soon. Though it seems I was wrong and we were, in actual fact, thinking along the same lines.'

'Oh my God, did you get me a new laptop?' Cally slowly took off the white ribbon and carefully unwrapped the pink paper to see a white box. She shook her head, pulled off the lid, and picked up a gold laptop. 'Wow! It's absolutely gorgeous.' Cally hissed as she turned it over and held it up as if to assess its weight. 'Goodness, it's on a different level to the one I've got. I can hardly even pick that one up. This is so light!'

'It is. I tried to use yours the other day and just lugging it from the table to the sofa was enough. Honestly, Cal, it really did need an upgrade.'

Cally ran her hand across the top of the laptop and then squinted as something caught her eye. 'Oh my goodness, did you get it engraved?' She looked closer to see that Logan had had the laptop engraved. She chuckled as she saw the word "Blackcurrant" just underneath the serial numbers on the back.

'I thought you'd like it,' Logan laughed.

'Like it? I love it. I can't believe you'd do this for me!' Cally swallowed as she traced her finger over the engraved word. She couldn't quite get her head around the gift. She felt *pathetically* grateful. An image of sitting in the spare room at her grandma's house in the early hours of the morning, wrapped in a duvet, trying to finish an assignment on her old laptop, flashed in front of her eyes. Her voice was thick with emotion. 'I don't know what to say. It's too much. You shouldn't have. It must have cost loads. I looked at these and, well, that's why Eloise suggested a reconditioned one.'

Logan shook his head. 'Nonsense. You need to stop saying that. You deserve this and so much more. I want to spoil you. Get it?'

Cally *didn't* get it. Not at all. Not even close. She thought about what her friend Eloise had told her about money blocks. This was clearly one of them right in front of her, wrapped in pink and topped with a bow. 'Right.'

'If a new laptop makes your life a little bit easier and brighter, then it's worth every penny as far as I'm concerned.'

Overwhelmed, Cally felt a prick at the corner of her eyes. She put the laptop back in the box, hugged Logan, buried her face in his neck, and breathed in the familiar Logan smell. 'Thank you. So much.'

'You are *more* than welcome.'

'I don't know what I did to deserve you, but I am so grateful to have you in my life.'

Logan squeezed her and then held her way from him. 'Are you getting soppy on me, Blackcurrant?'

'No, no, course not.'

'Ha, you are. I like it. Continue.'

'I'm just happy.'

'You deserve everything good in this world, Cal. I feel great to be the one who gets to share it with you.'

Cally was silent for a bit. She mused how she'd spent her

whole life before meeting Logan, caring for other people and holding up the sky. 'It's taking me a while to understand being treated.'

'Get used to it, chicken-licken. It's here to stay.'

'Thank you. I love you.'

'Right back at you. I'm so happy you came crashing into my world. Let me tell you, I *love* buying stuff for you.'

'Aww, thank you.'

'When I first laid eyes on you, I knew that you were special and a bit weird. Now I know you're *very* weird and I love it.'

Cally laughed, thinking back to their encounter at the manor, when she'd been covered in a huge blackcurrant stain. 'Ah yes, nothing says "soulmate material" like someone who throws chicken at you and turns up to a new job in a dirty great stained blouse.'

Logan grinned. 'It just goes to show that you have a talent for making a memorable first impression.'

Cally rolled her eyes and swatted his chest. 'Memorable is one word for it. I'd say "disastrous" or "cringe-worthy," but each to their own.'

'Well, I wouldn't change a single thing about that day or any of the days that followed. And I want more of them, though I might give the continually bumping my head on your flat's ceiling a miss.'

'You'll have to put up with it until I've saved enough money to start looking for my own place.'

'You're worth a few bumps.'

Cally carefully smoothed the wrapping paper, folded it into the laptop box, added the laptop, tied the bow, and then slid the box into the bag. She turned around and squinted across the harbour. 'Right, I feel an ice cream coming on. It's the weather for it.'

'Laptops, ice cream, coffee. Anything else?'

Cally giggled as they got up and she took Logan's hand.

'What a day, eh?' She looked up at the sun high in the sky as a few seagulls wheeled and cried overhead, and a salty sea breeze rustled through her hair.

'Yeah, we'd better make the best of it before the weather changes again. We are in Lovely, after all. We might get hailstones later.'

As they walked, Cally couldn't quite get her head around the laptop. Little did Logan know how much it *actually* meant to her. How, also, as she walked along beside him, she felt as if it was exactly where she was meant to be. She glanced up at him, her heart skipping a beat, and wondered if he really felt the same as she did deep down in her bones. From her side of the fence, without a shadow of a doubt, she felt as if they were meant to be. They just slotted together despite their different backgrounds and vastly different lives. So far, it had been marvellous. She couldn't wait to see where the journey would take them next. Little did she know what was coming. A little on the bumpy side sprang to mind.

2

It was the morning after Cally's day off and the laptop gift. Cally looked around her little flat, sighed happily, and shook her head at how her life was turning out. Part of her felt as if, at any given moment, her bubble would burst and she would find herself at the hospice waiting and watching her grandma and having the horrible rented house on the estate to go back to. It now felt as if that part of her life wasn't quite real. As if it belonged to someone else. She looked around at the flat and how nice she'd made it. The chalky white paint on the walls gave a soft, clean backdrop that made the place feel homely and clean and captured the morning light that filtered through the bamboo blinds.

The once dusty, old, brightly-coloured wall stacked with file boxes up to the ceiling was now adorned with a gathering of things Cally had found here and there: a collection of framed prints of the coast she'd found when doing a decluttering job for Nina, a mix of vintage botanical illustrations she'd come across in a charity shop not far from Eloise's house, a lovely photo of her grandma and her mum, and a couple of her own sketches from back in the day when she'd had the time. She'd spent ages arranging them so they fitted together in an organised jumble above the sofa. Somehow a story of little things she liked in her life.

Everything about the tiny flat was different from the day she'd first viewed it with Birdie when it had been packed to the rafters with junk. The flat's slow renovation had begun on the bottom with the floorboards, which were now stripped back to their original state and showed the natural grains and knots of the wood. Cally loved the way she'd got to know their creaks and sounds, as if they somehow spoke to her and made her feel safe.

She smiled at a large, soft, oriental rug in muted blues and creams, which sat underneath a coffee table she'd inherited from Lovely Manor. The coffee table had been on its way to the tip, but with its pretty turned legs, Cally had rescued it from the joys of the dump. Now it took pride of place, full of her things: a neat stack of books, a little glass vase with fresh flowers, a porcelain tray she'd found in a jumble sale with a huge scented candle Logan had turned up with one day, a small fabric-covered notebook and a little framed picture of her and Eloise taken when they'd been strawberry picking on a farm. Next to the frame, a smooth pebble with a heart shape drawn on it, a memento from one of her first walks along Lovely Bay beach. All of it strangely somehow a symbol of the new chapter in her life.

Sitting just behind the coffee table, Cally's sofa was the centrepiece of the small sitting room. Upholstered in a soft, linen fabric and adorned with a pretty assortment of velvet cushions in shades of blush pink, sea green, and dove grey, she loved settling into it at the end of the day. With a casual, lived-in look that invited one to sink in and relax and a chunky knit soft cream throw casually draped over one arm, it felt as if it had journeyed with her in her new life in the third smallest town in the country.

She stood for a minute and took in just how far she'd come. She loved it all, mostly because now, at the top of the building overlooking Lovely, she felt safe. For a long time, she hadn't felt as if she'd had roots. She'd floated around for ages, untethered and not quite sure who she was in her life or what she was going to do. Now, in Lovely Bay, she felt as if she was home.

She had made the whole place work for her and utilised just about every little bit of space. Wedged in the corner, by the balcony door, her neatly organised work desk with its weathered patina and strong legs spoke of years of use from days gone by. She'd found it on the first floor of the building under a pile of Birdie's pharmacy files. It was now doing a very good job of making her new laptop feel at home. All of it was a far cry from some of the places she'd logged on to the World Wide Web to get on with her work. Now, her desk and surroundings were easy on the eye: a lamp with a pretty floral shade, a couple of notebooks stacked up and ready to go, a framed photo of her and her grandma, and a pot full of nice pens. Above the desk hung a bulletin board covered in pinned notes, photos, and sketches. A collage of Cally's thoughts and inspirations, a visual representation of what was going on in her head. Scribbled ideas for places to visit, a map of Lovely Bay with marked locations, and a few photos of her and Eloise.

Cally turned around to see Logan coming out of the bedroom. He ruffled the back of his hair, smiled, and pointed to the bathroom. 'Morning. I'm going to go and have a shower. How are you? You must have been up early.'

'Yep, I was. I've been setting up my laptop. I'll make you a coffee.'

'Thanks, love one. Be out in a sec,' Logan replied as he opened the bathroom door.

Cally heard the shower turn on as she got the coffee ready, put two mugs on the worktop, poured boiling water into a coffee plunger, and went to her desk to continue with her new laptop.

A few minutes later, Logan came out of the bathroom. He nodded in the direction of the laptop. 'How is it?'

Cally leaned back and beamed. 'So good. It's like moving out of the dark ages. It's so much faster. We're talking chalk and cheese.'

Logan chuckled and kissed the top of Cally's head. 'I reckon it will save you time in the morning. You'll no longer have to get up earlier to wait for it to warm up and log you on.'

'Ha, I know.'

Logan gave her shoulder a squeeze. 'How is it with the apps and stuff? You couldn't get things on the old one, could you?'

'No. It's great. A whole new world of possibilities awaits.' Cally joked. 'I have moved on from the dark ages.'

'Indeed. Thank God.'

'I still can't believe you did this for me.'

'You don't have to thank me. It's just a laptop. I do think this little beauty is going to be a game-changer for you, though. No more fighting with outdated tech or frustrations.' Logan chuckled. 'The world is your oyster.'

Cally grinned. 'I know.'

Logan looked over in the direction of the kitchen. 'Right, where's this coffee, then?'

Cally swivelled in her chair, watching as Logan made his way to the kitchen. 'Coming right up,' she said, pushing herself to her feet. 'Just got to pour it.'

Logan leaned against the worktop as Cally pushed down the coffee plunger. 'So, how's the chatbot thing going anyway?'

Cally nodded as she poured coffee into two mugs. 'Yeah, same old, same old. It's nice to have something I can do from home, you know? Especially with hours that fit around the chemist.'

'Busy?'

Cally took a sip of her coffee. 'It's getting busier. More than I expected, actually. There are a lot of returns these days and in my opinion not as many problems with sales. I assume that's because there are less. Sign of the times, I guess.'

Logan nodded. 'Yeah.'

'Oh! I almost forgot. Croissants. Fancy one?'

'Yup. Love one.'

Cally moved to the oven, turning it on to warm up. 'They'll just take a few minutes to heat through. So, yeah, the chatbot job is not great, but for a home job, the money's not too bad. It all goes in the same pot at the end of the day.'

Logan raised an eyebrow. 'Not being funny, but it does annoy me how hard you work for that pay.'

Cally nodded as she placed the croissants in the oven. 'I know, but it's all going to my savings. It's amazing how quickly it's adding up now that my costs are lower. Between that and my regular wages from the chemist and the work I'm doing for Nina, I'm actually managing to save a decent amount each month.'

'Great.'

'I've been thinking about the money my grandma left me.'

Logan's eyebrows rose. 'The inheritance?'

Cally rolled her eyes. 'It's not quite an inheritance! But I've been doing some calculations, and I think I might almost have enough for a deposit on a flat.'

Logan's eyes widened. 'Really? Time to start looking at places?'

Cally shook her head. 'Not seriously, not yet. But I've been keeping an eye on the market in Lovely Bay. Just to get an idea, you know?'

'And?' Logan prompted. 'What have you found out?'

Cally sighed. 'Well, it's not cheap, that's for sure. Lovely's become quite popular in the last few years. But there are still some places that might be within my budget. Small places, mind you, but it would be a start.'

Logan nodded. 'A start is all you need. Getting on the property ladder is the hardest part. Once you're on, it gets easier.'

'That's what I've heard,' Cally agreed. She glanced at the oven. 'Oh, they're done.' She grabbed a couple of plates, removed the now-warm croissants from the oven, and put them on the plates. The buttery croissant smell filled the small kitchen, making her stomach rumble.

'So, any flats you've been eyeing up? Any particular areas you're interested in?'

Cally handed Logan a plate and they moved back to the sitting room, settling on the sofa. 'Literally anywhere I can afford. The harbour is nice. It's a bit on the pricey side, but the location is fantastic. Or, I don't know, anywhere near the river or over where Nancy is.'

Logan nodded, taking a bite of his croissant. 'Mmm, these are good. Yeah, where Nancy is is great. It would be a good investment, that area's only going to get more popular.'

'There are some older flats closer to the high street. They'd need a bit of work, but they're more in my price range. And I quite like the idea of doing up a place, making it my own, you know?'

'Yeah, this place is amazing now with what you've done to it.'

'Thanks.' Cally remembered when she'd thought she was going to find herself homeless. She'd come a long, long way. She'd been terrified at one point and eaten up with stress. Now, maybe the dream of her own flat wasn't as far-fetched as she'd feared. 'Having my own flat is actually becoming doable.'

Logan tutted as his phone rang. He pulled it out of his pocket and rolled his eyes as he turned the screen to Cally. 'Alastair. I know it will be the horses. Really? He's useless.' He sighed.

Cally gathered up the plates and took them into the kitchen as Logan spoke to Alastair. Her mind whirled with thoughts about flat hunting and mortgages as she rinsed the plates in the sink. It was all a bit scary at the same time as exciting. It felt weird to be happy and on the cusp of something that wasn't caring for someone else or sorting out finances for horrible things. A step closer to something that had been a dream for a long time. What she didn't know was that along the way, she had a few surprises to come.

3

Cally popped a straw in the top of a blackcurrant carton and tried not to feel guilty about the impact on the environment. She admonished herself and made a mental note to try and find something on YouTube to do with the cartons as she hustled along on her way to meet Eloise for a coffee. She'd spent the morning working on the chatbot, sorting out problems with customers, then had worked for a couple of hours in the back of the chemist helping with a huge order. Now, she was on the way to Lovely Bay library to have a little mooch and check out the resources section to see what courses were available locally. Not that she had any clue what course she wanted to do, but she wanted to put the feelers out and dip into furthering the education that had been on hold for a long time.

As she got to Lovely Town Hall, she took in the beautiful old building and looked left in the direction of the library. A very unusual circular-shaped building that, according to local lore, had been built by an architect back in the day who had totally ripped off the design of the Albert Hall. Lovely Bay's version was on a much smaller scale but just as beautiful. Cally had been to the library many, many times. In the days before her grandma had died, when she had been on a serious budget, she'd used the library as a free little resource to keep her mind active and allow the pages of a borrowed book to whisk her away from the realities of her carer role and the grind of her day-to-day life. She'd borrowed all sorts from the library's shelves, including the Regency dramas her grandma had adored so much. With a book bag full of library books, she would go and sit by her grandma's bedside and read every evening until her grandma had dropped off to sleep. In the end, when controlling the pain had been tricky, the narration of the Regency dramas had helped enormously. Cally tutted as she walked along and thought about her grandma, the old, familiar feeling of sadness still there right in the centre of her stomach. At least now she wasn't sad *and* guilty, too.

As she approached the library and took in its lovely old architecture, she realised just how far she'd come since the year before. Then she had visited the library at least biweekly, often more, with not just a heavy bag full of books but also a very heavy heart. Now, that same heart was far from heavy. In fact, she felt as if *she* and *it* had a new lease of life. Meeting Logan and moving to Lovely Bay had taken her heavy heart and lightened it and then some. Now, she floated along freely, almost as if she was up in the sky, very near to the clouds. No longer underneath, holding the darn thing up.

Arriving at the library, she stood by the door for a minute, read through a notice detailing new opening times, and scanned a poster informing about an author talk by a local writer. Once inside, she glanced at the long lines of books stretching away from her. In her element, she strolled slowly down the first aisle, peered at the staff picks lined up along the top shelf, and read the little cards alongside them, looking for something that might take her fancy.

After a bit of mooching and with an armful of books, she went upstairs to the non-fiction department and the area for courses and qualifications with the intention of mooching through and looking for a course that would somehow lead to a better job. There was no way she wanted to continue with the chatbot long-term. It wasn't what she wanted to do with her working life - would anyone love doing that job out of choice? Once she'd sorted a mortgage and her finances, she would train to do something more rewarding. As she got to the top of the old staircase in the centre of the building, she felt a bit of a sense of anticipation about the opportunity to change her life for the better. The upper floor of the library had always been her favourite. She'd loved just browsing it and imagining what she'd be able to do when she no longer had as many caring duties. In the library, she'd always felt as if surrounded by other people's knowledge and words she'd been somehow sheltered for a bit from the responsibilities of her life. Reaching the top of the stairs, she paused to take in the scene: beautiful old tall windows that let in light, circular walls lined with old timber bookshelves filled with an array of textbooks and reference materials. Several large tables in the centre of the room equipped with computers and reading lamps. A few students here and there, scattered around, surrounded by books and engrossed in their work. She loved the sound, too; a calm quiet with nothing much going on at all. Lots of decompressing.

Making her way to the section dedicated to courses and qualifications, she scanned the shelves, her fingers brushing the spines of books on everything from business management to creative writing. She then sat down at one of the computer stations and browsed a platform offering various online courses run by the council for free. She scanned through the options, her eyes widening at the sheer variety available. Digital marketing, graphic design, project management, hospitality. Cally clicked on a digital marketing course and began reading the description. It promised to teach her the fundamentals of SEO, whatever that was, social media marketing, and content creation.

After spending an hour down a well of all things courses and not really having found anything that had taken her fancy at all, she gathered her things and headed back downstairs. She checked out a marketing book and a couple of thrillers and left the library, her mind, at least, buzzing with possibilities. As she stepped out into the daylight, the sun shone brightly, and she felt a bit of a sense of purpose about herself. Not that long before, her future, her housing situation, and her whole life had been teetering on the edge of disaster. Everything then had seemed so uncertain and up in the air; now, *it* and *she* were on a different trajectory altogether. Cally de Pfeffer was, at last, in control. Oh, how good did that feel?

Half an hour or so later, Cally walked past the window of the coffee shop where she was meeting Eloise with her bag heavy with books and her head full of ideas. She was not sure about what she might do in the future once she was settled into a flat of her own, but she felt as if there was promise ahead of her. Promise and the future at last felt nice. Life was continuing to go on its way without her having to perpetually hold up the sky. She'd have some of that every day of the week.

Just as she got close to the coffee shop door, she could see Eloise hustling along, coming the other way.

'Hiya! How are you?' Eloise asked as she kissed Cally on the cheek.

'Hi. I'm great! Really good.'

'I'll say! You look amazing.'

'Do I? Thanks. Nice of you to notice. Ha.'

'Yes, you do. It must be the glow of romance.' Eloise joked.

Cally nodded and contemplated for a second. 'It's just that I'm happy, actually.'

'Aww, I love that. It's so nice to see.'

'Thanks,' Cally said as she walked into the café behind Eloise. The aroma of freshly brewed coffee and a hum of conversation enveloped them as sunlight streamed through large windows. After ordering two coffees and two Chelsea buns, they made their way to a small table in the corner.

Eloise plopped down into a chair. 'So, spill the beans, Cal. What's got you so happy and glowing? And don't try to tell me it's not Logan because I know that look.'

Cally laughed and blushed. 'I don't know. You're right, I suppose. Being with him makes everything feel brighter, you know? Like anything is possible. The future is bright.'

Eloise nodded. 'I'm so happy for you, truly. You deserve all the happiness in the world and then some.'

'Thanks.'

'You just seem, I don't know, full and buzzy. Not flat.'

Cally laughed. 'Well, yeah, I don't have time to be flat and I no longer spend most of my waking hours worrying about other people. It's so liberating.'

'Yeah, three jobs make one busy.'

'I've just been looking at courses. I feel like I'm on a new trajectory, like there's this whole world of possibilities opening up before me. And I want to explore that, to see where it might take me. That sounds a bit airy-fairy. Do you know what I mean, though? I never had the option for *anything* before. No time, no money and not a lot of inclination.'

Eloise's face lit up. 'Sounds good, and yeah, I totally get what you mean. You've been waiting around helping everyone out for too long and now's your chance to open your wings a bit.'

Cally nodded. 'One thing I know: I can't stay on that chatbot much longer. It's doing my head in.'

'I'm not surprised.'

Cally paused for a bit as two coffees and two Chelsea buns were put down in front of them. She looked at Eloise and sighed. 'I have no idea what course to do.'

Eloise took a sip of her coffee and shrugged. 'I guess the universe will tell you which one...'

'Yeah, I'll keep looking until I see something I fancy. Do you reckon it's a good idea to do a course?'

Eloise nodded emphatically. 'Yup, if you're getting that calling. Life's too short not to do things.'

'Exactly what I thought when I was in the library. I've spent so long playing it safe, settling for what fitted in around caring.'

Eloise nodded again. 'Tell me about it. And you don't need to do that anymore. Woohoo. How good is that?'

No words would ever be able to describe how good it felt for Cally not to have responsibilities. 'I can't even compute it sometimes. Sometimes I think the bubble will burst.'

Eloise smiled warmly. 'Anyway, how's it going with Logan?'

'Yeah, fine, better than fine. Really good.'

'You've got over the two different backgrounds thing?' Eloise asked, raising an eyebrow.

Cally rolled her eyes. 'Ha. No, not really. It's still there. I'm just *choosing* not to focus on it. It keeps coming up for me, but I have to suck it up. It is what it is.'

'Right. Good. Honestly, you need to get over that, though. You've found your person. You have that one-in-a-million connection,' Eloise said earnestly.

'Do we?' Cally contemplated for a second. 'Maybe that's it. Sometimes, I feel like there's still so much I don't know about him, though.'

Eloise frowned, tilting her head. 'Really? First I've heard of it. What? Like what?'

'I don't know. Like his past. I actually don't know a *huge* amount about that,' Cally admitted with a frown.

Eloise cocked her head. 'What? Haven't you talked about it?'

Cally shook her head. 'Not really, no. I mean, I know bits and pieces, little snippets here and there. But whenever I try to dig deeper, to ask about his childhood or his family, he sort of changes the subject or gives me these vague, noncommittal answers that don't really tell me anything at all.'

'You've not mentioned it before,' Eloise said, her forehead furrowed in concern. 'Where has this suddenly come from out of the blue?'

'I don't know, really. It came to me the other day and then I couldn't stop thinking about it. You know how once you notice something, it looks so obvious?'

'What are you saying?' Eloise asked, leaning forward and narrowing her eyes.

'No idea. It's not that I don't trust him. I just suddenly realised I don't know much about the nitty-gritty stuff. You know?'

Eloise shook her head. 'Right. I suppose everyone has their own pace in sharing stuff.'

Cally nodded slowly. 'Suppose so. It's not a biggie. I just realised it the other day. Or maybe he's not got as much baggage as me, ha!'

'I reckon just focus on the present. The rest will come in time. I'm sure of it,' Eloise added.

'Ever the voice of reason.'

'One of my *many* skills.' Eloise chuckled.

'Indeed. Right done with that?' Cally said, pointing to Eloise's coffee cup.

'Yep.' Eloise pushed the cup into the middle of the table.

'Right then, enough of this heavy talk. I say we go and find ourselves a proper Lovely Bay ice cream.'

'Ooh, just what I fancy. I need a chocolate flake in mine.'

'I can sort that. Then we can sit down by the pier and people-watch, like the nosy old biddies we are at heart,' Cally suggested.

Eloise laughed. 'Lead the way, Cal,' she said, standing up and grabbing her bag. 'You sure know how to show someone a good time.'

4

It was a warm, Lovely Bay kind of evening. Cally was on her way to the manor for supper with Logan. She strolled along with a Thermos cup full of hot blackcurrant in her hand, enveloped in the sights and sounds of Lovely all around her. Rounding a corner, she noted the change in pavement to cobblestones as she arrived in the vicinity of St. Lovely church. Its beautiful old spire pointed up into the evening sky and she stood for a moment, taking in its blue nave door and huge summer floral wreath attached to its front. Even Lovely's church seemed to just be that little bit prettier than any other she'd ever come across.

She held her head up to the sky and inhaled. The evening sun felt nice on her skin, a soft breeze rustled through the leaves and the sky above seemed to shimmer in pinks, golds, and all manner of orange hues as the sun began to go down. It was as if Lovely had been dipped in a golden glow that only seemed to exist in the third smallest town in the country. Each time it happened, it surprised Cally just how beautiful it was.

Taking a sip of her hot blackcurrant, she then inhaled another deep, long, luxurious breath full of the smells of long summer days as she listened to the backdrop of a Lovely evening going about its business. There was a far-off hum coming from the River Lovely, children playing in a garden next to the church, a lawnmower somewhere in the far distance, and the occasional bark of a dog. Everything about Lovely appeared as if it was revelling in the warm weather and showing off its finest: hanging baskets bursting with blooms every which way, saturated grass lawns in front gardens, window boxes dancing with petunias and lines of roses tucked up beside white fences and spilling over old stone walls. Cally would take Lovely when it was showing off its summer coat, that she knew for free.

Starting her walk again, she chuckled to herself as she remembered back when the weather had been bitterly cold and she'd been on her way to the manor to work for Nina and her company A Lovely Organised Life. That morning, she'd been full of strife and stressed up to her eyeballs about trying to find somewhere to live. She'd been so worried about the potential of finding herself homeless that with her head spinning with worry, she'd taken an almighty tumble on a frosty cobblestone and ended up face down on the pavement covered in mud. Now, both the chilly temperatures, slippery pavements, and her head full of stress were but a distant memory. She wasn't going to be welcoming them back anytime soon, or so she thought. She was on an upward course away from a life of caring for other people and on the cusp of lots of new happy things, she hoped.

About ten minutes later, as she approached the manor, as she usually did, she stopped for a few seconds, absolutely in awe of its magnificence. The spectacular house sat regally raised in the distance as if casting its eyes down on the mere mortals of the world. Cally remembered how she'd felt that first cold-as-ice morning when she'd arrived at the gates with a blackcurrant-stained top. Then, she'd taken in the size of the house and had not quite been able to compute that people actually lived somewhere as palatial. Now, she came and went as if it was completely normal. A tiny little bit of her had become part of the woodwork.

As she got closer to the house and the panel beside the huge black gates, she remembered that first morning when everything had sparkled in frost. She'd pushed one of the buttons and wondered what might happen next. A fancy-pants posh voice had spoken to her out of the tinny speaker in the brass panel in the wall. She recalled how she'd been mistaken for a new cleaner from the agency, and had not wanted to correct the posh voice. When the gates had opened, she'd felt quite literally as if she had been entering another world. As she'd walked up the long driveway, said hello to a gardener, and looked up at the house in awe, she'd felt as if she'd been cast in a BBC period drama. That morning had been the second time she'd ever laid eyes on Logan. He'd appeared behind her on the drive in his car and had stopped to say hello. It had turned out to be the continuation of the sliding doors moments that had ended up in the two of them becoming a thing. A thing she liked very much indeed. A thing she wasn't going to let go.

Since that driveway meeting, the prevailing few months had been a wild ride of *things* Cally had never even dreamt about. Some she'd not even *known* about. Her eyes had not only been well and truly opened to the manor house but a whole new way of living. All of it had been different and eye-opening compared with the sheltered life Cally had led, most of which had involved caring for her mum, her brother, and her grandma and not doing much else at all. Out of everything that had happened since she'd walked slap-bang into Logan's world, the most astonishing thing was that she now realised how the other half lived. Part of her wasn't sure what to think about it or how it made her feel.

As she pushed Logan's code into the pad and waited for the gates to clunk and clang and slowly open inwards, she smiled to herself at how, firstly, she was now part of the actual comings and goings of Lovely Manor and, secondly, at how quickly she'd got used to it. She'd liked how the other half lived and had decided to have a slice of it.

Not to say that she felt as if she belonged. *Nothing* like that at all. When she was around the manor and Logan's family, she felt like a duck out of water most, if not all, of the time, but she had learnt to get on with it. She'd spent way too much brain power stressing that she and Logan were worlds apart and eventually had just sucked it up and decided to see where the journey took her. Logan had told her in no uncertain terms that he loved her for who she was, not where she came from, and she'd decided to tuck that into her heart and run with it. Sometimes, though, when hobnobbing with the upper classes, it was *much* easier said than done.

Lost in thought as she walked up the drive with the manor house silhouetted against the brilliant oranges and pink hues of a Lovely sunset, she made her way past various gardens, followed the sweeping drive to the right, then strolled to the left of the house, past the stables and eventually to one of the residential cottages dotted in the grounds. The cottage, surrounded by beautifully tended roses with climbing pale pink Austins around the door, was where Logan lived part-time when he wasn't in town. With its exquisitely tended hanging baskets and a gravel pathway lined by blooming plants buzzing with bees, the feeling that Cally was in a picture book continued as she got to the front door.

Letting herself in, she slipped her shoes off on the doormat and took in, as she had many times before, the stealth wealth of the place and made her way through the hallway to the kitchen. Logan was standing leaning on the worktop with his phone in his hand when she pushed open the kitchen door. His face lit up when he looked up and saw her. 'Hey, how are you? Looking gorgeous as per usual.'

'Great, thanks. You?' Cally inhaled the smell of garlic and herbs as it wafted through the air. Her stomach rumbled in anticipation as she pulled out a chair and sat down. 'How was your day?' Cally asked, resting her chin on her hand.

'Busy, as usual,' Logan put down his phone and fully turned his attention to her. 'I had back-to-back meetings, but I got through them without too much trouble. The highlight was definitely the weather, though. I managed to sneak out for a bit and enjoy the sunshine at lunch. Long may it last. How come everything seems better when the sun shines?'

'I don't know but somehow it does. The town looked stunning in the evening light. It took my breath away over by the church there. The colours in the sky are amazing.'

Logan nodded. 'It's one of the things about Lovely you can't really put your finger on until you see it—how everything seems to shimmer. One of the gardeners said it's something to do with the position on the coast and how the land lies. Not sure about that, but it probably is. I mean, what do I know about stuff like that?'

Cally chuckled and tucked away her thoughts about having gardeners. *If only. More than a few pot plants on a rented balcony would be nice.* 'Who knows, but whatever it is, it works for me. I still pinch myself that I get to live in Lovely, to be quite honest.'

'How was your walk?'

Cally nodded. 'Close to perfect. It did the trick.'

Logan lifted his chin in the direction of the window and the garden. 'It felt as if the whole garden was bathed in that pinkish Lovely glow about ten minutes ago.'

'Yes. I saw it, too. I love that glow.'

'Works for me. Your head is clear, then? The workday is well behind you?' Logan asked.

'Yup. The fresh air has done me the world of good.'

Logan walked around the kitchen table and kissed her on the cheek. 'Good.'

'What's cooking? I'm starving.'

Logan chuckled. 'You always are.'

'I know.'

'You put away more than anyone I know.'

'Always been the same.' Cally joked, 'It costs a lot to feed me like the horses.'

Logan laughed and joked. 'You're up there with the horses as Lovely Manor costs these days. It's a good job I can cook a few things. I need to budget for you.'

'I'm such a lucky duck. I get the delights of your cooking as well as the shimmering light over the manor. I mean, what more could a girl ask for?' Cally bantered.

Logan reached for a wooden spoon and stirred a pot on the stove. 'You are *very* lucky. I've made something special, too. Remember our first dinner date here?'

'The risotto! You've made it again? I thought it smelt familiar.'

Logan grinned. 'Exactly. I thought it would be nice to revisit that memory. Plus, it's one of the few dishes I can make without setting the kitchen on fire, so that's always a bonus.'

Cally laughed. 'Rubbish, you're a great cook.'

'It should be ready in about ten minutes. Drink?'

'Love one.'

As Logan poured them each a drink, Cally rested her elbows on the table. 'Tell me more about your day.'

Logan leaned against the worktop, facing her. 'Aside from the meetings, not much to speak of. You?'

'Busy as well, but not with anything that interesting. Boring, really. I looked at a few flats online but that was about it other than work stuff.'

'Any good flats?'

The sound of the risotto simmering filled the room, accompanied by the clinking of utensils as Logan moved around the kitchen. Cally's stomach growled as he handed her a glass of wine.

'Nothing in my budget.'

'Sit tight. Something will come up.'

'Hope so.'

'Right, this is almost ready. I hope you're hungry.'

'I can't wait to taste it again.'

'As I said, I don't know where you put it.'

Cally laughed. 'My grandma always reckoned I had hollow knees. They used to say that in the old days, didn't they?'

'I make her right.' After Logan put out some plates and cutlery, they chatted for a bit and then he popped the cooking pot on the table, added a green salad and they both served themselves the risotto. 'Bon appétit,' Logan said as he raised his glass.

'Bon appétit,' Cally echoed, clinking her glass against his. 'Thanks for cooking. You can stay.'

'Ha. I'm so honoured.'

Cally tucked in and took a bite of the risotto. 'Mmm, perfect. You're very good at risotto.'

'Here's to many more evenings with sunsets and food like this.'

'Cheers.' Cally nodded with a smile. 'Here's to us, more like.'

'Oh, speaking of us.' Logan reached around behind him to the dresser. 'I forgot to show you this.' He slid an expensive-looking cream envelope with scalloped gilt edges across the table.

'What's this?' Cally asked as she put her fork down.

Logan rolled his eyes. 'Our first Henry-Hicks family outing together.' He grimaced. 'I can't get out of this one. It's an annual thing. *I*, I mean, *we* have to attend. No getting out of this one, I'm afraid.'

Cally frowned. 'Family outing?'

'The races. It's almost as serious as Christmas in this family. You do *not* not attend.'

Cally went a bit cold inside. She didn't like the sound of the races at all. Not one little bit. She shoved her feelings aside, took the envelope, opened the back, and pulled out a thick cream-embossed card with scalloped gilt edges that matched the envelope. She swallowed as she read the invitation twice. "Lovely Manor Races", it read, followed by a date and time. She slipped the card back into the envelope and propped it up against the pepper pot. A shiver of apprehension went down her spine as she stared at the thick, luxurious paper and the elegant, gilded script. Very, very fancy. Way out of her league.

She swallowed hard, trying to push down a rising tide of panic. The races. A high-society event that she had only ever seen in movies, on the telly, or read about in glossy magazines back in the day. A world so far removed from her own that it might as well have been on another planet. As she shoved another forkful of risotto into her mouth, she flicked her eyes to Logan and then back at the invitation. The embossed gold edges and the thick, luxurious paper screamed opulence, a stark contrast to anything she was used to. She tried to keep her face neutral to prevent the rising jitters from showing, but inside, her thoughts were going around so fast she almost felt as if she was spinning. In a flash, she remembered how she'd felt in a charity shop dress when Logan had surprised her with a trip to the theatre. She'd told herself she wouldn't ever let herself feel that way again, but here she was with the same inferiority complex racing around her veins.

The doubting voice in her head started to chat away to her. *What on earth do I wear to the races? Shoes? What the actual?* Her mind whirled with images of fascinators, women riding in open carriages, top hats and tails. All sorts.

Logan's voice cut through her thoughts. 'What do you think? Sound good to you? It's a really fun day, actually.'

Fun? Pah! Yeah, right. My left foot. Didn't sound like her idea of fun in any shape or form. Cally plastered on a smile, nodded, and flicked the switch in her voice she used when she pretended she was okay. She was an *absolute expert* at the voice. It betrayed none of her inner turmoil. 'It looks lovely. Really good. Yes, great.'

Logan didn't seem to notice her slight hesitation. The voice had clearly done its job. 'It's a bit of a to-do, but it'll be great. We can make a day of it.'

Cally forced a laugh. 'Mmm. Yes. Sounds good.'

It did not sound at all good. Not even close. It sounded more or less awful as far as she was concerned. She would have been fine to go to the races with just Logan or perhaps with Eloise, but not as part of a grand Henry-Hicks family outing. She had no idea how to behave, or what she was meant to do. She knew not a sausage about horses or racing for that matter and bottom line, she didn't really *want* to know, either. All around, she wasn't really interested. Plus, from what she'd seen on the telly, she felt sorry for the horses.

Then there was the absolute calamity of what someone like her would wear. It wasn't as if she had oodles of money to splash out on a solution, either. It was alright for Logan. He would just whack on a suit, have a shower and shave, and be done with it. She, however, would have to spend way too much thought and brain power on what to wear and would be weighed down in the preparation. One thing she knew for sure was that she would not be turning up at the races in a second-hand dress. Not on your Nelly. Been there and it hadn't been pretty for anyone involved. Even though it was trendy and all the rage to save the environment by recycling and wearing previously loved clothes, from her neck of the woods, it didn't quite have the same environmental clout. Where she came from, hand-me-downs came out of necessity not to make one look as if they cared.

Logan returned to his risotto, oblivious to the storm raging inside Cally's head. She took a way too big gulp of her wine, trying to steady herself. Her mind raced, and her thoughts tangled in their own little private mess for one. *What if I look completely out of place? What if they can tell I don't belong?* She imagined herself stumbling over her words, awkward with sophistication all around her.

Logan looked up and smiled. 'Mum wondered if you might want to go out with her to shop for a dress and hat. She said she has nothing to wear.' Logan rolled his eyes. 'She has more clothes than anyone. I said I'd mention it.'

She's not the only one, Cally thought grimly. She made an odd, tight-lined, not-very-happy smile. 'Sure.'

There was *no way* on earth she was going dress shopping with Logan's mum. In her mind, she pictured a boutique with intimidatingly stylish clothes, each more expensive than the last. She could feel the eyes of stuck-up sales assistants judging her. They'd be all friendly and beaming on the outside, but inside, silently assessing that she wasn't one of their usual clients. The whole thing filled Cally to the brim with *absolute* pure and utter dread. No way, José. She'd rather stick pins in her eyes than go shopping with Logan's mum.

Logan continued. 'Mum and Cecilia have a whole room full of hats for occasions like these.'

Cally already knew about the hat room. She'd been the one in there decluttering it when she'd first started working at the manor with Nina. She and Nina may have secretly tried on a few of the fascinators and made funny faces in the mirror. Cally nodded mechanically, her mind still racing. *A hat. Of course, I need a hat. What kind of hat? Wide-brimmed? Fascinator?* She had no idea.

Logan picked up on her body language, reached over, and squeezed her hand. 'Hey, you okay?'

Cally quickly masked her anxiety, flicked her voice switch

again, and added a bright I-don't-care smile. 'Yes, absolutely. Just a lot to take in.'

'You're not okay. You're doing the voice thing.' Logan stated flatly.

'And here I was thinking I'd hidden it so well.'

'Not a chance, Blackcurrant. It'll be fine. You'll see. And you'll get to meet everyone properly. The extended family will love you.'

Cally's stomach twisted at the thought. Meeting the whole family. *What if they don't? What if I make a fool of myself?* She took another overly large sip of wine, trying to quell the doubts. 'I'm sure it will be, err, fun as you said.' She tried to keep her voice steady, be normal, and not flick the switch. 'It's just that I've never been to anything like this before. Like I have zero clue what to do or how to behave.'

'Behave? What? What do you mean?'

Logan just simply didn't get it. He *knew* how to behave because he had been bred to do so. That was the whole point. 'I've never been before.'

'No drama. I'll lead the way. Honestly, I want you to be part of it. Just like the theatre, I think you'll *love* it. It's just entertainment. Fun.'

Cally's heart ached. Logan didn't understand, but it was sweet that he tried to get it. Part of her wanted to be excited for him and to share in his world without feeling like an imposter, the other part of her couldn't really give a flying fart about parading around in a fancy dress with a dodgy thing bouncing around on top of her head. She took a deep breath and squeezed his hand back. 'I'm just a bit nervous about stuff like that, I guess. I'll be fine, though. In at the deep end, as they say. It's good to try new things…'

'You'll be amazing, Cal. Trust me.'

Well played, Henry-Hicks, but you don't know the half of it.

Cally nodded, but her mind overflowed with doubt. *Amaz-*

ing? How can I be amazing when I don't even know where to start? Her thoughts spiralled as Logan chatted away and filled her in with what happened at the races, in particular, the event sponsored by Lovely Manor. The more he talked about the races themselves, the traditions, the dressing up, the more her inner voice questioned everything.

She pushed the horrible thoughts away as she realised she had little choice but to get on with it. The manor and what went on in it, including its social calendar, was part of Logan's life. If she wanted to be with him, even if it meant stepping far outside her comfort zone, she had to suck it up and crack on. She might even enjoy shopping for a dress—who knew? But there was no way she was going with Logan's mum. That would be a step too far. Shopping was bad enough without throwing Logan's mother into the mix.

Cally tried to let Logan's enthusiasm wash over her. She forced herself to focus on the positives. Maybe it would be an adventure. She had never done anything like it before, and while daunting, perhaps she should stop fretting and change her narrative. She'd try to look at it as an opportunity to experience something new, widen her mind, and broaden her horizons.

Logan handed her the invitation. 'Keep it in your bag so we don't lose it.'

Cally took the envelope, noting the weight of the expensive paper, and slipped it into her bag. She resolved to show it to Eloise and Birdie and get their take on it. They'd know what to do. Eloise would bestow her wisdom on her and yabber on about how she needed to stop being ridiculous.

'You're going to be great, Blackcurrant. I promise. Now, how about we finish this wine and then relax for the evening? Movie and the sofa? I feel they're calling.'

'That sounds perfect.'

With a box of Lovely chocolates on the coffee table, Cally settled back and tried to stop herself from making a mountain out of a molehill about the races. Here she was in a beautiful cottage with a man who adored her. She needed to remember that. Logan put his arm around her, she tucked her feet up under her, popped a chocolate in, and chose not to worry. Snuggled up beside Logan, she decided she would figure it out. She had to. She'd done a lot harder things in life. Tending to her grandma and raising herself sprang to mind. If she could work three jobs at the same time as studying for a degree whilst being in charge of wheelchairs, bed hoists, and the intricacies of her grandma's liquid diet, she could jolly well prance around in a dress and a silly hat, shaking hands and smiling at people. She would face the races, the fancy outfits, and the high-society event, and she would do it with her head held high and be confident. Or would she?

5

Cally walked out of her flat, down the steep stairs, and scooted across the first floor on her way to meet Nina. They were meeting to discuss another job at a property near the harbour and an extension to the decluttering job at Lovely Manor. As she made her way through the back of the deli and into the shop, she smiled at Alice and took in her surroundings. She loved living over the deli; the flat was close enough to be near to the bustle of Lovely, and she benefited from fabulous aromas of freshly baked bread and brewed coffee, but she was far enough above to be tucked up away from it all. She stood and looked around for a second at how nice everything was: the shelves lined with an assortment of bits and bobs, jars of home-made preserves, and beautiful teas, and everything else in between.

It wasn't only the aesthetics of the place, though. Cally slotted right in with the Lovelies and adored the warm atmosphere, the friendly buzz of conversation from the regulars, and the just general all-around comfiness of the place.

'Morning, our Alice,' Cally greeted. 'How are we? Keeping out of trouble?'

Alice looked up and returned the smile. 'Morning. How's your day going so far?'

'Just getting started with my *actual* day. I've been holed up on my laptop since the early hours, although it was very quiet. I think lots of people must be on holiday at the moment.'

'Yeah, they are. Every other person on Facebook is in Majorca or somewhere just as hot.'

'I reckon.'

'And I'm stuck here.' Alice rolled her eyes.

'There are worse places to be stuck in the world.' Cally noted with a chuckle.

'Yep, I guess so. What are you up to?'

'I'm meeting Nina to discuss a new job,' Cally replied, her tone cheerful.

Alice nodded. 'Busy as ever, our Nina. I don't know how she does it. She's always so organised and on top of everything and she does it all with Faye in tow half the time.'

Cally agreed. 'She's very good at what she does. Walks the talk, as it were. She puts me to shame.'

'So I'm told. I need her to organise my whole life. Coffee?'

'Yep. One for me and one for Neens. Lattes, please. Maybe a couple of scones, too, thanks. I'll get a table. Thanks,' Cally said, heading towards the front of the deli near the window.

As she settled at a table, she spotted Nina pushing her daughter Faye's pram past the window. With her shoulder up, wedging her phone against her ear, Nina, as usual, was multi-tasking. Nina looked in and waved as she went past. Cally went to the front door, opened it, and helped squeeze the pram around the little bistro-style tables. Nina finished her call, popped her phone on the table, navigated the pram into the corner behind Cally's chair, and sat down.

'Phew.' Nina gestured to Faye's pram. 'She was grizzling for England earlier. Overtired, I think. She really did get ratty. I didn't think she would ever drop off and then suddenly she was far away in the land of nod. So we can speak in peace, thank goodness. How are you?'

'I'm great.' Cally turned around and pointed to the pram where Faye's head was to the side, her eyes closed, one leg was resting up over the side of the pram and her pink dress was squidged up at the front. 'What a little sweetie. Aww, that dress.'

'I know. She's so funny. I'm so lucky she came along. It's weird I can't imagine life without her now.'

'Ahh. You are.'

Nina sighed happily and joked. 'I also like it when she's sound asleep. She picks her moments sometimes when she's ratty. I thought she was going to whinge all the way through this.'

'I bet.'

Nina looked over at the counter, 'Did you order?'

'Yeah, I got you a coffee.'

'Great. I need it. Right then. Ready to tackle another project?'

'Absolutely. What's the scoop?' Cally replied, eager to hear about the new job.

Nina gestured out the window. 'There's a beautiful old house near the harbour. The owner is an artist, and the place is filled with years of accumulated stuff. She wants to create a more organised space to work and live in. I scoped it out a good few months ago and heard nothing, but she wants to get going on it now. No exact date yet, though, so we'll see. Have you got any time coming up? Got much on?'

Cally nodded. 'No more than usual. The only thing in my diary really is the Chowder Festival.'

'You've not started on a course or anything yet?'

'Nope. I'm still not sure what I want to do. I may actually wait on that front and do it once I get a flat sorted. *If* I get a flat sorted.'

'Oh, right, okay. That's music to my ears then.'

'Ha.'

Nina shook her head. 'I have so much work. It's coming out of my ears. Who would have thought? It's just all grown by word-of-mouth. Can't complain.'

'Your reputation goes before you. That has a lot to do with it. What about the manor? I heard there's an extension there?'

Nina sighed, rolling her eyes slightly. 'Yes, more rooms to declutter. Apparently, Cecilia decided to open up the other wing. Did you hear that from Logan?'

'Yeah, more Doreen, really. I think she's concerned it will cause a lot more work for her.'

'I don't think she's wrong. Honestly, there is so much junk in there. Have you been in?'

Cally shook her head. 'No.'

'I wanted to run it past you. Are you up for it, or is it too weird for you to be working there now you're, well, an item with Logan? No worries at all. I wanted to ask you first. I'll put a post on Facebook if you're not interested.'

Cally mused for a second. It was a little bit tricky working at the manor now that she was going out with Logan. However, she was more interested in continuing to add to her savings account than feeling awkward. The equation was pretty simple: the more she worked, the quicker she'd be able to add to her savings for a deposit so that she would be able to buy a flat of her own. Saving and the deposit were driving just about everything she did, and she wasn't going to stop until she got what she wanted. Her decision was a quick one. 'I'm in.'

Alice brought over their coffees, placed the steaming mugs on the table, and added a plate of freshly baked scones. 'Here you go, ladies. Fresh out of the oven,' Alice said with a smile.

'Yum. These smell amazing.'

Alice winked. 'Enjoy!'

Nina took a sip of her coffee, sighing with contentment. 'Ah, I needed this. What a morning, already.'

Cally nodded. 'There's nothing like a good cup of coffee to kickstart the day, even though mine started at the crack of dawn.'

Nina leaned forward and frowned. 'So, you think you'll be fine working at the manor, even though you're now involved differently with it?'

Cally nodded and waved her hand dismissively. 'It'll be fine, yeah, not a problem. It is what it is and I love working with you.'

'Nobody even goes over to that side, do they? To that wing, I mean?' Nina clarified.

'No, not that I've seen, no.'

'So you'd probably not bump into anyone. Anyway, how have you been getting on with Logan?'

'Yes, great. I've actually just had an invitation to go to some fancy races. My first real Henry-Hicks family thing, as it were.'

Nina raised her eyebrows in surprise. 'Oh, wow, that sounds good.'

'Yeah, I don't know, I'm not sure. I've never been to the races, I've never been to anything like that,' Cally admitted. 'I'll have to meet the wider family, etcetera…'

Nina sucked air in through her teeth. 'Right, yeah, so you're not sure what to wear and all that?'

'No, no, I haven't a clue at all,' Cally confessed, shaking her head.

Nina smiled reassuringly. 'Yeah, it'll be good though, won't it? A new experience and all.'

Cally nodded, trying to muster up some enthusiasm. 'Yes, it will be. Just need to figure out the outfit situation. Logan mentioned his mum could help, but I think I'd rather do it on my own, to be quite honest.'

Nina chuckled. 'Understandable. You'll have to dip into the hat room.'

'I thought that! That was a funny day when we secretly tried on those hats.'

'Yup. Imagine having a whole room full of hats.'
'I know, right? I don't even really know where to start.'
'Don't worry about it. You'll look stunning.'
'I hope so.'

Cally picked up a scone and broke it in half as she wondered about the races. The more she thought about it, the more she felt as if her outfit was the least of her worries. Fitting in was going to be a whole different ball game altogether. Things were about to get interesting.

6

With a huge bag over her shoulder and her hands full with carrier bags, Cally was on her way to see Nancy at Lovely Lighthouse. Via Nancy's job at the railway, Nancy was involved in a fundraiser for the homeless in the city and was collecting equipment for a shelter. Cally had gathered loads of things from her place, from Birdie, and from her decluttering work at the manor. As she approached the lighthouse, she looked up as she always did and, as usual, was surprised by its vastness. Tall, eye-poppingly white, and towering over the town, it still managed to take her breath away every time she got close. She stood for a second with her chin raised and stared at the top, taking in the full height of its beauty.

Going around the back, she shifted the weight of the bags, made for the old hall and pushed open the door. The lighthouse smell greeted her as she stepped into the entrance area. Seeing not a soul around, she called out. Her voice echoed slightly in the open space. 'Hello. Anyone around? Nance?'

There was a shuffling sound from the back of the hall, and then Nancy's face appeared around a doorway. 'Our Cally!

We're out the back here in the kitchen. Come on in. I'm just putting the kettle on.'

Cally smiled and made her way towards Nancy, navigating around piles of boxes and bags.

'Blimey! Looks like you've had quite the haul of donations. I might have to have a root through and see what I can find.'

Nancy beamed, taking one of the bags from Cally's arms. 'Oh, you know how it is. Lovely Bay folks are always generous, but they've really outdone themselves this time. I think the upcoming Chowder Festival has got everyone in a giving mood. Now I just need to get a van and get this lot to the shelter. That will be a job and a half. Robby's lot are going to help out, hopefully.'

As they made their way into the small kitchen at the back of the building, Cally was impressed with Nancy's efforts.

'So, what have you got for us?' Nancy asked as she busied herself making a cup of tea.

Cally put her remaining bags on the floor. 'A kettle, I wasn't sure if you'd need to have that tested or not. Linens and a few other bits and bobs.'

As Nancy dipped teabags into mugs, the back door opened. Nancy gestured to Cally and the woman coming through the door. 'Pen, do you know our Cally? I wasn't sure if you two had met or not.'

Cally smiled at the woman. She held out her hand. 'No, we haven't met.'

The woman, Penny, smiled. 'No, but I feel like we should have met. I've heard so much about you.'

Cally had also heard about Penny mostly through Birdie and Alice. 'Same.'

Nancy chuckled. 'Cally, this is our Penny. She lives next door to me. Penny, this is our Cally. She's over the deli for now.'

'Oh, I didn't realise you were just by the green there.' Cally said, referring to the area of St. Lovely green where Nancy lived.

Nancy chimed in. 'Sorry, she is my neighbour, but she's not on the green but along the back there. You know the little lane that brings you out at the church? Amazing views there down to the river and the bay. True blue Lovely. We were at school together.'

Cally nodded. 'Ahh, right, yes. Nice spot.'

Penny smiled. 'It is a good bit of Lovely, where I am now.'

'Been there long?' Cally enquired.

Penny laughed. 'Ahh, just about all my life. Not this actual house.' She turned to Nancy. 'How long have I lived there now, Nance? Do you know? I couldn't tell you.'

Nancy blew air out of her lips. 'Has to be at least ten years. You were there well before me.'

'Yep, true.'

'Well, lucky you,' Cally said with a smile. 'I'm hoping to get a place in Lovely one day. I keep my fingers crossed at all times.'

Nancy smiled. 'Anyway. What have you been up to?'

'Nothing much and busy at the same time. I've been doing loads of stuff for Nina.'

'Oh, yeah. How's that going?'

'Fine. It's a job. Clearing out rich people's clutter has to be one way of making a living. How about you? Busy?'

Nancy rolled her eyes. 'What with doing this shelter volunteering and being in charge of the Chowder Festival, I don't know if I'm coming or going, to be quite honest with you. I'm a glutton for punishment. It keeps me busy.'

Penny widened her eyes. 'It sounds like it's going to be some festival this year. Colin is beside himself about it.'

Nancy nodded enthusiastically. 'He is. There's nothing quite like the buzz of festival day, though.'

Cally nodded. 'I've heard. There's been so much talk about it in the chemist.'

Penny continued addressing Cally. 'The people you meet at the festival – honestly, you'll get a crash course in Lovely Bay culture. So many locals come out of the woodwork or come back if they've left Lovely. It brings all sorts. I love festival weekend and the lead-up to it.'

'I'm looking forward to it. It will be different now I actually live here.'

'Yeah, it will be good.'

Nancy turned to Cally and joked. 'So, how are things going with that handsome fella of yours? How's Logan, or should I say lord of the manor?'

Cally attempted to sound casual. 'It's going well. Actually, I've been invited to a fancy family event at the races.'

Penny's eyebrows shot up. 'The races? Oh my, that is posh.'

'I'm a bit nervous, to be honest. It's not exactly my usual scene.'

Nancy let out a low whistle. 'Well, aren't you moving up in the world, our Cally? Rubbing shoulders with celebrities before we know it. We'll need to curtsy to you next.'

Penny nodded. 'They all have that air about them. That Henry-Hicks lot.'

Cally grimaced. 'It's a bit intimidating, if I'm honest.'

Nancy eye-rolled. 'You're every bit as good as those fancy folk, and don't you forget it.'

'Ha. I don't feel it.'

Penny chuckled. 'All you need is a huge hat. The hats are half the show, from what I've heard. Remember that year the Queen wore that bright yellow number? It was all over the telly.'

Cally's eyes widened. 'The Queen? Oh god, I hadn't even thought about that. What if I run into royalty?'

Penny chuckled. 'Don't you worry. Don't they tend to keep to themselves? Unless...' she trailed off, eyeing Cally speculatively.

'Unless what?' Cally asked, panic creeping into her voice.

'Well, where exactly are you going? There are different enclosures. Some posher than others, I think. Some you can't actually pay to get into. Invite-only.'

Cally wracked her brain, trying to remember what Logan had said. 'I think he mentioned something about the Royal Enclosure. Is that bad?'

Nancy and Penny exchanged looks of surprise. 'The Royal Enclosure?' Nancy repeated. 'Blimey, Cally. That's the crème de la crème.'

Penny nodded, looking impressed. 'Very exclusive.'

'Oh God. What have I got myself into? I don't know the first thing about horse racing or posh etiquette or anything!'

'What are you going to wear?'

'I haven't the foggiest! My usual wardrobe isn't exactly races-ready.'

Nancy shook her head. 'I reckon just don't go too over the top. You don't want to end up looking like you've got a garden party on your head. Some of those hats, I swear, must weigh a tonne.'

'Part of me thinks I might have to come up with an excuse. Maybe I should just tell Logan I can't go.'

'Don't you dare!' both Nancy and Penny exclaimed in unison.

'Just be yourself, wear a gorgeous dress and a fabulous hat, and be done with it. Make the most of it'

'And if all else fails, just smile and nod a lot. Works wonders in posh company, I find.'

Cally gulped. She wasn't sure if she wanted to find out.

7

Cally clicked the red button on the top left hand side of her new laptop's screen, sighed, pushed back her chair, and rolled her head from left to right. She'd spent a long six-hour shift working as Alex, the chatbot responder and it had not been one of her better experiences. The day had been a big, long loop of the same old problems she'd been dealing with for years and years. Sometimes, she just wanted to put a rude response on the screen just to see how it would kick off. However, needing her wages at the end of the week always put paid to doing that. One day, though, she'd do it just for a laugh. How funny it would be to tell one of the customers that she didn't give a hoot and couldn't care less that their silk blouse had shrunk on a hand wash. She chuckled to herself at the thought.

Pushing her chair back, she went into the kitchen, poured a fair old helping of blackcurrant cordial into a glass mug, flicked the switch on the top of the kettle, and waited for it to boil. Once she had her cup of hot drink, she shuffled into the sitting room, moved her laptop from the desk, propped it up on a pile of books on the coffee table, and prepared to video chat with Eloise. She clicked Eloise's number and waited for it to connect.

A few seconds later, Eloise's face appeared on the screen. 'Hiya. How are you? What's up?'

'How do you know something is up?'

'You wanted to video call. I always *know* that's serious.' Eloise joked.

'Sometimes I think you know me better than I know myself.'

'Yup.'

'So...'

'Oh dear, oh dear. Do I need a gin for this? Intravenous vodka?'

'I have this invite.'

'To?'

'The races and not just any old races.'

'Ouch.' Eloise sucked air in through her teeth. 'I know where this is going.'

'Precisely.'

'It's like sponsored by the manor, as in not just a race but the whole shebang.' Cally flashed the invitation in front of the screen.

Eloise swore. 'This is huge. Your feet are well and truly under the table. It'll be wedding bells next.'

Cally made a funny shrieking noise. 'Ahh, don't say that!'

'You need outfit assistance, I assume?'

Cally nodded. 'Tell me about it. Which is why I'm video calling you.'

Eloise made a wincing face. 'I'm not sure I can help you with this. I'm not qualified on what to wear to the races.'

'You have to! I'm desperate, or I will be.'

Eloise chuckled. 'Okay, okay. First things first, do you have any idea what kind of thing you might like?' Eloise raised her eyebrows. 'And not your usual school uniform look.'

Cally shook her head. 'I *like* my uniform. It's nice and safe. Not a clue. Something elegant but not too over the top.'

'Sheesh.'

'I don't want to look like I'm trying too hard, but I also don't want to look like I don't belong.'

'Right, balance is key. Colours. Don't they always wear pastels and suchlike? Princess Kate always nails it. Follow her lead. Google the heck out of her.'

Cally shuddered. 'Honestly, don't even go there.'

'Or something with a floral print?'

'I'll look like my grandma's curtains,' Cally stated morosely.

'Trouser suit?'

'Nope.'

Eloise nodded. 'As I said, I reckon pastels are always a good choice for the races. Nothing too busy.'

Cally sighed. 'This is already feeling overwhelming. Why? Why do I have to put myself through this?'

'Don't worry, we'll sort it out. Do you need a hat?'

Cally groaned. 'Logan mentioned his mum and her hat collection. Little does he know that I had the job of decluttering it a few months ago. Oh, the irony. It's like Cinderella goes to the ball, but in my case, it's the races.'

'Hats are tricky.'

'I think it's a given that I'll be wearing something on my head. I need to google the dress code.'

'Go subtle.'

'Subtle, definitely. I don't want to feel like I have a satellite dish on my head. You see some horrors in the Daily Mail.'

Eloise laughed. 'Too easy then. Heels?'

'Probably heels, but nothing too high. I need to be able to walk without wobbling.'

'Do you have any shoes that might work already?'

Cally shook her head. 'Me? God no! I have ballet flats, boots and a few pairs of past-their-best trainers. Nope, I'll need to get a new pair of heels. I need everything new! Which is why I'm panicking. It's going to dent my savings and then some.'

'Okay, so we're looking for a dress, a hat, and shoes. We can do this. Have you got any ideas where to shop?'

'No.'

'You should go somewhere nice. Start early, have a nice lunch, and make a day of it.'

'Yeah, maybe.'

'Show me the invitation again.'

Cally pulled the invitation from her bag and held it up to the camera. 'Here it is. The races, sponsored by Lovely Manor. It's all very fancy.'

Eloise examined the invitation on the screen. 'Very fancy indeed. Leave it to me. We'll go somewhere nice and come back with the whole thing done and dusted. Make a day of it. Honestly, don't stress.'

'I hope you're right. Yes, okay we'll organise something.'

Eloise nodded. 'Trust me, I'm a doctor.'

'No, you're not.'

'I know. Sounds good, though.'

Cally wasn't quite as sure. The closer it got, the less and less she fancied the races at all.

8

A couple of days or so later and after another particularly long and gruelling chatbot shift, Cally made herself a cup of hot blackcurrant, ran a very deep bath, poured in a long stream of bubble bath under the tap, sloshed a measure of gin in her drink for good measure, dropped her clothes on the bathroom floor and lowered herself down in the water. Nice.

Up to her neck in posh bubbles bought for her by Logan, she sipped on the alcoholic blackcurrant and googled what to wear to the races. She skimmed the first ten entries and then swallowed and re-checked the invitation. So much for worrying about what to wear. The dress code was so tight there wasn't much room for manoeuvre. There would be no fascinator in the enclosure Cally would be entering. The dress code was *that* strict that it only allowed hats, and not any old hats either, but hats of a certain diameter. Ditto the length of one's skirt. Clicking on the second search result Cally looked at the pictures of what outfits were suitable and which were very much not. She ran her eyes down the list of prohibited outfits and let out a strange blow of air through a weird, crooked shape in her mouth. Yikes.

Sinking deeper into the fragrant bubbles with steam rising around her in spirals she learned all about the ins and outs of what was acceptable to wear to the prestigious event she didn't really give a stuff about going to. The glow of her phone illuminated her face as she scrolled through it in the odd little cramped bathroom, with its slightly chipped tiles and dated fixtures, which seemed a world away from the glamour and prestige of what she was reading about.

She took another sip of her blackcurrant and gin concoction, wincing slightly at its strength and as she delved deeper into the strict dress code, her eyes widened and she shook her head. The list of requirements seemed endless: dresses and skirts of modest length falling just above the knee or longer; no shoulder straps or of at least one inch in width; jackets and pashminas could be worn, but the dress had to comply with the rules. And then there were the hats - proper hats with a solid base of four inches or more in diameter. No fascinators allowed whatsoever.

Cally let out another weird, windy groan, her head tilting back to rest against the edge of the tub. The ceiling above her had a small patch of mould in the corner, a stark contrast to the opulence she was reading about. Not for the first time, she found herself wondering if she truly belonged in Logan's world.

The water began to cool, and Cally reached out with her toes to turn on the hot tap, careful not to splash her phone as she plonked her leg back in. As the steaming water poured in, she scrolled further, her heart sinking with each thing she read. The enclosure, she discovered, as Penny, Nancy's neighbour, had said, was invitation only. It wasn't simply a matter of rocking up, buying a ticket, and dressing up a bit to make yourself look fancy. Oh no, this was a world of tradition, of unspoken rules and social nuances. Cally already felt uppity about the situation, now her nerves had *quadrupled*. She feared she might never fully grasp any of the stuff she was reading about. She pictured herself surrounded by the crème de la crème of British society. Not really her cup of tea at all.

Putting her phone down on the bath caddy, she watched as a droplet of water rolled down the side of the bath and then took another swig of her drink hoping it might quell the growing unease in her stomach. It didn't do anything of the sort.

Sitting up, her hazy reflection, partially fogged from the steam, caught her eye in the mirror. She saw herself and shook her head. She was so far from one of the polished, sophisticated women she'd just read about, it wasn't even funny. With her baby-blonde fuzzy hair piled messily on top of her head, face free of makeup, surrounded by bubbles in a bathtub that had seen better days, polished was not a word that sprung to mind. How could she possibly fit in and move in the circles of Logan's world? Not only that, was she interested? Not in the slightest.

She thought back to their first meeting, how charmed she'd been by his confidence and easy manner. Logan had swept her off her feet, introducing her to a life she'd not only never seen but not even glimpsed from afar. Fancy restaurants, weekend getaways to picturesque countryside hotels, and now, going to the races dressed up to the nines had not been on her radar in any shape or form. It had all seemed a bit like a fairy tale at first, but sitting in her bath, in the flat above the deli, Cally did not now feel like Cinderella. Rather, she felt woefully unprepared and *way* out of her depth.

The dress code swam before her eyes as she picked up her phone again. Formal daywear, it insisted. Dresses and skirts of modest length. Trouser suits permitted, but must be full-length and of matching material and colour. No culottes, no shorts, no off-the-shoulder, halter neck, spaghetti straps, or strapless dresses. The list seemed to go on and on forever. So many do's and don'ts. A multitude of things to get wrong.

She sank lower in the bath, letting the warm water lap at her chin and tried to picture herself in one of the outfits she'd seen:

a fitted dress to her calf in a pastel shade, a wide-brimmed matching hat perched, carefully styled hair. A square peg in a round hole. Turning heads for all the wrong reasons.

The doubts that had been simmering beneath the surface for ages that she'd been able to squash now bubbled up with renewed vigour. She shook her head. Was she really cut out for this life? Would she ever truly fit into Logan's world, with its unspoken rules and expectations that everyone else would clearly just know, having been brought up with it all? And more importantly, did she want to?

Cally looked around at the shabby little bathroom, which wasn't even hers. It was more her world: unpretentious, lived-in, real, and a bit raggedy around the edges. Topping up with a bit more fresh, hot water, she inhaled deeply. The scent of the expensive bubble bath Logan had bought her filled her nostrils. Even that, she realised, was a reminder of the world she was trying to adapt to. A world of luxury and excess, where even something as simple as bath products came with a hefty price tag and an air of exclusivity. She now circulated with people who had rooms full of hats.

She sighed and decided to change her narrative otherwise she'd end up driving herself around the twist. She needed to flip the way she was thinking. Yes, the dress code was daunting. Yes, the thought of mingling with the upper echelons of society was intimidating. Yes, she wasn't really that interested. But she decided to look at it in a different way. Let it in and see where it would take her. If she met it head-on, she might, in fact, enjoy it. See what doors opened. If Cinderella could do it, why couldn't she? She was about to find out.

9

Two days later, Cally had thought a lot about the races. On the one hand, she was all over the show, but on the other, she'd decided that, for once in her life, she would take the bull by the horns and go all-in in her preparation and actually try to make the run-up a good thing. Cinderella would, in fact, scrub herself up and jolly well go to the ball. Not only that, if it was the last thing she did, she was going to enjoy it.

In light of that, she'd decided to get her nails done as a trial run to see what was what. She'd found herself sitting in a nail bar with her feet dangling in water, a pair of flip-flops beside her, and a cup of hot blackcurrant in her hand. What looked to her like coloured water bubbled and fizzed around her ankles. A woman shoved a white tub full of long plastic strips with nail varnish colours on the ends towards her and said something to her she couldn't quite understand. Cally had never had her nails done before and surrounded by millions of bottles of polishes, bright lights, and a lot of activity, she didn't really have a clue what was going on. It was a whole other world to her and she wasn't quite sure what to think about it at all. She took her surroundings in as a gigantic bronze massage chair pummelled her back and a girl in a mask yanked a tiny red stool on wheels from another station, plonked herself down, snapped latex gloves over her hands, grabbed the tops of Cally's feet out of the water, placed them on the towel-covered edge of the foot bath and studied Cally's toenails with a frown.

The girl then gesticulated to the little plastic sticks in the tub with her eyebrows raised. Cally shook her head, grabbed the tub, looked through a few of the plastic strips and, plumping for the least offensive, safest colour, pointed to the number underneath a pale pink dab on the end of a white plastic stick. The girl then shouted the number to someone on the other side of the room, flicked a towel from a trolley, and pulled out two bright yellow foam toe dividers that she pushed in between Cally's toes.

Cally smiled as the woman dabbed a huge tube of white lotion on her cuticles, then sat back and looked around. Various people in front of her sat at stations with their hands out in front of them and foam spacers between their toes. After a few minutes, she tuned into the woman sitting to her left who was speaking way too loudly into her phone.

'Yeah, I went to the gym this morning, and then I went out for a walk and sat by the rocks looking out over the sea. Then I went for a massage and to the sauna because I just needed to chill out, you know? After that, I had a really nice lunch at the bistro there. I might have slipped in a quick glass of wine. Ha! You know how it is.'

Inside, Cally rolled her eyes. She may have tutted.

'It's so stressful having children. I mean, I know they're in school all day, but you know?'

There was a pause for a moment as the woman listened and then continued. 'I know, right? Let me tell you, Gabs, I have all my meals delivered these days. No way do I have time for food shopping and cooking, you know?'

Another pause.

'Yeah, right. I need to rush out of the house doing school runs and ballet and stuff, you know?'

The conversation moved to where she was going that evening.

'I've got this lace bodysuit. I was going to wear that with a leather skirt and boots which are high but comfy. I've got my black shoes too, which I could wear.' The woman waved foil-wrapped fingers around in front of her. Cally stole a glance further to her left and took in the woman's filled lips and bladed eyebrows as she continued to yabber on about how hard her life was. She then stopped talking for a minute, leant forwards, squinted at her toenails, and proceeded to admire her pedicure. Cally shook her head to herself as she listened to the woman whining about how stressed she was. Cally sighed; she'd clearly gone wrong somewhere in life. She turned a bit further to her left and took in the golden tan, perfectly coloured hair, the workout clothes with the obnoxiously expensive logo, and the diamond flashing underneath the downlights.

'Oh, we're going to get a boat in the harbour.'

Cally growled in her head. Sometimes, she felt as if entitled people were purposely trying to not only irritate her but also illuminate just how different their lives were from hers. Here was this woman, not knowing she was born, sitting there complaining about her life in the same breath as talking about having her meals delivered and her visits to the sauna, all whilst sitting in a nail bar with someone tending her feet while on her thousand-pound phone. First-world problems.

Cally didn't *want* to feel envious, unkind or, let's be honest, downright catty, but listening to the whining made her want to grab the woman by the neck and tell her to get a grip. That would go down like a sack of potatoes. She leant back on the nobbly bits kneading her mid-back, closed her eyes for a second, and inhaled as the woman continued to blab on so that the whole salon had little choice but to listen in to the trials and tribulations of her oh-so-very-hard life.

Trying to tune out the conversation, Cally opened her eyes, stared out the window, and watched as a large, black, shiny Mercedes pulled into the curb. A woman with her phone to her ear got out of the car, closed the door, grabbed a bag from the back seat, clicked a button and scooted inside. Every single one of the workers in the shop sat up a bit straighter as the woman hustled in. The girl who was sweeping brushed a bit faster and two girls came running out from the back. The woman, clearly the owner, appeared busy, rich, successful and very much in charge.

Cally watched in fascination as even whilst speaking in a language Cally couldn't understand, the woman's voice dripped power and confidence. She listened as the woman switched to English and spoke quickly into her phone. She was clearly instructing someone in another nail shop about something to do with a payment dongle. As the conversation went on, it was clear there was a chain of shops under this businesswoman's command. Cally looked her up and down. Nail bars were clearly a good business venture. She'd underestimated the sort of wealth that could be accumulated from them, or the place was doing another sort of business underneath the table and not the application of fancy American gel polish.

As Cally sat there, her feet again submerged in the bubbling, fizzing water, she was impressed at the scene unfolding before her. She watched as the woman who had just entered the salon swept through the room like a queen, her head held high and her eyes sharp and focused. She moved with a sense of purpose and authority, her every gesture radiating a fab woman in control.

Cally felt a twinge of envy as she observed the woman, taking in her impeccable appearance and the way she commanded the attention and respect of everyone around her.

From her perfectly coiffed hair and flawless makeup to her designer clothes and expensive accessories, everything about her screamed success and achievement. Cally couldn't get enough of it even though it felt like a stark contrast to her own life. She leant her head back against the rest and thought about the years she'd spent putting her own dreams and aspirations on hold as she'd cared for her grandma. She'd struggled to make ends meet and endeavoured to keep all the balls up in the air. She'd always told herself that it was temporary, that once her responsibilities were fulfilled and she had some money behind her, she'd finally be able to focus on herself and pursue the things that mattered most to her. But it felt a little bit as if time had run away with itself. She'd been stuck not only in a rut, but as the years had stretched on and the challenges had mounted, she'd stagnated, too. She'd felt as if her life was passing her by while everyone else moved forward and achieved their goals. In actual fact, the sad reality was that not only had she not achieved goals, she hadn't even had any in the first place. She'd *not* gone off to university, *not* started a career, *not* had a decent relationship, *not* thought about settling down, *not* really done anything except care and wait. All the while, she'd remained frozen in place, trapped by circumstance and obligation and holding up that blooming sky every day of the week.

And now, sitting in a nail bar, surrounded by women who seemed to have it all figured out, she felt a flush of embarrassment. She knew it was more than futile to compare, but she did it anyway. Well aware that comparisonitis never ended well and that she shouldn't measure her own worth and value against material possessions and outward appearances, she ploughed on. A vile, nagging voice in the back of her mind whispered that she was so far behind that she'd never, ever catch up.

She thought about the woman on the phone, with her designer workout clothes and her meals delivered to her door, complaining about the stresses and strains of a life that seemed like a dream to Cally. She pondered the nail bar owner and how nice it might feel to run her own business, be in charge of her life.

The girl in front of her flicked her hand as if to say she was finished and brought Cally back to the room. She looked down at her now very pretty toes and wiggled them, marvelling at how different they looked. She couldn't quite get her head around it. She'd treated herself to a bit of self-care, and her feet now looked as if they belonged to someone else. Polished and put-together even. She nodded to herself, fairly impressed. How bizarre; an hour in a nail bar had resulted in great things. Yes, she had spent most, if not all, of her life putting her own dreams and desires on hold and sacrificing her own happiness and well-being for the sake of others. But somehow, one little pedicure had shown her that it was time to start living for herself. It was time for our Cally to start chasing dreams of her own. There was just one little hurdle to get over before she did.

10

After the night in the bath taking in everything about the races and initially getting herself in a right old two and eight about her outfit, Cally had forced herself to stop panicking and overthinking. Instead, as Eloise had suggested, she had planned to make a day out of shopping for the races outfit. Why ever not? Her experience in the nail bar had made her adamant about making the preparation for the races a good thing. She was determined to make it something to enjoy. Therefore, she'd invited Eloise on a day out and they had planned to turn outfit shopping into an expedition, including a nice long and possibly boozy lunch. Things had been worse. Cally had meticulously planned out a day for them both, worked out her finances and couldn't quite believe it when she'd actually started to look forward to it.

After meeting Eloise at a train station, they took a fast train to a pretty Georgian spa town and headed for a historic shopping area renowned for its unique boutiques and picturesque setting—a perfect place to shop for a fancy outfit. After walking around the lovely streets for a while with a takeaway coffee from Gail's, they headed to a heritage colonnade walkway with elegant columns and old-fashioned tiled pavements.

Walking along next to Eloise, Cally looked down at the map on her phone, worked out where to go, and they made their way to a heritage-listed shopping arcade. After her research in the bath, she'd decided to go all in and spend some of her hard-earned savings on a dress, matching hat, and shoes to ensure that she was properly attired. She'd found a few places that catered specifically for the occasion and had decided to throw caution to the wind, for once in her life, not worry about money and get the shop to kit her out from head to toe. Job done.

She felt quite apprehensive about trying to find an outfit but kept her mouth shut and felt determined to stick to her plan. She would no longer be defined by what her old life had given her. Goodbye doubt and overthinking, hello newfound confidence. As they got to the shop Cally had found online, she hesitated at the entrance, her hand hovering over an ornate brass door handle. Taking a deep breath, she steeled herself, pushed the door open, held it open for Eloise, and stepped in.

The shop was quieter than she'd expected. Plush carpeting muffled their footsteps, and a rainbow of pastel colours lined the walls. Soft music played, and everything felt calm, peaceful almost. Oh, how the other half shopped. Pound shop retail, this was not.

'Hello, how are you today?' An assistant asked with a friendly smile and hushed tone.

'Good, thanks.'

'Anything I can help you with, or are you just having a look around?'

'Just having a look. Actually, no, we're not. I'm going to the races and I'm really not sure what to wear.'

'You're in the right place,' the woman smiled. 'By the way, I'm Sophie.'

'I'm Cally and this is my friend, Eloise. She came along for a bit of moral support. I've never been to the races before.'

The assistant rubbed her hands together. 'Ooh, you're in for a right treat then. What section will you be in?'

'Section?'

'Sorry, I meant what enclosure? So we know the dress code.'

Cally suddenly went blank for a second or two. She fumbled in her bag, pulling out the slightly crumpled invitation. She squinted at it before looking up. 'The Royal Enclosure.'

The woman gaped. 'Wow, right, okay. Hold on a minute, I'll get Barbara.'

A few minutes later, an older, impeccably dressed woman emerged from the back. Her silver hair was coiffed perfectly into a chignon, and she carried herself with an air of quiet authority. Barbara beamed and put a pair of half-moon glasses on as she approached. 'Hello, there. I hear you're going to the Royal Enclosure. What an absolute treat. Lucky you!'

'Yes.' Cally gulped. She felt far from lucky. 'I have nothing to wear and no idea.'

Barbara raised her eyebrows, looked Cally up and down and smiled. 'Oh, don't you worry about that. You have nothing to worry about in the slightest.'

'No?'

Eloise smiled. 'See, I told you.'

'We do all the worrying for you,' Sophie added.

'Right.'

Barbara squinted over the top of her glasses. 'And you, my lovely, you, are going to look amazing. Trust me. I know a good start when I see one.'

Sophie beamed. 'Barbara is an absolute expert at this, aren't you?'

Barbara nodded. 'I am, indeed. If there is one thing I know, it's what to wear to the races. I've been doing this job for a very long time. Too long, some might say!'

Eloise rubbed her hands together. 'Let the fun begin.'

For the next ten minutes, Cally found herself in a whirlwind of fabric and fashion advice. Barbara and Sophie knew what they were doing. They were so nice about it, too, and worked together seamlessly, pulling dresses from racks and discussing colours and cuts in a language that seemed foreign to Cally. She sucked it up and went with the flow. Newly confident Cally was quite enjoying the ride.

Barbara handed Cally the first dress to try on. 'The Royal Enclosure has very strict rules. Dresses and skirts should be of modest length, falling just above the knee or longer. We know the ins and outs of it. Everything here is designed to conform.'

Cally nodded, disappearing into the plush changing room. She emerged a few moments later in a pink dress with cap sleeves, feeling like a sack of potatoes with a belt in the middle.

Eloise clapped her hands together. 'Oh, that's lovely!'

But Barbara shook her head. 'Gosh, no. Dreadful. The colour washes you out and that is not the shape for you. Let's try something else.'

Back into the changing room, Cally went. This time, she came out in a navy blue dress with a high neckline and long bell sleeves.

Eloise shook her head and Barbara pursed her lips. 'Too severe,' she said, shaking her head. 'We want to accentuate everything about you. You are very easy to work with, isn't she Sophie?'

Sophie nodded and chuckled. 'Very.'

The next dress, a yellow, fairly flowing affair, was promptly vetoed for being too casual. A black and white polka dot number Barbara felt was trying too hard on Cally's small frame and a flowing maxi dress in emerald green had Cally tripping over the hem.

'This is hopeless,' Cally sighed, slumping onto a velvet

ottoman outside the changing room. 'Maybe I'm just not cut out for this.'

Barbara rolled her eyes. 'Nonsense. We just haven't found the right dress yet. Dresses are like love – when you find the right one, you'll know.'

Sophie appeared then, a garment bag draped carefully over her arm. 'This just came in yesterday. I have a good feeling about this one. I was unpacking them earlier.'

Cally trailed along behind Sophie with a weary smile and disappeared once more into the changing room's entrance. As Sophie unzipped the bag, Cally gasped. The dress inside was white with a high-neck lace-covered bodice with fitted sleeves, a narrow nipped-in waist, and full skirt. She took it into the changing room and slipped it on, immediately noticing how it felt good in all the right places. The neckline was modest yet flattering, and the hem hit just below her knees. Taking a deep breath, she stepped out of the changing room.

The reaction was immediate. Sophie gasped, her hands flying to her mouth. Eloise squealed, Barbara's eyes widened and she beamed. 'Why didn't I go with white in the first place? Now, that is a dress fit for the Royal Enclosure. Stunning on you. I know we aren't allowed to mention our bodies these days, but what a figure. Amazing!'

Cally turned to look in the full-length mirror, barely recognising herself. The dress was elegant and sophisticated, yet it still felt like her. She stood straighter, already feeling more confident. The delicate dress, with its high neckline, long sleeves, and fitted bodice, gave her a demure but goodness-knows-how sophisticated look. The lace detailing added a dainty and feminine touch. Her waist looked teeny-tiny. She loved it and possibly even herself, too.

'It doesn't look like me. But it's perfect,' Cally breathed.

'Not quite. We still need to find you a hat.'

What followed was another whirlwind of trying on, this time with hats of all shapes and sizes.

Eloise laughed out loud at the first one. 'It makes you look like you've been eaten by a UFO.'

Cally giggled, peering out from under the enormous brim and Sophie laughed. They then tried pillbox hats ("Too Jackie O," according to Barbara), elegant straw ("Nice, but not quite right for the Royal Enclosure"), and everything in between. Just as Cally was beginning to despair about ever finding the right hat, the last one was the winner, with a gently curved brim and a delicate flower detail sitting on the hairline underneath.

'This is it,' Cally said confidently as she placed it on her head. 'This is the one. I can feel it.'

Barbara nodded approvingly. 'Yes, that's it. Nude shoes and bag, and we're done here. Too easy.'

For the first time since receiving the invitation, Cally felt a flutter of excitement about attending the event. She even twirled in front of the mirror, watching as the dress swirled around her legs. She turned to Barbara and Sophie. 'Thank you. I came in here feeling so lost, and now, I do not at all. In actual fact, I feel amazing.'

'You look it for sure.' Sophie trilled. 'I love it when it goes like this.'

'Yes, me too.' Barbara agreed.

Eloise nodded. 'And me. You look so pretty, Cal. I love it. This has been one very sweet day already and we haven't even had our boozy lunch yet.'

Cally chuckled. 'We can go and actually enjoy it now.'

'Yup, and you, my friend, are going to the races dressed up to the nines. Just wait until Logan sets eyes on you in that. He's going to die.'

11

Cally and Birdie had just finished working at the chemist. They'd locked up the shop and were on their way to the old hall nestled behind the lighthouse for a Chowder Festival town meeting. As they approached, they could hear the sound of a few people talking inside and a couple of groups were standing on the pavement chatting. They made their way around the front of the lighthouse, into the backyard and let themselves in the back of the hall where rows of chairs were lined up in front of the stage and various people were standing around talking.

They weaved in and out of a scattering of Lovelies, exchanging a few words here and there, and said hello to Alice from the deli. Cally looked around at the old hall as she stood next to Birdie as Birdie conversed with one of the regulars from the chemist. The beautiful old lighthouse hall was another thing Cally loved about the little town. With its exquisitely crafted wooden floors, high ceilings and walls adorned with faded photographs and paintings depicting the town's maritime history, it seemed to encapsulate the history of the place in a nutshell. The hall was warm and busy with Lovelies and began to fill up as Cally and Birdie made their way to a couple of seats in the middle in the second row from the front.

Cally settled herself down and looked up at the small stage where a few chairs had been set out in front of thick, heavy, blue velvet curtains. Nancy, with her Lovely coat draped over the back, sat in one of the chairs, and Colin stood in front of a timber lectern, fussing with a tablet and a bunch of papers. Colin was very clearly in charge, not only that he revelled in it. His twin brother Clive, with his glasses on, was sitting adjacent to Nancy, looking down at his phone. As the last few stragglers took their seats, Colin rose to his feet and pointedly tapped on the top of the lectern with a stick at the same time as peering out at the hall. The room fell silent almost immediately, all eyes turning to the front. Let the Lovely show begin.

'Right then. I think we can get started. Welcome, everyone, to another planning meeting for this year's Chowder Festival. We've got a lot to cover, so let's dive right in, shall we? This year is going to be our biggest and best yet, isn't it?'

There was a ripple of agreement through the hall, a rustling of papers and scraping of a few chairs. Cally slipped her phone out of her pocket, opened her Notes app and balanced her phone on her bag, which was resting on her knee. Colin looked down, consulted his notes for a second and then looked back up with raised eyebrows. 'First item on the agenda: the chowder competition. As you all know, the speakeasies are the heart and soul of the festival, but the competition is a fun addition. We need to make sure we have a diverse range of chowders represented, from the traditional to the innovative. Nancy, I believe you're in charge of this again this year.' Colin looked over at Nancy with his eyebrows raised in question.

Nancy nodded. 'I'm happy to report that we've got a record number of participants this year.'

Colin looked pleased. He tapped the top of his tablet and nodded. 'Excellent. Brilliant work, our Nancy. That's fantastic.'

He squinted out in the direction of the hall as a side door opened, and a latecomer came rushing in. He waited and then continued. 'We're expecting a record number of visitors to the third smallest town in the country this year. I, along with the committee, thank you, Birdie, have been working with the local tourism board to promote the festival, and the response has been overwhelming. We're going to have people coming from all over the place, so it's going to be great for Lovely! It's all about putting our town on the map, as it were.'

As the discussion turned to logistics and the nitty-gritty details of event planning, everything from parking arrangements to closing the roads to the council toilets, Cally found herself tuning out for a bit.

Birdie leaned over and joked in a whisper. 'I heard a rumour that the BBC might be sending a film crew this year. We'll make the national news.'

Cally smiled. 'I hope not. I want this place to stay a secret. At least until I've bought a flat. Ha.'

Birdie raised her chin in Colin's direction. 'I don't think the BBC could cope with our Colin's rules and regulations.'

About an hour later, as the meeting wrapped up, Cally stood, stretching her legs and rolling her shoulders. The hall filled with a buzz of conversation and the scraping of chairs. Cally smiled at Birdie as she gathered her things and put her bag over her shoulder. 'Well, that was comprehensive. Colin is a force to be reckoned with.'

'I think he covered everything short of the molecular structure of chowder.' Birdie joked.

Cally chuckled. 'Don't give him ideas, or we'll never make it out of here.'

They made their way to the refreshment table at the back of the hall, where a spread of biscuits, tea, a few bottles of wine and beer had been laid out. Nancy was standing pouring a glass of wine and looked a bit frazzled.

'All good?' Birdie asked.

Nancy rolled her eyes. 'You have no idea. Colin's on form. Say no more. He'll be taking our inside leg measurements next. He needs a chill pill.'

Cally glanced over to where Colin was still at the front, surrounded by a group of Lovelies, gesticulating wildly as he no doubt expounded on some minute detail of festival planning. Just then, the side door opened, and Cally saw Logan step into the hall. Looking slightly out of place in smart work clothes, she watched as his eyes scanned the room. He smiled and waved when he saw her. She felt a flutter in her stomach as she waved back.

As he made his way through the crowd, nodding hellos to a few people, Birdie nudged Cally with her elbow. 'Looks like someone's come to sweep you off your feet. Or at least rescue you from another hour of Colin. Prince Charming has officially entered the building.'

'I think he might have to save us all.' Cally said with a smile.

Logan charmed as he reached them. 'Ladies. Good evening. How are we all? I hope I'm not interrupting anything important?'

Nancy chuckled. 'We were just discussing how we can get Colin to calm down about the festival. Care to weigh in with any advice on that?'

'I wouldn't dare! How's it all going?' Logan asked. 'Everything under control?'

'Yeah, fine. I think everyone has had their roles assigned. We've been planning since last year. It's all downhill from here on in.'

'All that's needed then is to make sure Lovely delivers on the weather.' Logan noted.

'The one thing our Colin cannot guarantee.' Nancy said with a chuckle. 'Though, if he could find a way, I am sure he would try to make it happen.'

Birdie laughed. 'He would. If he could order sunshine and warm weather, it would be on his list.'

Logan smiled. 'I heard he's going all out on the bunting and lights this year.'

Nancy frowned. 'How do you know that?'

'There may have been a call to the manor for assistance.'

'He's a one, isn't he?' Birdie laughed.

'Lovely Manor may have donated a thing or two.' Logan noted.

'Makes sense.' Nancy nodded. 'I wondered about that. He doesn't leave a stone unturned.'

'Nope.'

Birdie joked. 'You wouldn't want to make an enemy of him around here.'

'Definitely not.'

Logan widened his eyes. 'I wouldn't want to make an enemy of anyone around here.'

'True that.' Nancy nodded.

Birdie agreed. 'Yep.'

Nancy looked directly at Logan and joked. 'You don't want to be upsetting any Lovelies, especially our Cally here.'

They all chuckled, and Cally felt a warm, Lovely fuzz at being included in the little community. Shame she didn't quite know what was around the corner. It would soon take more than a Lovely fuzz to make her feel better.

12

It was a few weeks following the expedition to get the dress. Cally had risen at the crack of dawn for chatbot work and made her way to the manor, not as Logan's girlfriend but working for Nina's company, A Lovely Organised Life. She had wanted the job for the financial reward, but, to be frank, she hadn't quite fancied bumping into Logan's mum or his aunt Cecilia as she went about her business. Bottom line, she was basically doing their dirty work for them and it was rather tricky all around. Cleaning out the stuff of over-indulged people who lived a very different life to her had its downsides. As she arrived at the manor, she felt a pang of awkwardness. There was a glaring contrast between her role as a worker at the manor and her occasional presence in its social settings. She again felt doubt about her place as if there was a huge elephant in the room that would only be amplified a millionfold at the races. Determined not to jump down that rabbit hole, she stuck her nose in the air and clutched her new confidence tightly to her chest.

Just as she was checking her phone for the code to punch into the pad on the door of the east wing, Doreen, the housekeeper, with a huge trug of hydrangeas in her arms, came the other way.

Doreen smiled. 'Hey, our Cally, how are you?'

'Great, thanks. You?'

'Yeah, good, thanks. Coffee?' Doreen asked.

'Love one before I get going.'

'Good to see you.'

'You too.'

'How do you think you'll get on with the storage rooms?' Doreen asked as Cally fell into step beside her and they made their way to the old, original part of the manor house.

'Not too bad as long as we crack on.'

As they entered the huge old kitchen, the aroma of freshly baked bread wafted through the air. Doreen bustled around and inhaled. 'Nothing beats the smell of fresh bread, don't you think?'

Cally smiled, inhaling deeply. 'It smells heavenly. You're so clever.' She looked up at the gleaming copper pots hanging from a rack above the large, central kitchen table and the huge old Aga on the far wall. Sunlight streamed through the windows, landing in a puddle on the well-worn wooden floorboards and loads of bunches of lavender scented the room.

'Sit yourself down. I'll put the kettle on,' Doreen said, gesturing to the large, farmhouse-style table.

Cally sank into one of the chairs and chatted as Doreen filled the kettle and put it on the Aga.

'What time will Nina arrive?' Doreen asked.

Cally checked her phone. 'Not sure.'

'Will I make her a coffee?'

'Yep, she might just need to warm it up.'

'She'll need coffee for her work this week. That's a big job, that is. Those rooms haven't been touched in years, as far as I can remember.'

Cally nodded, watching as Doreen gathered mugs from a

cupboard. 'I think there is a lot of history over there, just waiting to be discovered.'

Doreen smiled. 'Oh, I'm sure there are plenty of secrets hidden away in this old house. If these walls could talk, they'd have stories to tell. You don't know what you might find…'

'Hopefully nothing bad.' Cally chuckled.

Doreen set two mugs of coffee down on the table with a clink. 'Now, what's this I hear about you going to the races with the family? That's quite the occasion.'

Cally's stomach turned over and steam curled up into the air as she took her coffee. 'Oh, yes. It's a bit overwhelming, to be honest.'

'Ah, well, it's the highlight of the social calendar around here. Not long now. All the posh folks come out in their finest, sipping champagne and showing off for the Lovely races.' Doreen chuckled.

Cally hoped her face didn't show as much alarm as she felt. She couldn't think of anything to say. 'Right.'

Doreen clearly read her thoughts. 'Don't you worry. You'll fit right in. Just be yourself, and they'll love you just as much as we do.'

Cally felt grateful for Doreen's words, but nerves fluttered in her stomach. She lowered her voice. 'It's so different from anything I've ever experienced. I don't know the first thing about horse racing, or what to wear, or how to act.'

'You'll be fine,' Doreen said as she moved to the large farmhouse sink, where the bunch of hydrangeas from the garden sat in a bucket of water. 'Just follow your nose.'

Cally was reminded of her grandma as Doreen started to pull the bottom leaves off the hydrangeas and deep purples, soft pinks, and vibrant blues swirled in front of her eyes. 'I don't have much choice. Gosh, those hydrangeas are so pretty. They remind me of my grandma.'

'I know, same here. My mum had a big bush in our garden when I was a girl. I used to pick them for her and bring them inside to brighten up the kitchen. Just like I'm doing now, actually.'

Cally smiled. 'That's a lovely memory.'

Doreen nodded. 'Funny, isn't it? How a scent or a flower can transport you back in time.' Doreen finished arranging the vase and stepped back to admire her handiwork. 'There. That's better. A bit of colour to liven up the place.'

'They're beautiful. You're really good at arranging them too. I just plonk flowers in willy-nilly.'

Doreen waved away the compliment. 'Oh, it's nothing. Just a bit of practice, that's all. You have to turn your hand to everything working here.' Doreen rolled her eyes and then moved to the oven and peeked inside. 'The bread's coming along nicely. Should be ready in a bit. Anyway, back to the races. Have you got your outfit sorted?'

Cally didn't want to talk about the races. 'Yes.'

'I remember the first time I went to the races,' Doreen reminisced, a faraway look in her eyes. 'I was just a young thing, barely out of school. My mum had saved up for months to buy me a new dress, and I felt like a princess. Those were the days.' She chuckled, shaking her head. 'Of course, I had no idea what I was doing. I picked the horses based on their names if you can believe it. But I had the time of my life, just soaking up the atmosphere and the excitement. You'll love it.'

Cally smiled. 'I hope so.'

'Just remember to enjoy yourself, and don't get too caught up in trying to impress anyone.'

The Aga oven timer dinged, and Doreen jumped up to retrieve the bread. She pulled the loaves out and set them on a cooling rack. 'Another coffee?'

Cally looked at the time on her phone. 'I should get to it.'

Just as Cally was polishing off the last of her coffee, Alastair,

Logan's cousin, came hurrying in from the main house. 'Morning, all,' he said in his usual posh-boy voice.

'Morning, Alastair,' Doreen and Cally said in unison.

'How are you, Doreen?' Alastair asked, flashing a charming smile.

'Yes, good, thank you.'

'I'm after a coffee, please,' Alastair said, then turned to Cally. 'How are you, Cally? All good with you?'

'Good, thanks. Yep.'

'What are you doing here? Where's Logan?' Alastair asked.

'I'm not with Logan.'

'No? What are you up to then?' Alastair probed with a frown.

'I'm with Nina. I'm doing a job over in the east wing.'

Alastair raised an eyebrow. 'Oh, decluttering, is it? Good luck. That's quite the task, sorting through all that old junk. You need a medal. Oh, no, actually, you're getting paid for it, so there's that.'

Cally felt her cheeks flush. Alastair had a way of putting his foot in it and making her feel bad, even though it was completely unintentional. She didn't know what to say. 'It's a big job.'

Alastair's voice was not unkind, but to Cally's ear, it dripped with condescension. 'A big job of sifting through a load of crap, old newspapers, and broken furniture. As I said, good luck with that. Best of British. Rather you than me. Someone has to do it, though.'

Cally tried to keep her voice steady. 'Thanks.'

Doreen handed Alastair his coffee. 'Here you go, Alastair. Freshly brewed.'

'Thank you, Doreen,' Alastair said, taking the cup. 'You always make the best coffee.'

Alastair sipped his coffee, seemingly oblivious to the fact that his words had made Cally feel awkward. 'So, do you enjoy working here? It must be quite different from, you know, that little job thingy you were doing in the chemist.'

Cally took a deep breath. 'It's good. It's given me an appreciation of the manor's history.'

Alastair nodded. 'Well, I suppose it's good to find joy in the little things. We always say that, don't we, Doreen?'

Cally felt her jaw clench. 'Yes, I suppose it is.'

'Well, I guess I'd better get back to it. Time waits for no one. Enjoy your morning ladies.'

As Alastair left the kitchen, Cally let out a breath through tight lips. 'Yes, see you later.'

Doreen rolled her eyes. 'Ignore him. He's something else. Completely in a world of his own.'

Cally laughed. 'That's one way to put it.'

'Always been the same. Absolutely harmless at the end of the day. He doesn't understand the value of hard work because he's never done a day of it in his life. It is what it is. He means no harm.'

Cally nodded. 'You said it.'

Doreen patted Cally's hand. 'You're doing great, love. Don't let anyone tell you otherwise.'

'I should get on. Thanks for the coffee.'

'Anytime.'

Doreen raised her eyebrows. 'And don't you be fretting over what big mouth did or didn't say. Not being funny, but he's not quite all there, so don't worry about it. Got it?'

'Yeah, thanks,' Cally affirmed, but as she walked out of the kitchen, she made a wincing face. Alastair had pushed her buttons hard and fast, and she didn't like how it made her feel. She heard a very strange, out-of-context cross between a growl and a croak come out of the back of her throat. Big mouth Alastair had not made her feel very good at all. Trouble was, how she felt was going to get worse. Bumpy ride upcoming. Hold onto your race hat Cally de Pfeffer. Strap yourself in girlfriend. Things are not going to be that fun.

13

Cally walked back to the east wing, her mind buzzing with thoughts. The encounter with Alastair had rattled her, to say the least. He'd not even done anything *that* bad or *that* wrong even, the problem was mostly, actually *all*, hers. She tried to keep herself in check as she pondered his comment about her "little job".

Letting herself in via the code Nina had sent her, she switched on lights and did a walk-through of the rooms. There was more dust than she'd ever seen, piles of crates everywhere, stacks of old paintings, antique furniture left, right, and centre, boxes of forgotten treasures, and loads of old packing cases full of knick-knacks. Ornate chandeliers hung from the ceilings draped in cobwebs, old shutters were locked closed, and curtains were dusty and needed a good air. The smell wasn't great either. As Cally walked around the wing, it was as if, along with the mustiness and dust, she could feel the weight of history in the air.

'It's like stepping back in time,' Cally said to no one at all.

She moved further into one of the rooms off the main corridor, pulled a few dust covers off furniture and peeked into boxes. Flicking through an old photo album, its leather cover cracked and faded, she peered at black-and-white photographs of the manor and its inhabitants from decades past. She found an old journal tucked away in one of the boxes and carefully opened it. The pages were filled with elegant handwriting, detailing the daily life of Lovely Manor from decades before. She read about grand parties, quiet moments, and the lives of the people who had called the manor home.

Opening her phone, she navigated to the job spec Nina had sent her, retraced her steps to the main door, and opened the first door on the left. A lot of junk greeted her. She coughed as she walked across the room and dust blew up into the air. She pulled open the curtains, then unlocked the shutters, flung open the windows, and took her bag off as fresh air blew into the room. Fifteen minutes later, with her jacket hung on the handle of the door and a carton of blackcurrant accompanying her, she'd yanked out most of the boxes in the middle of the room and was starting to get to the nuts and bolts of what was what. She pulled open a door to one of a long row of built-in cupboards lining the entirety of one wall. Her chin dropped to her chest at what looked back at her from the shelves of the cupboard – many, many, many vintage Louis Vuitton handbags, which had clearly been someone's very expensive collection at some point in time. She proceeded to open more doors and more bags appeared to double in front of her eyes.

'How the other half lives,' Cally said to herself as she gingerly picked up one of the handbags and blew off a layer of dust. She chuckled, turning the bag this way and that. Squinting in the cupboard, she counted bag after bag after bag. She couldn't quite fathom how much the bags in front of her might be worth. After a quick eBay search, she was staggered, floored even. Vintage designer bags were clearly a thing. It was a whole other world she had no idea about, but via the listings on her phone, the collection of bags alone would buy her a flat. Not that it was an option for her, but it was an interesting thought: an old out-of-use room where, just in the contents of its cupboards alone, there was more money than her savings account. As Cally started to pull out the bags and then suitcases, she found it mind-boggling as she came across more and more bags, folios, luggage, and cases.

Sorting methodically through everything and attempting to put it into some sort of order, she thought about how life at Lovely Manor was very different from the world she'd been brought up in. The opulence and the sense of history were overwhelming, and the house itself, of course, was completely different, but it was more the little things that made the contrast just so stark. Things like having staff, rooms full of old bags worth a fortune, and gardens with names of their own. All of it made Cally's own past, indeed her whole life, seem like a different reality altogether.

Once all the bags were out of the cupboards and she'd added vintage Gucci and Yves Saint Laurent to the humongous pile, Cally assessed her work in the room. She spent ages painstakingly running the vacuum around and dusting until the shelves shone. She then devoted a lot of time curating the bags into styles and shapes and popping them back neatly into the cupboards. Just after she had pressed the button to wind the vacuum cable in, she was stretching her back and pulling her arms over her head when she heard the front door open and Nina appeared in the hallway.

'Hiya. How are you?'

'Good. Busy!'

Nina looked around the architrave and raised her eyebrows. 'Wow, you've really cracked on here.'

'To be honest, it looked a lot worse than it was.'

'No, you're a whizz!'

'Thanks. You're not going to believe this. Look over here,' Cally said as she started opening cupboard doors. The designer bags were now curated and sorted on the shelves by size and shape. Now, no longer in a jumble, clean and tidy, they were even more impressive than when Cally had first found them.

Nina's jaw dropped. She swore and whisper-hissed. 'Omg. Are they what I think they are?'

'Yes indeed,' Cally replied. 'Can you even?'

Nina walked closer, her eyes wide with astonishment. 'These must be worth a fortune! Some of these brands...'

Cally nodded, smiling. 'I was amazed when I started pulling them out. It's like a treasure trove in here.'

Nina reached out and gently touched a vintage Chanel bag. 'I can't believe this is hidden away like some discarded junk. And we thought the hat room was something...'

'I know. I looked them up on eBay...'

'And?'

'Put it this way, you're looking at a flat or a deposit for one.'

'Wow!'

As they stood there, marvelling at the incredible collection of designer bags, Cally shook her head. Nina reached into the cupboard and carefully pulled out a vintage leather suitcase. Despite its age, the leather was supple and smooth. 'Look at this,' she sighed. 'The craftsmanship, the attention to detail. I wonder if they still make them like this?'

Cally nodded, running her fingers over the locks and clasps. 'You have to wonder about the places it's been and the people who've carried it.'

'Yeah, a glimpse into a world that's so different from our own. At least, mine anyway.'

'And mine!'

Cally thought about her own battered, second-hand luggage, the cheap, flimsy bags that had always seemed to be falling apart at the seams. Not that she'd ever used them much. The idea of owning something as luxurious and well-made seemed a bit like a fantasy from another life. 'It's crazy to think about the kind of money these bags must have cost when they were new,' she mused, shaking her head in disbelief. 'I mean, I've never even seen that many zeros on a price tag before.'

Nina chuckled. 'Can you imagine walking into a shop and just casually dropping that kind of cash on a handbag? Like it was nothing?'

Cally snorted, the idea so absurd that it was comical. 'I can barely wrap my head around spending that much on a car, let alone a bag to carry my lipstick in.'

'In a way, it's kind of sad to see them sitting here like this, gathering dust and forgotten about. These bags were meant to be used, to be loved and cherished, and passed down through generations.'

Cally nodded. 'You're right. It's like they're just waiting for someone to come along and give them a new lease on life.'

'Maybe that someone could be you, Cal, once your feet are under the table.' Nina winked.

'Hilarious. I don't think so.'

'Never a truer word said in jest, my friend.'

Cally chuckled. 'Let's hope you're right. I wouldn't mind a collection like this.'

14

Later that day after eating their lunch sitting out overlooking the grounds of Lovely Manor, Nina led Cally down one of the long corridors in the east wing to a room that had clearly seen better days. The door creaked as it opened, revealing a space crammed with boxes, a desk buried under papers, and vintage filing cabinets standing against the walls, their drawers bulging with documents.

'Another room full of old stuff. Looks like this is yet another one that has been neglected for far too long,' Nina said with wide eyes. 'I only briefly looked in here before. It's mind-boggling how many rooms there are.'

Cally surveyed the scene. 'Wow, there's a lot to go through. Any idea what's in all these boxes?'

'I had a quick look through when I scoped the job. Mostly old files, paperwork from years back. Some of it might be important, but honestly, Cecilia said that nothing in here is that important.' Nina shook her head and lowered her voice. 'Not that I think she has a clue what's important or not anyway.'

Cally nodded. She wasn't going to start giving her opinion about Cecilia, Logan's aunt, but, truth be told, she was with

Nina all the way to the bank. 'Alright. First things first, I'll need to go through everything and sort it into categories. It'll help to know what we're dealing with. Yeah?'

Nina looked relieved. 'I reckon. If you need me, I'll be down the hall. Just shout if you find anything interesting or need any help.'

'Will do.'

As the door clicked shut behind her, Cally took a deep breath and began the task at hand. She started with a floor-to-ceiling pile of cardboard filing boxes, pulling them down one by one and sifting through the contents. Old invoices, receipts, and letters filled the room with the scent of aged paper. To be quite honest, she had no clue really what to keep and what to throw, but as she worked, she made a little pile of anything that seemed particularly significant or interesting. A good few hours passed in a blur of sorting and organising, and soon, the piles of papers began to make a bit of sense. The room, once chaotic and cluttered, slowly started to take on a more orderly appearance.

Just as she was beginning to make headway with the desk, Nina popped her head back in. 'How's it going in here?'

'Good, actually,' Cally said, looking up with a smile. 'I'm making progress. There's a lot to go through, but it's not as bad as it first seemed. So much stuff!'

Nina stepped inside, looking around. 'I can see that. You're getting on better than I am.'

Cally laughed. 'There are definitely some interesting things here. Look at this from back in the day.' Cally held up an old letter.

Nina took the letter and glanced over it. 'Wow, you don't really see things like this these days. What beautiful writing.'

Cally nodded. 'There are loads more like it. It might be worth setting them aside.'

'Good idea. Okay, I'll get back to it, then we'll stop for tea.'

'Sounds like a plan.'

After opening another carton of blackcurrant, Cally got stuck in and uncovered forgotten memories, piles of accounts from the stable management, and reams and reams of old documents. The desk, once buried under clutter, was gradually cleared and organised.

Hidden among the papers she found a few old trinkets here and there; a vintage watch, a set of collectible silver spoons, and a few pieces of random jewellery. Among the papers, they found old business records, property deeds, and personal letters.

Once the desk was clear and Nina had arrived with two cups of tea and a packet of Bourbons, which they'd had on a little patio area outside the east wing, Cally went back into the room and started to pull piles of papers off the tops of the old timber filing cabinets. She plonked them onto the desk and as she was moving back to get more, she knocked a pile on the floor with her hip as she shimmied around a small side table. The pile teetered for a moment before falling onto the floor in a flurry of documents. Papers scattered all around and as she tutted and bent down to scoop them up, a green leather folio whose contents had fallen out caught her eye. Mostly because, in contrast to everything else in the room, the folio was bright green and more modern.

Crouched down on the floor, she started to gather the contents of the folio and stuff it back into the main section. Reaching forward to scoop in some papers, a semi-folded marriage certificate caught her eye. Not really realising what she was doing, she flicked it out to its full width and then frowned. As her eyes scanned the names, she froze. Right after that, she wanted to vomit.

She read it again and her whole face crumpled as she sat back on her heels and stared at the piece of paper in front of her. She closed her eyes and shook her head. Surely not. It didn't make sense. But there it was in front of her in black and white. According to the official signed paper, many moons before, Logan Henry-Hicks had married someone called Cassia Allegra Brommington.

Cally went cold to her core. She frowned and squinted. It couldn't be her Logan, surely.

Logan Henry Hicks. Cassia Allegra Brommington.

How many Logan Henry-Hicks were there in the world? As far as she knew, not that many at all. And the one she knew, the same one she was currently in love with, had forgotten to tell her a tiny little detail about his life. This was not going to end well. At all.

15

Cally's heart pounded in her chest as she sat and stared for ages at the piece of paper. She felt a rush of nausea, her mind racing with questions and doubts. She squinted at the certificate, trying to convince herself she had read it wrong, but the names remained unchanged. It was there, right before her, telling her in no uncertain words, that Logan had, in fact, at one point been a married man.

Her hands trembled as she took out her phone and snapped a photo of the marriage certificate. She wasn't even sure why she was taking the picture. The words on the paper were imprinted on her brain anyway. Not sure what to do she started to rifle through the rest of the contents of the green leather folder. But as she looked and flicked from one to the next, she found nothing else that hinted about anything. No photographs, no letters, and no additional documents to provide context or answers. No fancy invitation, mementoes, order of service, nothing at all. It was all quite odd. There were a few old receipts from a shop in Scotland, a handwritten list that appeared to have been written by Cecilia detailing flights to Edinburgh, and a random picture of Logan's uncle in a kilt.

Cally's mind swirled with confusion and hurt. Why hadn't Logan mentioned anything? Was it a secret he had intended to keep forever? Surely, he must have reasoned that, at some point, she would find out. Was the whole family keeping the secret, and if so why? Pushing herself up from the floor, she sank into the chair at the desk, leant forward, put her head in her hands, and pressed her fingers into her forehead not sure what to think or, more importantly, what to do. Feeling as if someone had ripped out a rug from under her and she was lying on the floor flailing, her emotions zipped around her in absolute turmoil. The certificate had cast everything into doubt. More, it hinted at what she didn't know: who even was Logan? Had he been hiding an entire life from her? What a nasty, mean, horrible thing to do.

She remembered their conversations, the way he had spoken about his past. There had been no mention of a wife, no hint of this Cassia Allegra Brommington. Her brain raced at a hundred miles an hour and swirled in a tsunami of doubt. Was there some other explanation, some reason for this marriage that he hadn't shared?

The questions came thick and fast as Cally seemed to be paralysed by thought and nailed to the chair. Hurt gnawed, followed by anger, with betrayal nipping at its heels. She couldn't quite believe it and kept frowning down at the certificate as she wallowed around. She was so very furious, too. Absolutely fuming. She'd trusted Logan and couldn't compute any reason why he might have felt it acceptable to have kept something so significant from her.

It was as if the whole Logan and Cally thing was now tainted as far as she was concerned. She had believed in their relationship, but now, everything seemed uncertain. All of it now a deep, murky pool of omission and doubt. Determined to find some clarity or something, but she didn't know what, Cally continued to rifle through the papers. Like a woman possessed, she searched every box, every drawer, hoping to find something that would explain the marriage certificate. But there was nothing, not even a sniff of anything else. She felt as if the room was closing in on her as she sorted at lightning speed until most of the documents were filed in piles. The neatly stacked papers from posh people's lives then seemed to mock her. She imagined that they had eyes following her around the room. Stupid little Cally with her short skirts and tights. Silly poor girl from the village dilly-dallying around thinking she was something else. No need to tell her about a marriage.

Cally sat down on the chair by the leather-topped desk, the weight of the discovery pressing on her. She looked at the marriage certificate again, trying to make sense of it. The elegant script, the official seals – it all seemed so real. It *was* real. There was no doubt at all about that.

Her mind flashed back to moments with Logan and she winced as she searched for signs she might have missed. Had there been hints of a secret life? Had he ever slipped, given away something unintentionally? Nothing. Try as she might, she couldn't recall anything that suggested he was hiding such a significant part of his life. The only little red flag had been the fact that he hadn't really said that much about the past at all. She kept shaking her head over and over again as if that might somehow help. It didn't, instead, she felt adrift, hurt, and oh-so-angry. She wanted to scream in frustration and yell at someone that she'd known all along that it was too good to be true. Just her luck. Her bubble hadn't just burst. It had smashed to oblivion, taking her along with it for the ride.

Yanking the vacuum from the corner of the room, she stuck the small upholstery brush nozzle on the end, pushed the button with her foot, and began to run the brush over the now clear desk, the thick, wide windowsill, and along the seats of the chairs. As she zoomed around, her thoughts turned inward, her mind a whirlpool going around and around. She remembered the first time she'd met Logan, the spark between them, the way he had made her feel special. How she'd told him so much stuff about the real Cally that no one else knew. How she'd shared with him about holding up the sky. She'd thought they had something real. She'd thought he was nice. She'd tucked him up in her life next to her heart. She was livid.

Had it all been a lie? She felt another surge of anger at the thought. Right beside the white-hot anger, though, was a deep, deep, *deep* sense of sadness because, bottom line, Cally had believed in Logan, and much more importantly, she'd *trusted* him. For the first time in her life, she'd let herself be vulnerable and opened up to him in ways she hadn't with anyone else. She'd let being with him mean she could finally let go of the sky. She'd so enjoyed seeing it coming crashing down.

Logan Henry-Hicks had not played a good game. He had proceeded directly to jail. He'd one million per cent shattered the trust. Cally shook her head. Henry-Hicks would never be able to claw his way back into the special little corner of her heart. He was done and very much dusted.

16

It was early evening the next day. Cally got out of the shower, wrapped herself in a fluffy towel, pulled the bathroom door open, tutted when it knocked against the bath and padded into her bedroom. She quickly admonished herself for even thinking about complaining about the cramped flat, knowing how lucky she was to have a roof over her head at all.

She tried not to think about her discovery, but her mind wasn't going to stop spinning about what she'd revealed about Logan. Marriage, marriage, marriage. Wife, wife, wife. She desperately tried to push away the thoughts that had been plaguing her mind all day, but it was no use. Her brain simply refused to let go of what she'd found. She couldn't wrap her head around the fact that, firstly, he'd been married and, secondly, that he'd not mentioned it. Admittedly, he hadn't actually full-blown lied, at least not as far as she knew. However, as far as she was concerned, he'd lied by omission and that was equally as bad, if not worse. In a way, much worse.

Logan not telling her a little thing like the fact that he'd been married made her question everything. If he could omit that, what else was he hiding? It did not bode well. It felt like a betrayal, a breach of the trust and honesty she thought they'd shared. If he could keep something as monumental as a previous marriage hidden, what else might he be concealing from her? The thought made Cally's stomach churn with unease and doubt. She felt almost as if she'd been winded by an actual physical body blow. As if someone had slammed into her with a boxing bag and kept on going.

The turmoil spun around her brain as, on autopilot, she pulled on her usual white shirt, short skirt, ballet flats and popped a cardigan over the top. Not only was her brain spinning way out of control, but she was also mind-bogglingly angry. Henry-Hicks was in so much trouble. Cally was so furious and so completely discombobulated by the whole situation that she felt paralysed, unsure of how to even begin to react. She was in such a complete fuddle that she didn't actually know what to do which is why she'd done absolutely nothing.

Her first thought had been to phone him and absolutely blast him all over the show and never speak to him again. Then she'd actually gone into disbelief and thought that perhaps what she'd seen on the marriage certificate wasn't actually true. Her mind had played all sorts of tricks on her and revelled in doing so. She'd even made up strange excuses and fancy things about what might have happened to Logan. She'd considered that perhaps there was another Logan Henry-Hicks in the family. That it was a fake marriage certificate that someone had made up for a joke. On and on her mind had gone, making up all sorts. Her thoughts had spiralled and spiralled, grasping at any straw that might have made the reality not feel quite as bad.

In the end, she'd not phoned and blasted him at all. In fact, she'd done nothing as if the whole revolting episode had crippled her somehow. She'd not told Eloise, not done anything except fall down into a pit and wonder how, in the name of goodness, she was ever going to get back up. Logan had also been away, she'd had a full day at work, so she'd just let it fester. As far as Logan was concerned, nothing had changed.

After popping her hair up in a clip and spraying herself from top to bottom in Cloud perfume, she went into the kitchen, put the kettle on to make a hot blackcurrant, poured way too much cordial in the bottom of a mug, plonked on the hot water, and stood with her back to the worktop, sipping the drink. Here she was, going about her day as if nothing had changed when, in reality, her entire world had been turned upside down.

Her mind galloped with questions, doubts, fears, and worst-case scenarios. What had Logan's previous marriage been like? Why had it ended? Why had he never once mentioned it to her? Did he not trust her enough to share something so personal? She grimaced as she wondered if there might be a more sinister reason for his secrecy, some dark and twisted truth that he'd wanted to keep buried. Cassia Allegra Brommington had been murdered. By him.

The more Cally thought about it, the more her anger and hurt morphed into a sickening sense of betrayal and violation. She felt like a fool, like she had been played for a naive and gullible idiot. How could she have been so blind and ignorant of the signs that must have been there all along? Looking back, had there been hints or clues that she had missed, red flags that she had chosen to ignore in the rush of falling for the Henry-Hicks thing?

Her heart and head rallied wildly between hurt and anger. How dare the little ******? How dare he let her fall so deeply? How dare he not open up about his baggage? Cally's grip on her mug was so tight her knuckles turned white. She closed her eyes, trying to steady herself against the onslaught of emotions.

She simply didn't know what to do. She *did* know that something was stopping her from confronting him. She felt almost as if she was unable to speak. As if first she needed to protect herself.

Time to process it before she acted. And she had the little card up her sleeve she'd always had: the flick of the switch in the back of her throat and the look on her face that told everyone she was fine when inside she very much was not. She would do what she had always done in the face of adversity. She'd flick the switch, put one foot in front of the other, go through the motions, and work out what would be her next move. Taking another sip of her blackcurrant cordial, she stood up a bit straighter. She'd just keep quiet for a bit, attend the races, then she'd dump Henry-Hicks from a very high height. See how he liked it. Give him a taste of his own medicine, only worse. Yes, she'd play a little game with our Henry-Hicks, that's what she would do. He thought he could mess her around. Oh she could do so much better.

About fifteen minutes later, her phone pinged to tell her that Logan was waiting outside the deli. They were off to The Drunken Sailor for a rare speakeasy held in one of the back rooms behind the pub. Before her discovery, Cally had been looking forward to not only the chowder and the Lovely event but also spending the evening with Logan. Now, not so much. To be quite frank, she could quite comfortably have wrung his neck and stuffed him and it down the nearest drain. Pop some very strong acid on afterwards.

Popping a carton of blackcurrant in her bag, she slammed the flat door shut, went down the steep stairs, made her way down the building and out to the front of the deli. She might have been fuming at him, but as Cally approached Logan, as he usually did, he took her breath away. He smiled at seeing her and kissed her. 'Hey, Blackcurrant. How are you? Being a good girl?'

Cally didn't laugh. Imaginary hot red smoke poured out of her nose. So up himself, too. She inwardly growled but outwardly mustered up a smile. She'd play the game for a bit, then dump him. She flicked the 'I'm Okay' switch, not the regular one but the emergency one. The one she hadn't used for a long time. 'Hiya. How was your day?' *Tra-la-la.*

'Busy but good.'

Married any brides today you forgot to tell me about? 'Nice.'

'What have you been up to?'

Cally flicked her hand upwards in the direction of the flat. 'Working, then I cleaned the flat and I did some admin stuff for Nina. I went to see Birdie about preparations for the Chowder Festival, too.'

'Sounds like you've been busy, too.'

Not as busy as you covering up secret wives. 'Mmm.'

'You okay?'

'Yes, yes, fine. Marvellous.'

Inside, Cally was far, so very far, from marvellous. As they walked along the High Street, the Lovely glow draped the quaint, cobblestone streets in its pink-orange shimmer. The air was filled with the gentle hum of conversation and laughter as locals and tourists alike wandered up and down the road. Cally, though, barely noticed her surroundings, too lost in the swirling, tumultuous thoughts in her mind. She couldn't stop thinking about the wedding certificate, the tangible proof that Logan had been married before and had chosen to keep that fact hidden from her.

The worst thing was that she kept on asking herself the same questions over and over again, as if, at some point, she might well come up with a different answer. How could he have lied to her by omission, if not outright deceit? How could he have kept something so significant, so life-altering, from someone he claimed to love?

Cally's stomach churned with a sickening mixture of anger, hurt, and confusion. She wanted to confront Logan, to demand answers and explanations, to unleash the full force of her fury on him. At the same time, something was somehow telling her to hedge her bets for a bit. Keep her cards close to her chest before she decided what to do. Keep quiet and wait. After all, no one knew she'd found the certificate. She could keep schtum and no one would be any the wiser.

Instead of saying anything, she walked beside him in silence, her heart heavy and her mind racing, as he chattered on about his day and the plans he had for their evening at the pub. He seemed so normal, so untroubled, as if he hadn't a care in the world. The more casual, relaxed and happy he was, the more agitated Cally got.

'I hear they've got a new chowder recipe on the menu tonight. Apparently, it's got a secret ingredient that takes it to a whole new level. They're trialling it in preparation for the Chowder Festival.'

Cally didn't give a stuff about the chowder or the festival. Even the old Lovely superstitions and customs were irritating her. She made a noncommittal noise and fixed her gaze on the pavement beneath her feet. She couldn't muster up the energy or the interest to engage in small talk, not when her entire world felt as if it was crumbling around her.

Logan glanced over at her, a flicker of concern in his eyes. 'Hey, are you sure you're alright, Blackcurrant? You seem a bit off.'

'I'm fine,' Cally snapped, the words coming out harsher than she intended. 'Just tired, that's all.'

Logan frowned but didn't push the issue. They walked on in silence for a few moments, the only sounds were their footsteps against the cobblestones and the distant cry of seagulls wheeling overhead. Cally's mind continued to whir and spin, cycling through a dizzying array of emotions and scenarios. She felt nauseous as it zoomed around her.

Part of her wanted to believe that there was some innocent explanation or logical reason as to why Logan had kept his previous marriage a secret. Maybe it had been a brief, youthful mistake, a fleeting moment of passion that had burned out as quickly as it had ignited. Maybe he was embarrassed by it, ashamed of his own naivety and impulsiveness. Another part of her, the part that had been hurt and betrayed, wanted to murder him, to be quite frank. What if there was more to the story than met the eye? What if Logan had deliberately deceived her, had hidden the truth of his past in order to manipulate and control her?

The thought made Cally's blood run cold and sent a shiver of dread down her spine. She had trusted Logan. Let him into her life, into her bed, into the most vulnerable and intimate parts of herself. And now she felt weirdly trapped.

As they approached the entrance to The Drunken Sailor, she felt a sudden, overwhelming urge to turn and run. She could just flee to the flat, race up the stairs, lock the door, and never look back. Henry-Hicks could go and get lost. She didn't run. The Drunken Sailor was full of the happy chatter of a busy evening. Logan led Cally through to the back function room where the chowder event was taking place.

Cally plastered a smile on her face as they made their way over to a table, greeting a few people with forced cheer and enthusiasm. Logan, his usual charming, confident self, made her more and more annoyed. How could he sit there so calmly, so easily, as if nothing was wrong? How could he joke and flirt and charm? Her blood boiled away. She kept squinting at him to see if she could make out any signs of a liar.

Logan had picked up on the fact that she was not herself. 'You seem a bit quiet tonight.'

Cally swallowed. 'I'm fine,' she said again, the words sounding hollow and false even to her own ears. 'Just enjoying the atmosphere. It's been a busy week.'

'It is a great spot, isn't it?'

Cally nodded, unable to speak past the gigantic lump that had risen in her throat. She'd give him good spot.

As the evening wore on and the drinks flowed, Cally became

more and more agitated, more and more restless. She couldn't sit still, couldn't focus on the conversation but couldn't bring herself to confront him. All she could think about was the wedding certificate and the way it had shattered her but still, she kept mute. As if staying quiet somehow bought her a little bit of time and let her ponder what she was going to do. The races were also on her mind. She'd be damned if she was not going to go after all the effort she'd put in.

She looked at Logan and inside did a very strange, wicked cackle. She'd go to the races, let him think he was so very clever, oh yes. Then she'd pull the rug out from under him quicker than he'd ever known and see how he felt when the boot was on the other foot. Sounded like a plan.

17

Cally certainly didn't have a spring in her step the next day. The night before, she'd made an excuse not to go back to the manor with Logan because he'd had to get up early for the horses and so she'd gone back to the flat without him. It had more than suited her. She hadn't wanted to look at him for a moment longer. She'd been quiet with the certificate going around and around her head in a horrible fat loop of distress.

Getting on the riverboat, she smiled at Colin as she stepped on, tried to avoid making conversation with him and went and sat up the top. She watched the river path on the other side of the water when the boat pulled away from the jetty and puttered along. As the boat meandered down the calm waters of the River Lovely, Cally did not feel calm at all. Sitting on the upper deck, her eyes fixed on the passing scenery without really seeing it she sighed. The breeze fluffed her hair and warm sun hit her skin, but she barely registered the sensations, too lost in her thoughts and emotions. She felt numb as if her entire being had been hollowed out and replaced with a dense, leaden weight. Absolutely, grimly, awful. The shock of discovering Logan's secret had made her sick to the bone.

Colin came up from below, raised his eyebrows and smiled. 'Hey, our Cally. How are you?'

'Great, thanks, really good.' Cally was definitely quite the little pro at lying. She was far from good. She couldn't be bothered to converse with Colin but attempted to look interested.

'How was last night?'

Awful. Dreadful. 'Yeah, fabulous. Did you enjoy it?'

'Oh, yes. How could one not?' Colin leaned against the railing. His face creased into a smile. 'That chowder was something else, wasn't it? Don't tell Birdie I said that, though. They use a special blend of spices in the pub, secret family recipe and all that. They all say that, though, don't they?' Colin chuckled. 'We'll hear it time and again by the time it gets to the Chowder Festival. Family recipes will be coming out of the woodwork left, right and centre.'

Cally nodded and forced a smile. She really couldn't be faffed with small talk. She just wanted to retreat in her own head. Colin jarred at her already-irritated edges. 'Yeah, it was delicious. Really tasty and comforting.' She gave him the get-lost vibes. He didn't take the hint.

'And the music, too. Those guitarist guys really knew how to set the mood, didn't they? Had the whole place swinging and swaying at one point. Nice to be part of it.'

Cally made a noncommittal noise. 'Yeah.'

Colin cocked his head, a flicker of concern in his eyes. 'You alright there? You seem a bit distracted.'

Cally blinked. That was putting it mildly. She felt as if someone had pushed her out of a plane without a parachute and she was free falling down to a very hard ground. 'Oh, sorry. Just a bit lost in thought, I suppose.'

Lost in a maze of betrayal more like. Taken in by the posh boy.

Colin nodded. 'I know that feeling. Sometimes, the mind just wants to wander, to drift off into its own little world. It's one of the reasons I like working on the river because it makes it easy to do that.'

Cally tutted inside and wished Colin would bog off. He simply wasn't getting the memo. Any other time, she loved it when he chatted away with her and made her feel as if she was part of the woodwork. Now, she wanted to be left alone. 'It does.'

Colin still didn't seem to have read the room. 'Such a good speakeasy in that location. One of my favourites. Can't ask for much more than that, can you?'

Cally felt her nostrils flare. 'You're right, Colin. It was a lovely evening, all in all.'

A lovely evening built on the foundation of a big fat lie.

Colin grinned. 'We've got to take the good moments where we can find them, eh?'

'Oh yes.'

'Life's too short to dwell on the bad stuff.'

Cally swallowed. She was doing more than dwelling on the bad stuff. She was *living* it. She always had done, and it felt *very* unfair. Her life hadn't been full of Lovely days. It had been hard, messy, complicated, full of twists and turns and unexpected things as she'd struggled to hold up the sky. She pretended to agree with a false chuckle. 'It is indeed.'

'Right, you are. Well, nice to see you.'

'Yep, you too.'

Cally retreated into herself, her mind spinning. She closed her eyes and tried to shut out the world as her brain continued to swirl and churn. Things were not good.

Cally walked up the path to Eloise's house and let herself in. She called out and found Eloise in the kitchen with a bottle of wine on the table and a glass in her hand.

'Hiya.' Eloise smiled.

'Hey. How are you?'

Cally hugged Eloise just a little bit too hard. Right away, Eloise frowned and squinted.

'What's wrong? You okay?'

'Yep, I'm fine.'

'Worried about the races?'

Cally rolled her eyes. The races were the last of her worries. It was what was going to happen after the races that was bothering her. 'No, not at all.'

She leaned against the kitchen worktop as she tried to gather her thoughts, and Eloise chatted about her outfit for the races. A warm, cosy scent of garlic and herbs filled the air as Eloise poured her a glass of wine.

Eloise frowned. 'What's wrong? You're doing the voice thing.'

'Am I?'

'You are.'

'Nothing's wrong.'

'I'm fine.'

'Just tell me.'

Cally considered whether or not to tell Eloise about the secret marriage certificate. She felt stupid and embarrassed. She sighed. 'I don't even know where to start.'

'Try me.'

Cally took a deep, shuddering breath and let the words come pouring out in a rush. 'I found something that changes everything. I can't believe it.'

'What? You found something? Like what? What do you mean? What did you find?'

Cally swallowed. 'I found a wedding certificate.'

Eloise wrinkled her nose. 'What of your grandma's? I thought you got rid of most of that stuff.'

'Not my grandma! Logan's wedding certificate. From a previous marriage that he never told me about!'

Eloise's eyes widened, her hand stilled mid-stir over the pot on the hob. 'Sorry? What? Are you serious? What the heck? Are you kidding me?'

'Oh, how I wish I were.'

'Sorry, wait, how did you find it?'

Cally let out a bitter, humourless laugh. 'The decluttering job.'

'Oh.'

'I was in one of the wings. It was in a folio that fell on the floor. It was tucked away like some dirty little secret.' Cally felt tears prick at the corners of her eyes, hot and stinging.

'Are you sure?'

'Yep.'

'You're *definitely* sure?'

'Yes!' Cally fished for her phone. 'I took a photo of it.'

Eloise squinted, picked up the phone and frowned. She swore. 'Looks legit.'

'I know. 'I can't believe he kept this from me. I can't believe he lied to me after everything.'

'I can't even imagine how you must be feeling right now.'

'It's quite simple, really. I feel like I'm going crazy, El. Like everything I thought I knew, everything I believed about him and about us was just a lie. A façade.'

'So, what has he said?'

'I haven't said anything.' Cally replied miserably.

'What?' Eloise shook her head. 'Are you nuts? You haven't said anything! Why ever not?'

'I'm going to wait until after the races, and then I'm going to call it off. See how he likes it out of the blue. I'll break up with him then.'

'What? Sorry? You've just kept quiet?'

'Yes.'

Eloise swore. 'I don't think that's a good idea. Ridiculous!'

'Probably not, but I've made my mind up. Two can play at his game.'

'This is so weird. Why would he do that?' Eloise asked. 'It doesn't make sense.'

'You tell me.'

'You need to talk to him! There might be more to the story; there might be a reason why he didn't tell you about this before.'

'What possible reason could there be? What excuse could he have for keeping something like this from me, for lying to me about his past?'

Eloise sighed. 'I don't know. Maybe he was ashamed. Maybe he didn't know how to tell you, didn't want to risk losing you over something that happened long before you two even met.'

Cally shook her head. 'Rubbish.'

Eloise nodded. 'He should have trusted you, should have been honest with you from the word go, but people make mistakes. It doesn't necessarily mean he doesn't love you.'

'Feels like it from my end. How can I trust him now?'

'Just talk to him, Cal.'

'I will once we've been to the races. It's so close now.'

'You really think that's a good idea? What, so you're just going to keep schtum all day?'

'Yup.'

'I don't think that's a good idea. You're bonkers! You're better off to just talk to him and find out what is what.'

'I've made up my mind.'

'Well, there you are then. He better have a good reason for keeping this from you, or I'll kick his sorry butt from here to next Sunday. Best friend's prerogative and all that.'

Cally let out a watery laugh. 'Too funny.'

'Let's have something to eat. That will make you feel better. I really don't think it's a good idea to bottle it up and go to the races with the secret, though. Why would you do that?' Eloise narrowed her eyes. 'I don't get that.'

Cally watched as Eloise ladled out two generous portions of pasta and garlic prawns into shallow bowls. 'I don't know. It's warped, but me knowing and him not knowing that I know…'

'Yeah, that *is* warped. You just need the truth, plain and simple. Or just finish it. Why put yourself through that?'

'Grandma always said to stick with the truth.'

'And we know she was *always* right.'

'That we do. I'll go to the races and then call it a day.'

18

Cally shifted another box along the floor in the dispensary, plonked it in the corner, and counted the line of boxes in front of her. It had been hard going in the chemist with Birdie having added another store to her empire. Cally's role had kicked in with her having to deal with extra deliveries, unpacking them, and getting them ready to be collected by a member of staff from the new store. Well used to the intricacies of the job and the fact that it looked very easy on the outside but that you actually had to keep your wits about you, she had been firing on all cylinders since she'd arrived early that morning. Birdie had been very good to her, but she sure got her pound of flesh in return.

Coffee and treats from the Lovely Bay chocolate shop had fuelled Cally quite nicely, but now she was ready to put her feet up and have a sit-down. She finished with a stack of boxes, called out to Birdie that she was going up to the flat to make a sandwich, hauled herself up the stairs, made a sun-dried tomato, cheese, and ham sandwich and a cup of hot blackcurrant and went and sat at her desk to check for any emails from her chatbot role. After scrolling through her inbox and answering a message from Nina about helping out with a decluttering job in a house not far from the RNLI station, her mind zipped straight back to the discovery of the marriage certificate.

Since her find, she'd managed to only see Logan twice and had kept her mouth fully shut while she attempted to regroup and work out what she was going to do. Her loose plan was to get the races done and dusted and confront him after that. There had been their usual texts and exchanges, but from her end of the stick, she was right off him. Being an expert in keeping up appearances, Logan himself didn't have a scooby about what was going on in Cally's head. Neither did she, really. He had no clue that Cally now knew he'd been married. Every time she looked at him or thought about him, she felt anger bubbling up in the pit of her stomach. So much for being in love. It no longer felt like that at all. For some unfathomable reason, though, she hadn't said anything. She'd kept telling herself that she'd dress up for the races and then cut him off just like that. Part of her wanted to wait and see if perhaps without her prompting, once she'd met his wider family, he'd tell her about it anyway.

She sat and ate most of her sandwich and blackcurrant, and before she knew what she was doing, she whipped out her phone, tapped on the photos, expanded the one of the wedding certificate, and zoomed in on the names. Cassia Allegra Brommington. Cally tutted. It even looked posh written down. She repeated the name a few times in her head, pushed her fingers up into the little grooves under her cheekbones, and pressed as if doing that might somehow help. No such luck.

In the space of about two seconds, before really thinking about what she was doing, she popped the name in the box under the six brightly coloured letters of the Google logo and had hit return. That had been our Cally's first mistake. As soon as she saw the entries in the search going on for what felt like ever, she knew she'd made a gigantic error in judgement by going anywhere near snooping on Cassia Allegra Brommington. She should have left well alone. As she read the first few lines, the old screaming voice of self-doubt and inferiority started to yell manically at her.

She tapped on a picture of Cassia and nodded. Cassia was not what one might have described as pretty if one was so inclined. But, oh, did she look noble. Indeed. With that sort of glossy, straight, blown-out hair with a just right curl at the very ends that looked, if a curl could, well bred. Ditto the skin. An almost aristocratic jawline and a very good nose. Teeth were good. Expensive.

Cally scrolled through the search results, the second half of her sandwich forgotten beside her as she delved deeper into the life of Cassia Allegra Brommington. The more she read, the more her heart sank. A heavy weight settled in her chest and she must have sighed out loud a thousand times.

'Fine art gallery in Kensington,' she muttered, her voice tinged with disbelief. 'Of course, she owns a blooming fine art gallery in Kensington. Probably sells paintings that cost more than my entire flat. Oh, wait, I don't own a flat.'

She took a sip of her blackcurrant, grimacing as she realised it had gone cold. She told herself to click on the red button on the left hand side of her screen and leave well alone, but she couldn't tear herself away from taking in more.

'Distinguished career in the art world,' Cally read aloud, her voice taking on a mocking tone. 'Curated exhibitions for some of the most prestigious museums in Europe. Well, la-di-da-di-da, Cassia. I've curated a pretty impressive collection of caring duties in my time, if I do say so myself.'

She clicked on another link, this one detailing Cassia's education. 'First-class degree from Oxford.' *Because, of course, she went to Oxford. Probably rowed crew and drank champagne for breakfast.*

Cally glanced around Birdie's small flat, taking in the slightly worn furniture and the stack of pamphlets from the adult education centre on the corner of her desk. Her three menial jobs flashed through her mind and she mused that her flat would probably fit in Cassia's walk-in wardrobe. She scrolled further, coming across a photo of Cassia at a charity gala. The woman was draped in a designer gown, diamonds glittering at her throat and wrists. To Cally, she might as well have been wearing the Crown Jewels.

Cally pushed back from her desk, looking at her reflection in the small mirror on the wall. Deflated was the word with a side of demoralised. Turning back to her computer, she continued her deep dive into Cassia's life and had a conversation with her laptop screen. 'Guest lecturer at the Sorbonne,' she read, her voice dripping with sarcasm. 'I don't even know where that is. Well, I once gave a very moving speech to the nurse's station at the hospice. We're practically equals.'

On and on it went. She came across an article detailing Cassia's family background which informed her that Cassia had descended from actual aristocracy. Taking an aggressive bite of her sandwich she continued to scroll to learn that Cassia spoke four languages fluently, was a published author, a noted philanthropist, talented pianist, and patron of the arts. *Speaks at international conferences. Advises on government arts policy. Vegan.*

Cally clicked on an image of Cassia at a polo match, looking effortlessly elegant in a polkadot dress. She scrolled further, finding more photos of Cassia at various high-society events: at a gallery opening, a charity ball, a royal garden party. Cally glanced at her own CV, a single sheet of paper next to the stack of pamphlets, and a Post-it note beside it with 'Don't forget bin day' stuck on the desk. She felt a bit sick and continued to scroll further, finding more and more evidence of Cassia's seemingly perfect life. She found herself looking at photos of Cassia's art gallery, a sleek, modern space in the heart of Kensington. Cally sighed out through her nose at the injustice of it all. She felt so outclassed it was actually comical. Shaking her head, she leaned back in her chair and addressed the room at large and mimicked a movie announcer's voice, 'Coming this summer: Extreme Makeover: Cally de Pfeffer Edition. Watch as we transform this common chemist worker into a high-society art dealer. Stay tuned for our new reality show: 'Chemist to Countess. Warning: may require actual magic.'

Cally sighed, pushing away from her desk and stretching her arms above her head. She'd been hunched over her computer for far longer than she'd intended, feeling worse and worse about pretty much her whole existence. She tried to talk herself up, telling herself that she was her own person, that she could do anything she wanted to. It didn't really work that well.

She grimaced at the irony of it all; she'd just read about a wonder woman and here she was about to go down to the back of the chemist for the remainder of her day to deal with the rest of the cartons of drugs and shop supplies. She wasn't a curator of art. Far from it. Oh, no, instead she had cardboard boxes full of antacids and haemorrhoid cream with her name on them.

As she closed the door of her flat and carefully stepped down the steep stairs she reminded herself that she'd promised she wouldn't give in to self-doubt. She'd plough on. No navel-gazing or pity. However, when you flattened cardboard cartons and decluttered other people's junk for a living, it was much easier said than done. She nodded defiantly. She'd stick with her master plan of going to the races and then she'd do what she'd planned and drop Henry-Hicks from a height. Take back control.

19

It was the day of the races. Cally had kept the marriage thing completely under her belt. Only Eloise had been privy to what was going on in her mind. And certainly Logan was none the wiser.

Unlike what Cally assumed most of the other guests who were going to be in the Royal Enclosure were doing, Cally had spent a very early morning short three-hour shift on the retail chatbot. Being Saturday, she'd expected it to be busy and she hadn't been wrong. She'd dealt with all sorts of problems, including but not limited to a woman in Saffron Waldron who'd ordered a size eighteen but been delivered an eight, a customer in Falmouth complaining that a dress she'd bought had come undone at the seams when she'd worn it horse riding, and a complaint from someone in Lancashire whose parcel had been lost only to turn up at a post office in Northern Ireland. Cally had dealt with the problems by her pseudonym, Alex, as she always did quickly and efficiently and on the outside with the patience of a saint. Inside, she could have quite frankly throttled someone, that was the severity of her mood.

Also, unlike most other people attending the races, she was

not going to the hairdresser or anything of its ilk. Because of the fact that she'd wanted to work the morning shift, her hair was being done by way of Alice from the deli popping up to put a low bun in and secure the hat to her head. After a very quick shower and not washing her hair as instructed by Alice, she was in her underwear, and super-fine stockings with her dressing gown over the top, and with more makeup on than she'd ever worn in her life. Her hair was moussed as instructed by Alice, and she had a mug of blackcurrant in her hand.

Her shoes were ready to go by the front entrance and as she opened the door to Alice, Alice smiled. 'Ooh, look at you with your make-up on! You look so pretty, our Cally.'

Cally scrunched her face up. 'Do I? I don't really know what I'm doing. I just slapped it on here and there and hoped for the best.'

'Well, whatever you did, it works. Really nice.'

'Thanks.'

'And you smell amazing! What is that?'

Cally chuckled. The Cloud perfume she'd worn for years always got comments. She shrugged it off. 'Oh, just a combination of a few, you know. I just spray willy-nilly.'

Alice looked at Cally's hair. 'You put the mousse on?'

'I did. Just as you instructed.'

'Excellent.'

'So, how come you know how to do updos and stuff?'

Alice shook her head. 'My sister was a ballroom dancer. I had the unenviable job of doing her hair. I can literally do a fancy low bun with my eyes closed. It is nowhere near as complicated as it looks.'

'The things you learn.'

'Tell me about it,' Alice said as she popped a gigantic can of hairspray, a big box of hairpins and hair elastics on the table. 'Right. Sit down and I'll get started.'

Cally looked at the equipment and swallowed. 'Should we have done a prerun?'

'Nah. That picture you showed me is so easy and the hat means it doesn't even have to be perfect on top. When I say perfect, my sister wasn't allowed to have one hair out of place, not a single one. We learnt the hard way. Gosh, the things I could tell you about the ballroom dancing world in those days. I think they'd call it abuse now.'

'Right. So this is easy for you?'

'Yes, walk in the park. We basically do three ponytails, one on either side, and one at the back, which turns into a huge low bun.' Alice held up a very fine hair net. 'This goes over the top, then the two ponytails loop over from each side in a load of swirls, making the bun look very fancy and very elegant.'

Cally wasn't sure, but Alice appeared to know what she was doing. 'I'll leave myself in your capable hands. You know me. My hair is usually shoved up in clips.'

Cally settled into the chair and tried to relax as Alice began to section her hair and spray for England. The unfamiliar weight of makeup on her face made her hyper-aware of every expression, and she struggled not to frown as doubts began to creep in.

'You're going to love this. It'll look so elegant, perfect for a day at the races.'

Cally managed a smile. 'I hope so. I feel a bit like I'm playing dress-up, to be honest. I'm not really sure if this is my scene.'

As Alice began to gather Cally's hair into the first ponytail, Cally's mind started to race. 'I hope this is going to look okay. My hair is weird at the best of times. It has a mind of its own.'

'Nope. Trust me. I know what I'm doing.'

'At least one of us does.'

'I've never been to the races. I've only ever seen it on telly. Is it as posh as they make it out to be?'

Cally chuckled nervously. 'I honestly have no idea. This is

my first time. I'm half expecting to be turned away at the gate for not being fancy enough.'

Alice tutted, securing the first ponytail with an elastic. 'Nonsense. You're going to fit right in. Especially with this hairstyle. Now, hold still while I do the other side.'

As Alice worked on the second ponytail, Cally's inner monologue attempted to taunt her. She was determined not to let it win.

'I reckon it's all smoke and mirrors, really.'

Cally latched onto Alice's words. 'Really? How so?'

Alice grinned. 'Well, take this style we're doing. It looks all intricate and fancy, right? But it's really just three ponytails arranged cleverly. The hat does half the work, hiding any little imperfections.'

Cally nodded, hoping to high heaven that Alice was correct.

'Right, no drama there. Now for the big low bun, which is going to be the base for everything else.'

As Alice began fiddling with hair at the nape of Cally's neck, Cally's mind wandered again. She tried not to but couldn't stop thinking that she was going to somehow make a fool of herself by using the wrong fork or saying something stupid. She was well aware that everyone else in attendance would probably have grown up around it and would know precisely what to do. On top of that, there was the marriage situation. In an odd way, she now felt a spot of guilt that she knew and Logan didn't know that she did. The whole thing had got away with itself. As usual, she should have taken Eloise's advice, plumped for the truth and confronted him right away.

Alice appeared to pick up on Cally's mood. 'Nervous about the day?'

Cally forced a laugh. 'Is it that obvious? I'm trying not to be, but I've never been to anything like this before. I'm worried I'll stick out like a sore thumb.'

Alice met Cally's eyes in the mirror in front of them. 'I

reckon the secret is to act like you belong there. Fake it 'til you make it, don't they say?'

Cally watched in the mirror as Alice began to secure the bun with what seemed like an endless supply of bobby pins. 'Yeah, I'm going to run with that.'

Alice stuck in a few more clips and started to spray the back of Cally's hair back and forth with an industrial-sized can of hairspray. 'I'll let you in on a little secret. Half the fancy hairdos you see? They're held together with enough hairspray to be considered a fire hazard.'

'Really?'

Alice nodded. 'By the end of the day, my sister could have used her hair as a helmet.'

As Alice continued to work, chatting away about everything from the weather to the preparation for the Chowder Festival to the latest gossip from the deli, Cally found herself relaxing slightly. The constant motion of Alice's hands in her hair was almost hypnotic, and she started to feel a bit more optimistic about the day ahead. She wasn't even going to think about Logan's marriage. She'd get through the day and deal with that afterwards.

'Right. That's the basic structure done. Now for the fancy bits and you're good to go.'

Cally watched, fascinated, as Alice began to manipulate the side ponytails, looping them over the central bun in a way that looked far more complicated than it actually was.

'See? Looks dead impressive, doesn't it? But it's really just clever positioning.'

As Alice worked, Cally's thoughts drifted back to Logan and how, right after she'd got through the races, she was going to confront him about the marriage certificate. Her mind flicked back and forth. Every time she'd thought about him since the discovery, she'd felt a furious mix of anger and sadness and utter indecision about what to do.

Alice broke her thoughts. 'Okay. Almost done. Just need to get this last hair net on.'

Cally watched as Alice carefully positioned the very fine hair net over the elaborate bun. It was nearly invisible, but Alice assured her it would keep everything in place.

'Time to make sure this masterpiece stays put. Close your eyes and hold your breath!'

Cally did as instructed, listening to the prolonged hiss of the hairspray can. She could feel the fine mist settling on her hair and face and fought the urge to sneeze.

'That should hold through anything short of a hurricane. You could probably go skydiving and that hat will stay put when you put it on.'

Cally laughed, opening her eyes. 'Let's hope it doesn't come to that. I think I'll stick to watching the horses.'

'Now for the pièce de résistance,' Alice said with a flourish, picking up the hat.

Cally nodded as Alice carefully positioned the hat, angling it slightly as she'd seen in the pictures Cally had shown her. Cally turned to the mirror, her eyes widening in surprise. The woman looking back at her was... Well, she was still Cally, but a version of Cally she'd never seen before. The elegant updo, combined with the carefully applied makeup and the stunning hat, created an image that took her breath away.

She turned her head slightly to see the hairstyle from different angles. 'I can't believe that's me.'

Alice beamed. 'Told you it would look amazing. You're going to fit right in, our Cally. They won't know what hit them.'

As Cally continued to stare at her reflection, her doubts began to fade. Maybe she could do it after all. Maybe, just for one sweet day, she could step into the world of high society and hold her own. She certainly looked the part, so that was a start.

Alice began to pack up her supplies, and Cally stood, carefully moving her head to test the weight and stability of the hairstyle. To her surprise, it felt secure and not nearly as heavy as she'd feared when she'd seen the number of pins and hairspray.

'How does it feel?'

'Good.'

Alice nodded. 'The trick is to make sure it's secure enough to last all day but not so tight that you're in agony. I think we've nailed it.'

'Thank you. I love it.'

Alice waved off the thanks with a smile. 'Happy to help. It's not every day one of us Lovelies gets to go to races, is it? We've got to stick together.'

'Yep, true.'

Alice paused at the door. 'Hold your head high, smile, and if all else fails, just nod and say "indeed" a lot.'

Cally chuckled as she stood by the door at the top of the stairs and saw Alice off. As she closed the door, she nodded to herself. She would be fine. Whatever the day had in store, she would meet it head-on, armed with a bomb-blast-safe-exquisitely-crafted low bun. And anyway, Henry-Hicks and his lot were soon going to be toast, so part of her didn't give a hoot anyway. She just had another little bump to navigate along the way.

20

Cally wasn't anywhere near as nervous as she'd thought she might be. After Alice had gone, she'd popped on the beautiful dress, slipped the shoes on, and stood in front of the mirror. What looked back at her, even *she* had to admit, was on the nice side. In fact, she'd been totally and utterly transformed. It was as if someone had waved a sparkly, twinkling wand over her head and turned her into someone else. Cally de Pfeffer's fairy godmother had done quite the job. Maybe it was the fact that she was used to looking at herself in the same old uniform she always wore, or maybe it was the fact that she'd scrubbed up well. Either way, even if she said it herself, she looked rather good. More importantly, though, she felt *fabulous*. *Strictly level fabulous*, in fact. A very strange feeling for Cally, but, oh, what a nice dress, a hat, and a fabulous updo could do for a girl.

She nodded to herself resolutely as she just about managed to squeeze a mini carton of blackcurrant into her bag; she was going to shove all the doubts of Thomas to the back of her mind and jolly well enjoy herself like every other person on the planet did when they went to events. Stuff putting herself and her background down all the time for a game of soldiers.

An hour or so later, she was sitting in the back of a car next to Logan with butterflies in her stomach and a smile fixed perfectly on her face. She'd used the switch at the back of her throat a few times, but not anywhere near as much as she'd thought. As the car pulled in through a fancy-looking gate, she couldn't quite believe where she was. Not only was she at the races but in the posh end, no less. It hadn't taken her much to work out that she was not only in the posh section but the upper elite end for people who had prefixes attached to the front of their names. Not that she cared about that, but still. Perhaps she could add one to hers for a laugh. Lady Cally de Pfeffer didn't sound too bad. Maybe she'd introduce herself as such. Inside, she chuckled. What a funny old turn-up for the books. Who would have thought she would be sitting in the back of a car in a very fancy outfit, ready to hobnob with the upper echelons of society? She was a very long way from the chatbot window on her laptop.

Logan reached over, put his hand on her leg and squeezed. 'Okay?'

Cally didn't like the squeeze. She nodded. She was far from okay where he was concerned. She shoved it under the carpet and stomped on the top. She fully intended to deal with him and the situation once the races were over. 'Yep. I'm looking forward to it. Exciting.'

'Good. Me too. You're going to love it.'

Cally looked out the window where women in beautiful outfits filed this way and that, and men in top hats and tails stood around chatting. She was surprised that instead of her earlier trepidation she actually felt okay as she took on the regalia going on out the window. 'I love all the pomp.'

Logan touched his hat. 'Ha. I won't be saying that when I've been lugging this around all day.'

As the car rolled to a stop, Cally took a deep breath, steeling herself. The butterflies in her stomach seemed to have multiplied tenfold, but she was determined not to let her nerves show. She resolved to have a nice day.

Logan stepped out first, offering his hand to help Cally from the car. As she emerged, the noise, the colour and the full spectacle of the event hit her all at once. The sight was almost overwhelming – a sea of colour, a swishing movement of pomp and extravagance, ladies in elaborate hats and men in morning suits milling about in every direction.

Cally gripped Logan's arm, suddenly feeling very small and out of place. 'It's, err, quite something, isn't it?'

Logan smiled. 'Yep, wait until we get inside.'

As they made their way through a gate where even the people at the gates looked fancy, they strolled through what felt to Cally like crowds of people. She felt as if she was in a show, a movie, or a dream, almost as if she were looking down on herself in a role. In the beautiful but very high nude shoes and the swishy dress, and with the hat balanced on her head, she wobbled a bit. A very, very pretty fish out of water. She tried to walk with grace and confidence and her head held high. She may have practised walking in the shoes and the hat going back and forth in the sitting room of her flat, but in situ, it was very different. Each step felt a bit precarious in her high heels as she looked out from under the hat and held onto her bag as if her life depended on it. Man, did she need a blackcurrant.

All around her, a riot of colour and style stretched off into the distance. Hats of every conceivable shape and size bobbed through the crowd, dresses ranged from classic, tailored looks in muted pastels to bold designs in eye-catching prints, and men all around her were topped with hats. Cally took it all in as she picked up snippets of overwhelmingly posh-accented conversation around her. As she stood next to Logan, waiting to go up some stairs to a stand and restaurant area, she tuned into a couple in front of them.

'Did you hear about Fitzgerald's Folly? They're saying he's

the one to watch in the third race.' The woman in a bright pink dress, with matching hat, shoes, and bag said, her voice dripping with confidence.

'Oh yes, but I wouldn't discount Thunderbolt. His bloodline is rather impeccable.'

Cally felt a moment of panic. She didn't know the first thing about racing. What if someone asked her opinion? She swallowed and resolved not to worry. It was a horse race at the end of the day. She could get the hang of that, couldn't she? It couldn't be that hard.

Logan guided her through the entrance, presenting their badges to a steward. As they stepped into the enclosure, Cally felt as though she'd entered another world entirely. Everything was immaculate: lawns stretched out before them, elegant white marquees dotted the landscape, the sound of champagne corks popping mingled with refined laughter, and there was a gentle clinking of glasses and music playing somewhere in the background.

'Shall we get a drink?' Logan asked, already steering them towards one of the bars.

Cally nodded, not trusting herself to speak. She watched as Logan ordered two glasses of champagne with the easy confidence of someone who belonged in the world. As she accepted her glass, she caught sight of her reflection in a nearby mirror and nearly fell over. The woman looking back at her looked *absolutely* stunning. She squinted, not really believing it was her, and moved her head a bit closer and peered for a few seconds. She might be *feeling* like a fish out of water on the inside, but on the outside, she stunned. Cally de Pfeffer nodded. Oh yeah, oh yeah, oh yeah. She adored how that made her feel. Talk about beautiful.

Logan clinked his glass against hers. 'To a wonderful day at the races.' He leaned closer to Cally's ear and lowered his voice.

'Bloody hell, Blackcurrant. You look absolutely breathtaking. I have to be the luckiest man in here. On the planet, actually.'

Logan's marriage certificate flashed in front of Cally's eyes. Grrr. He wouldn't be feeling lucky when she'd finished with him. His world might well crash down as had hers. She smiled, nodded, didn't say anything in return, and took a sip of the champagne. The bubbles tickled her nose, the crisp, dry taste a contrast to her usual drinks. She swallowed and enjoyed her drink and continued to get lost in the sea of fabulous outfits.

As they moved further into the enclosure, Cally was quite enjoying herself. Her senses were assaulted from all directions; freshly cut grass mingled with the aroma of the racetrack itself, floral arrangements adorned every surface, the sound of a band drifted on the breeze, and all around them, people were engaged in animated conversation and very much appeared to be enjoying themselves. The pomp was doing its thing and she lapped it up.

Logan seemed to know everyone, stopping every few steps to shake hands or exchange pleasantries. Cally stood by his side, smiling and nodding but not really contributing to the conversation. Each time Logan introduced her, she felt a moment of panic, worried that her accent or pretty much anything, like, you know, moving, would give her away as an outsider. A part of her didn't give a hoot as she stunned in her outfit.

'And this is Cally,' Logan told a distinguished-looking couple. 'Cally, this is Lord and Lady Farrington. Friends of the family.'

Cally bobbed in a weird curtsy-type bowing movement and immediately realised she'd done the wrong thing. 'Lovely to meet you.' She squeezed her eyes together as she heard her voice come out in a strange, squeaky sort of chirp.

Lady Farrington smiled. 'Lovely to meet you, dear. Is this your first time?'

Cally nodded, relieved to have a simple question to answer. 'Yes, it is.'

'Oh, you'll get used to it in no time,' Lady Farrington assured her. 'Why, I remember my first event. I was rather terrified I'd trip over my own feet and make a spectacle of myself! It's the shoes on the grass that get you.'

Cally managed a genuine smile. 'That's exactly how I feel!'

Lord Farrington chuckled. 'The secret, my dear, is to act like you own the place, even if you don't, though if you're with the Henry-Hicks lot, you more or less do.'

As the conversation continued, Cally found herself relaxing ever-so-slightly. She even managed to laugh at Lord Farrington's jokes, even though most of the time, she couldn't fully understand what he was saying. Between his mumbling, his accent, revolting throat clearing and gigantic moustache, most of the time, it seemed as if he was conversing in a completely different language.

As they moved on, Logan leaned in close. 'All good?'

Cally flicked the switch and ignored the fact that very soon she would be blasting him with his own marriage certificate. 'Yep, fine.' She actually *was* fine-ish, though, which was a revelation. She was having a much nicer time than she thought she would. Strolling around in an expensive hat and swishy dress was actually not too bad at all. The good life did her well. She could get used to it. Thing was, she didn't quite know what was coming next.

21

After another glass of champagne and something to eat, Cally and Logan stood in a viewing area, watching the scene on the track.

'Want to place a bet?' Logan asked.

The idea of gambling was an unfamiliar concept to Cally. She'd never quite been able to understand how gambling equated to fun. The truthful answer was no; she had little to zero interest in placing a bet. She wrinkled her nose. 'I don't know. No, not really. I wouldn't know where to start.'

'It's easy.'

Cally nodded. Of course it was easy for Logan. He clearly knew exactly what he was doing. 'Yeah, actually, no, I don't think so...'

Logan picked up on Cally's hesitation right away. 'We'll just put a small bet on Midnight Dancer to win. It'll make the race more exciting to watch. Trust me.'

The irony, Cally thought to herself. Trust was not something she was feeling in spades at that precise moment. Before she could protest further, Logan was leading her towards the betting stands. She blinked rapidly as she tried to work out what was going on. The process was a blur of unfamiliar terms and numbers, but soon enough, she found herself holding a betting slip.

As they made their way back to the stands to watch the race, Cally again felt as if she was enjoying herself. It was an odd feeling: a mix of excitement and trepidation together with being dressed up to the nines and tottering around on heels under a huge, pretty hat. The atmosphere was electric, with people jostling for the best viewing positions and discussing the merits of various horses. Cally stood squinting at the track and then down at her ticket when the sound of the starting bell cut through the chatter. She found herself caught up in the excitement despite herself, cheering along with the crowd as the horses thundered past.

When Midnight Dancer crossed the finish line first, Cally let out a whoop of joy. 'We won!'

Logan beamed, pulled her into a celebratory hug, picked her up, and spun her around. For a moment, Cally forgot about how angry she was with him and how the next day she would be telling him about what she knew, letting him know that she was aware that he'd been married and hadn't told her. That he was a liar.

As the excitement of the win settled, they made their way towards a small circle of people where Logan's mum and his aunt Cecilia stood chatting.

'Cally, dear, you look absolutely stunning!' Cecilia gushed as they approached. 'That dress is simply divine on you. Rather gorgeous hat, might I add.'

Cally blushed but very much liked the compliment. 'Thank you, Cecilia. You look lovely as well.'

Logan's mum smiled warmly, then turned to introduce a few family members. Beatrice, an elegant woman in a pale pink suit and wide-brimmed hat, stepped forward to air kiss Cally's cheeks. 'It's wonderful to finally meet you, my dear. We've heard so much about you.'

'Indeed. It's a pleasure to have you join us today,' Logan's mum added.

Cally smiled politely. 'Thank you. It's lovely to be here.'

The group fell into conversation, discussing the recent race and their plans for the rest of the day. Cally mostly listened, trying to follow the unfamiliar jargon and references to past events.

'I must say, that was quite a thrilling race,' Beatrice commented. 'Midnight Dancer certainly lived up to expectations.'

Logan's uncle, Reginald, nodded, swirling amber liquid in his glass. 'Yes, he's been in excellent form this season. I had a feeling he'd pull through today.'

Cally glanced at Logan. 'Cally and I actually placed a bet on Midnight Dancer to win,' Logan said, wrapping an arm around Cally's waist.

Cecilia raised an eyebrow, looking impressed. 'Did you now? Well, congratulations on your win, both of you.'

As they chatted, Alastair arrived. Cally bristled internally. Alastair had a habit he wasn't even aware of, of rubbing her up the wrong way. Alaistair kissed everyone and grabbed himself a drink from a passing waitress. He then turned to Cally and beamed. 'You look beautiful! Wow! Do you often attend the races?'

Cally felt her stomach flutter with nerves, unsure how to respond. 'Oh, no, this is actually my first time,' she admitted. 'I'm quite new to all of this.'

Alastair frowned and wrinkled his nose. 'First time! What? Really?'

'Yes.'

'Sorry, I thought you were joking! You've never been to the races before! What? Rather odd.'

Cecilia joined in. 'She's loving the excitement, all the glamour, and the thrill of it all.'

'Bet you are.' Alastair laughed. 'Can't actually believe it's your first time.'

Cecilia touched Cally on the elbow. 'I have a feeling Cally here might be our good luck charm. It's not often that Logan wins a bet.'

Logan feigned offence. 'Hey, I've had my fair share of lucky streaks in the past.'

Cecilia rolled her eyes good-naturedly. 'Of course. But you have to admit, having Cally by your side makes you rather luckier than usual.'

Cally felt a pang in her chest at the mention of luck and fortune. These people didn't know they were born. Or they did. They very much knew where they were born. On the right side of a big fat silver spoon. One that dripped in liquid gold.

She flicked the switch and smiled at Cecilia, and played along with the banter, hoping what she felt didn't show on her face. 'I'm happy to be anyone's good luck charm.'

Logan squeezed her arm. 'You're certainly mine.'

Grr, that's why you lied to me, Cally said to herself. She had to stop her nostrils flaring and a hiss of steam coming out of her ears. What an actual scumbag. He was making out they were so tight when he'd lied. She bristled inside. If only the stupid Henry-Hicks family knew that she knew the secret. A knife twisted in Cally's gut. How could he say nice things and woo her when he had been hiding such a monumental secret from her? She simply didn't get it. She smiled, played the part of the happy, carefree girlfriend and thought about how she was going to be the one with all the cards the next day.

'You two make such a lovely couple,' Beatrice said. 'Rather lovely to see.'

Cally swallowed hard, forcing a smile. 'That's very kind of you to say.'

As the conversation flowed on around her, Cally found herself drifting, her mind consumed with thoughts of Logan and the secret. She tried to focus on the present, but the nagging betrayal lingered. Part of her realised her plan to keep schtum until after the races was complete stupidity. What had she been thinking? She glanced around at the sea of colourful hats and tailored suits, at the gleaming horses, and at the immaculate grounds of the racetrack. It was all so different from the world she knew—such a contrast to her simple, unassuming life.

Beatrice rested her hand on Cally's arm. 'You must visit us at the estate sometime. We would love to show you around the gardens and introduce you to the rest of the family.'

Cally blinked, surprised by the invitation. 'I'd love that.'

Beatrice nodded enthusiastically. 'Yes, please do come and visit. We could make a whole weekend of it, perhaps have a little dinner party for you and Logan.'

Cally glanced at Logan, who was smiling broadly. 'Mmm. Thank you.' She nodded, trying to muster up some enthusiasm for the idea, even though inside, she thought that she wouldn't be around after the next day.

As the group continued to chat, Cally looked around at her surroundings. A beautiful building looking out over a racetrack surrounded by high society where she actually wasn't doing too badly at all. She observed Logan for a bit and how he was completely at ease. How he navigated this world and had brought her into it entirely comfortable and confident amongst the wealthy and the privileged. He was fine carrying on when he'd not been truthful. She couldn't shake the feeling that there was a part of him she didn't know, as if he had a secret life hidden from her. The thought made her heart ache and question everything. Cally did not like that at all. She touched the edge of her hat and pursed her lips. Henry-Hicks would soon be toast. The little façade he'd created would come crashing down around his ears, and she would go back to holding up the sky. Just as she always had.

22

Despite Cally's feelings, she'd quite enjoyed the races and had held her own well. She'd been fine chatting here and there, and it hadn't taken her long to work out that her outfit was on point. It was mid-afternoon, and the weather had turned cloudy. Logan had gone off with Alastair to bet, and after standing with Cecilia and Beatrice for a while, Cally had decided to take herself off for a walk. Considering that she had never in her life been interested in fashion or anything like it, she was fascinated by the outfits, hats, and generally just the pomp and dress-up going on around her. She'd made her excuses and fully intended to have a little stroll around, get herself a cup of tea, and have a bit of a people-watch at how the other half lived.

Strolling out of the enclosure towards the marquee area, she immersed herself in a sea of vibrant colours and extravagant fashions. A stunning kaleidoscope of outfits and aristocratic elegance that seemed almost too perfect to be real surrounded her. Everywhere she looked, women were dressed up to the nines in stunning outfits, their hats adorned with feathers and flowers and delicate, intricate designs, standing around looking fabulous. Cally lapped up the atmosphere and marvelled at some of the hats. She was enjoying the spectacle of the niceties of life more than she thought she would.

Making her way to one of the refreshment stands in a marquee, a smartly dressed attendant greeted her with a polite smile and a nod. 'What can I get for you?'

'Just a cup of tea, please.' Cally gestured to the rest of the marquee, 'Can I sit anywhere here?'

The attendant looked at Cally's badge and chuckled. 'With that you can go just about anywhere you like and get someone to serve you whatever you want.'

Cally smiled, 'Ha, okay, thanks. I'm going to take a pew somewhere over there.'

'I'll bring your tea over. Go and find yourself a nice spot.'

Cally liked the treatment. She could get used to it in her life. 'Thanks.'

A couple of minutes later, she sat at one of the only empty tables waiting for her tea. Right next to her, a group of older women had their heads bent together in conversation. Dressed in elegant, timeless pieces that spoke of old money and aristocratic breeding, their hair swept up into intricate, perfectly coiffed styles, Cally vacuumed up the people watching. The women dripped wealth in an understated, quiet way; one in a pale, buttery yellow, another sported a hat adorned with a spray of pale lilac roses, another in a dress of deepest, richest blue, the colour so intense that it seemed almost to vibrate with energy. Another with a gigantic cream hat nearly as big as the table chuckled as she sipped on a flute of champagne.

As the attendant bustled over with a tray and handed Cally a cup of tea in a delicate china cup, she settled back into her seat, felt her shoulders drop, and let her gaze wander over the whole colourful, animated scene playing out before her. She sat and soaked it up as if she'd stepped into a dreamy, fantasy world where everything was perfect, elegant and impossibly breathtakingly happy. No bed hoists, money worries, liquid diets, early morning laptop shifts, just a frothy world full of pomp and spectacle. She *adored* it.

After another cup of tea, which had been delivered with a plate of tiny miniature pastries, Cally continued to sit, ostensibly watching the racing going on outside the marquee but really earwigging the conversation going on at the table beside her and gawping at the various outfits walking past. Just as she was thinking about getting up and heading back to where she'd come from, her attention was suddenly caught by someone approaching the table of women beside her. She peered for a second, racking her brain about where she knew the person from. Then she realised. Oh. Her heart skipped a beat as recognition dawned. There, just a metre or so away was no other than Cassia Allegra Brommington in the flesh. And boy, was she an eleven out of ten.

Cally's breath caught in her throat as she took in the sight of Logan's ex-wife. Cassia was, if possible, even more regally beautiful in person than in the photographs Cally had obsessively looked over. Tall and graceful, her posture perfect as she laughed at something the woman in the gigantic cream hat said. The light caught Cassia's hair, styled in an effortlessly elegant sweep of an updo that made Cally's own carefully crafted bun-by-Alice feel heavy and overdone by comparison. Cassia's hat was a work of art, a wide-brimmed creation in a soft blush pink that complemented her complexion perfectly. Delicate silk flowers cascaded down one side, their petals seeming to flutter as she talked. Cally's eyes travelled down, taking in Cassia's outfit. Her bespoke creation fit her slender frame like a glove. Pale pink silk shimmered in the sunlight, the cut somehow modern and classic at the same time with a slash neckline and three-quarter-length sleeves. Everything about her was just right: a string of tiny pearls, flawless makeup, little studs, and nude nails. Understated elegance.

Cassia bent down to air-kiss a couple of the women at the table, pulled over a spare chair, and sat down. Now so close that if Cally had moved to the next chair on her table, she'd be able to touch her, Cally couldn't get enough. A tidal wave of inadequacy topped off with pure envy engulfed her. She reached up to feel her hat self-consciously and suddenly felt all wrong.

Her inner monologue rattled on like crazy. *If it isn't la-di-da Cassia Allegra Brommington herself.*

Cally watched as Cassia laughed at something one of the older women said. Even the way Cassia sat seemed elegant, one hand resting lightly on the table while the other held a flute of champagne, poker straight back. Cally shifted her weight, sat up straighter, and lifted her chin. She sighed; she wasn't even on the same planet, let alone in the same league.

A distinguished-looking older man approached Cassia, bowing slightly as he greeted her. Cassia's face lit up with a dazzling smile, and she engaged him in what appeared to be an animated conversation about the upcoming race.

Of course she knows everything about horse racing, Cally thought, rolling her eyes internally.

Whipping her phone out of her bag and shoving the carton of blackcurrant further inside, she tried to work out how she could get a photo without being caught. Her mind was going nineteen to the dozen as Cassia and the man chatted.

I bet she was born on a thoroughbred stud farm and learned to ride before she could walk. Probably has her own stable of championship horses hidden away somewhere.

Cassia laughed and the flowers on her hat ruffled. Cally half-expected to see a miniature rainbow appear and unicorns dance around Cassia's head. Sitting upright, Cally tortured herself further by staying rooted to the spot and listening to everything that was being said. The only good thing about the whole situation was that Cassia and everyone at the table had no clue who Cally was. Her anonymity and not being part of the tight little upper-class world meant that she could overstare and earwig as much as she liked. She fully indulged and continued to watch and listen. Cassia chatted with the older woman in the gigantic cream hat.

'Darling, you simply must come to visit us in St. Tropez this summer. The weather is divine, and the yacht parties are not to be missed.'

The woman in the cream hat nodded. 'Oh, I have no doubt. But I'm afraid I'll be spending most of the season at the estate in Scotland. You know how Hugo gets when the grouse shooting begins.'

Cassia laughed. 'Ah, yes. The call of the wild. I do envy you, Margaret. There's something so invigorating about tramping through the heather, rifle in hand.'

Cally nearly choked on her tea. Rifle in hand? She tried to picture Cassia, with her perfect hair and delicate features, tromping through the Scottish moors in pursuit of game. It seemed about as likely as Cally herself being invited to one of the yacht parties in St. Tropez.

Margaret lowered her voice. 'Well, between you and I, I'm looking forward to a bit of a break from the social scene. All these parties and polo matches can be rather exhausting, don't you think?'

Cassia replied, 'Oh, absolutely. Sometimes one just needs to escape to the country, to reconnect with nature and recharge the batteries.'

Cally bit back a snort. Escape to the country? More like escape to a sprawling, centuries-old estate complete with a full staff and every luxury imaginable. She couldn't even begin to fathom what it must be like to have so many options, to be able to jet off to the French Riviera or the Scottish Highlands on a whim.

As the conversation continued, Cally's mind drifted to the stark differences between her own life and the lives of the women around her. She thought about her tiny flat, with its cramped kitchen and creaky floorboards, and compared it to grand mansions and estates. She thought about the long hours she spent at the chemist's, dealing with carton after carton of drugs and always having been on a budget. Cassia and the women around her had no idea about any of that. No doubt they whiled away their days at garden parties and charity galas. She was so lost in her own thoughts that she almost didn't notice when Cassia turned slightly in her chair, her gaze drifting in Cally's direction. For a quick second, their eyes met, and Cally felt a jolt of panic run through her. But Cassia smiled politely, not even remotely interested and turned back to her conversation with Margaret.

Cally glanced down at her phone, realising with a start that she had been sitting there for far longer than she'd intended. Logan would probably be wondering where she'd gone, and the last thing she wanted was for him to come looking for her and find her eavesdropping on his ex-wife's conversation like some kind of creepy stalker. She watched as the older women started to gather their things and she heard one of them say that they were going out to watch the next race as the clouds had darkened and it might start to rain. Cassia said that she'd got chilly standing by the racetrack and stayed put, took out her phone, and sat scrolling with her head bent down.

Draining the last of her tea, Cally gathered her things with the intention of popping to the loo before heading back to where she'd left Logan and the Henry-Hicks contingent. She stood up, smoothed down the front of her dress, and with a nod of her head, decided that she wasn't going to allow Cassia to bother her. She wasn't about to let some posh toff with a fancy hat and a trust fund make her feel like she was not worthy. The surprising thing that was emerging from the races was that Cally overall felt okay, not flick the switch okay but *really* okay. Yes, she felt a bit unsure, but at least she was honest, knew a day's hard work when it hit her in the face and had always looked after herself. She was no longer prepared to let things from her past, or lack thereof, define or diminish her. In a funny way, being dressed up to the nines and having to hold her own had shown her she was no different from anyone else. That she could do it. On top of that, it had shown her that she was happy with who she was. It was a revelation that had been a long time coming.

23

Cally walked away from the table she'd been sitting at and strolled between tables behind where Cassia still sat with her head bent to her phone. Looking for a sign to the toilet, she stopped by the bar and asked the attendant, who told her that the nearest toilets were out the side door of the marquee across the open grass area and to the far side. Looking in the direction he'd pointed and realising that the toilets were in the opposite direction to the way she wanted to go, but busting for a wee she decided to go anyway.

Peering upwards as she got to the side door, she frowned at the colour of the sky. The morning had dawned a clear, bright day with blue sky and sunshine. The forecast had mentioned a slight possibility of it clouding over, but it had done more than that and heavy black rain clouds looked as if they might drop their load at any time. Cally grimaced at the clouds, peered over to where she thought she could see a sign for the women's toilets, and stepped out gingerly, trying not to let her heels sink into the grass. About halfway to the toilet, the sky above suddenly darkened further. The chatter around her faltered as people glanced upwards and started to move away from the fence.

A man with an American accent in front of Cally muttered as he peered at the ominous clouds rolling in. 'Looks like we're in for a proper downpour. English weather. Gets me every single time.'

No sooner had the words left his mouth than the heavens opened. Huge, fat, heavy droplets of rain began to fall, quickly intensifying as Cally lifted her dress and looked up at the sky. The elegant crowd erupted into a flurry of activity, people scurrying for cover left, right, and centre. For a moment, Cally stood frozen, a bit shocked by the sudden deluge momentarily overriding her ability to move. The rain then started to pelt down. Her beautiful hat started to get wet and the lace overlay on the arms of her dress felt damp. She attempted to hustle over the grass, concerned that her hat would be ruined and that the elaborate updo that Alice had so painstakingly crafted would droop. She muttered and swore to herself, realised that the toilets were far too far away, and looked around frantically for shelter. Logan was nowhere to be seen and people were cramming themselves into every available covered space. The nearest marquee was already bursting at the seams, a sea of colourful hats and suits visible through the entrance. Cally started towards it but quickly realised she'd never squeeze in.

She spotted another small gazebo marquee off to the side, partially hidden behind a carefully manicured hedge. Without a second thought, she made a dash for it, her heels hampering her movements and her hat feeling as if it might slip off entirely. Reaching the gazebo, breathless and a bit wet, another woman was doing exactly the same thing just behind her. As Cally ducked under the marquee porch and let out a sigh, she turned around and her eyes widened in shock as she recognised the other refugee from the rain. Cassia Allegra Brommington stood right next to her, looking far less composed than she had earlier.

Her own hat was askew, the delicate silk flowers now drooping sadly. The pale pink of her dress had darkened where the rain had soaked it, and her perfectly styled hair wasn't looking quite as fabulous.

For a moment, the two women stared at each other, the comedy of the moment palpable over the sound of the rain hammering on the gazebo's roof. Cally felt her cheeks flush, mortified to be face-to-face with Logan's ex-wife.

'Ghastly weather, isn't it?' Cassia said, her voice as cultured and refined as it had been when Cally had been earwigging. Cassia nudged Cally's elbow and peered behind Cally. 'Can you shove back a bit?'

Cally nodded mutely, stepping fully into the gazebo. She stood as far from Cassia as the small space would allow, but with little more than a few inches between them, Cassia laughed. 'What a nightmare! I'm Cassia.'

Cally swallowed. 'Cally.'

'I daresay this isn't quite how either of us expected to spend our afternoon at the races.' Cassia said with a roll of her eyes. 'Weather, eh? Best of British.'

Cally nodded, unsure of what else to say. Cassia, however, didn't seem to notice and obviously had no clue whatsoever who Cally was. Why would she?

'I feel rather like a drowned peacock.'

Cally glanced down at her own bedraggled state and chuckled. 'Join the club. I look like I've gone for a swim in the Thames.'

As they stood there, Cally felt some of her earlier awe and intimidation ebb away. Cassia, for all her poise and beauty, was just as dishevelled as she was. There was something oddly comforting in that realisation.

'Do you know how long it's meant to rain for?' Cally ventured, gesturing towards the rain still pelting down outside their shelter.

Cassia shook her head, reaching up to adjust her hat. 'I'm afraid meteorology isn't one of my areas of expertise.' She joked. 'Though, given my luck today, I wouldn't be surprised if we're stuck here until next Tuesday.'

Cally raised an eyebrow. 'Your luck?'

'Luck isn't one of my strong points.' Cassia looked at Cally's hat. 'How's your hat holding up?'

'Fine, I think. My friend Alice spent ages on this updo. It seems to be doing okay, too.' Cally said, touching the back of her hair.

'Alice did a marvellous job,' Cassia said, eyeing Cally's hair with approval. 'It's holding up remarkably well, all things considered. My hairdresser would have a fit if he could see me now.'

Cally heard herself rambling. 'Alice isn't actually a hairdresser. She works at the deli near my flat. She just happens to be good with hair. She used to do her sister's hair for ballroom dancing competitions.'

'How wonderfully versatile.'

The absurdity of the situation suddenly struck Cally. Here she was, trapped in a gazebo with Logan's ex-wife, discussing hairstyles as the rain poured down around them. Cassia appeared to have no idea who Cally was and definitely not that Cally had Googled the life out of her. It was like something out of a surreal comedy sketch. Or horror story.

Cassia looked down at Cally's badge. 'Oh, you're in the same area as me.'

Cally panicked inside. 'Ahh, right, yes.'

'Who are you here with then?'

'Oh, you know, just a few various people.' Cally moved her head and looked up at the sky, peering out from under the shelter. She changed the subject as quick as a flash. 'Looks like it's easing off a bit.'

Cassia put her hand out. 'Not really.'

Cally nodded. She needed to get away and fast. 'I think I might make a dash for it.

'Really? Rather you than me! Good luck.'

Cally gathered up the skirt of her dress. 'Thanks.'

She peered out of the marquee, took a breath in and hoped she wouldn't end up in the mud. As she hustled away from the marquee in the direction of the toilets, she didn't look back. No way was she going to be stuck with Cassia Allegra Brommington talking about who she was with, that she knew for free.

24

As the rest of the day wore on, the rain eased up. Cally had blasted herself under a hand drier for a bit and successfully made it back from the loo in one piece. She'd subsequently dried out without too much mishap to her outfit and her hat had held up well. She did, however, inevitably think about Cassia way too much. The whole interaction had been quite bizarre. The fact that Cassia had no clue who she was, the dashing through the rain, Cassia being posh-confident and chatting away as if she belonged there. Cally nodded to herself as she thought about their interaction. Cassia *did* belong there.

She stood next to Logan in a circle of people she didn't know and listened to chit-chat going on around her. Talk of racehorse investments, holiday homes, and boarding schools for children Cally didn't have fizzed around her. She smiled and nodded in what she hoped were the right places and occasionally offered a non-committal "indeed" when she felt it was expected. She'd loved the day, had felt fine hobnobbing in her beautiful outfit and overall, had unexpectedly enjoyed herself despite what she knew about Logan.

As the last round of races began and everyone watched, she

didn't watch but instead found her mind wandering. She thought about her three jobs, her constant saving for her deposit, the flat above the chemist, Birdie and the regular customers she saw every day. That world seemed a million miles away from what was currently going on around her.

'Penny for your thoughts?' Logan said and gently nudged her on the elbow.

Cally startled slightly. 'Oh, you know, I'm just taking it all in,' she said, forcing a smile.

Logan squeezed her hand. 'Everyone I've introduced you to has been charmed.'

Cally wished so much that she hadn't found out about his secret. She felt like a fraud, play-acting at being someone she wasn't. She smiled and nodded anyway, thinking that it wouldn't be long before Logan was no more in her world once she confronted him about his marriage. It was all going to go sliding downhill from there. As the next few races went by, Cally couldn't quite wait for the day to end. Although she'd enjoyed it, she was feeling it: the constant small talk, the effort of maintaining everything, the heels, the pins in the back of her head. All of it exhausting. Her feet ached, her face hurt from the perpetual smile and her brain was a complete and utter jumble of she knew not what.

Standing by the window looking over the racetrack where the dark clouds had lifted a little bit, she was counting down the time until she could get into the car and slip off her shoes. She certainly wouldn't be confronting Logan until the next day; she barely had the energy to keep her eyes open. As the last race finished, Logan turned to her with a smile and waved a few of his betting slips. 'Ready for the after-party?'

Cally's heart sank. More socialising, more pretending. She nodded, summoning what little energy she had left. Making their way to another elaborate marquee, the sounds of a live band drifted out to meet them. Elegantly dressed guests were filing in through the doors and she caught glimpses of faces she'd seen throughout the day - Lord and Lady Farrington, the woman who'd been discussing Fitzgerald's Folly, the French couple they'd had lunch with. All of it began to blur together in Cally's mind. As they stood with the Farringtons, she smiled and laughed in what she hoped were the right places, but inside, she wanted to go home. All she really wanted to do was pull the mountain of pins out of her hair, get out of the dress, have a nice long bath, scrub off the make-up, get her pyjamas on and settle into her own bed. Swig a quick hot blackcurrant, maybe with a nip of gin.

After another glass of wine, Cally didn't want to look at another person, let alone have small talk with them. She smiled mutely, half listening to Logan chat to Alastair about one of their horses.

Logan lowered his voice, put his hand on the small of her back and leant into her ear, 'Had enough? You seem like it.'

Cally nearly jumped down his throat. 'I have, actually.'

'Shall we get going?'

'If you don't mind, that would be great. I'm exhausted.'

'Of course not.' Logan slipped his phone out of his pocket. 'I'll call the driver.'

Cally felt a wave of relief. 'Okay.' She nodded in the direction of the toilets. 'I'll just pop to the loo.'

Logan looked around. 'I'll do the rounds and say our goodbyes if you don't want to go through all that rigmarole.'

Cally definitely didn't want to have to go through saying goodbye. She felt more than relieved. 'That would be great.'

Logan joked. 'We'll do a runner. An exit plan.' He indicated in the direction of the toilets. 'You go to the loo and I'll see you out the front where we got dropped off. We'll be home before you know it. You can put your feet up. I'll run you a nice bath.'

Cally nodded, but there was no way Logan was staying at the

flat. She'd cook up some excuse about having to get up for work. 'By the main gate?'

'Yep, then we'll walk to the side entrance where the cars are.'

'Great, see you there.'

Cally then shimmied through people and made her way across the marquee in the direction of the toilets. When she got to the entrance, an attendant shook her head. 'Sorry, this one is out of action. There's a leak because of that downpour.'

'Ahh, right, where's the nearest one?'

The attendant pointed out the door. 'Out there, across the grass, and via the other marquee. Right over the back there.'

Cally nodded. It was next door to the marquee where she'd sheltered from the rain with Cassia. 'Thank you.'

A few minutes later, she was going through the next marquee. Just as she was near the toilets, someone tapped her on the shoulder. She turned around with a frown and closed her eyes for a second as she saw Cassia. 'Oh, hello again,' Cally stuttered.

There was a strange look on Cassia's face. 'Hi! I just had to come up and say something.'

'Yes, yes, fancy bumping into you again.'

'Ha. Not about that!'

'Sorry. What?'

'You're with the Henry-Hicks family, that's right, isn't it?'

Cally's jaw tightened. What was Cassia going to say? Cally nodded, trying to keep her expression neutral even as her heart raced in her chest. She tried to make her voice sound breezy. 'I am, yes.'

'I saw you from the stand. Your hat caught my eye. Have you dried out now?'

Cally wanted to bolt. 'Ahh, yes. That was some downpour earlier. It did brighten up in the end, though. I made good use of the drier in the loo, too. Amazing what those super-duper news ones can do.'

Cassia smiled warmly, but her face was different from before, with something Cally couldn't quite put her finger on. Cassia's smile widened, and she leaned in slightly. Her voice dropped to a whisper. 'I couldn't help but notice you with Alastair earlier. Are you two...?' She let the question hang in the air, her eyebrows raised suggestively.

Cally blinked, momentarily thrown by the assumption. Alastair? Logan's cousin? She almost laughed at the absurdity of it. She wouldn't touch Alastair with a barge pole. Or any kind of pole whatsoever. Nor a log. Cassia didn't know who Cally was and didn't realise that she was actually there with Logan, her ex-husband. For a moment, Cally considered correcting Cassia and setting the record straight. But something held her back, a sense of self-preservation mixed with a morbid curiosity about what Cassia might say next about Alastair. She simply shrugged, her voice carefully nonchalant, 'Oh, Alastair and I are just friends. We were just chatting earlier, that's all.'

Cassia nodded. There was a strange, knowing look in her eyes. 'Not if he invited you to the Henry-Hicks private area. He'll be after something. Well, be careful with that one, darling. Alastair is a bit of a playboy, if you know what I mean. They all are. Never settled down any of them. Use and abuse is the Henry-Hicks motto, and many of us have unfortunately been on the end of it one way or another.'

Cally felt her stomach clench. 'What do you mean?' she asked, trying to keep her voice steady.

Cassia sighed, glancing around as if to make sure no one was listening before leaning in even closer. 'All the Henry-Hicks men are the same, really. They're known for using women, for having lots of different girlfriends at once. Logan, Alastair, even the old boy Reg... and when they're done with you, they drop you like a tonne of bricks or, you know, just pay you off to keep quiet and make you go away. Seen it time and time again over the years.' Cassia gestured with her hand in the direction of the space outside the marquee. 'All of us know what they are like.'

Cally felt as if she'd been punched in the gut. She stared at Cassia, her mind reeling as she tried to process what she'd just heard. Using women and then paying them off to disappear? Was this another thing she didn't know about? Clearly, it was. For some unknown reason, Cally felt as if there was more to Cassia's words than just idle gossip. At the end of the day, Cassia was Logan's ex-wife, the woman who had been married to him. If anyone knew about the Henry-Hicks clan, it would be her.

Cally's mouth suddenly felt as dry as sandpaper. 'I had no idea,' she managed to croak.

Cassia reached out to pat Cally's arm. Her face looked sympathetic. 'I'm sorry, darling. I didn't mean to upset you. I just thought you should know before you get too involved with *any* of them. Seeing as I've never seen you before and all that. They're obviously having to cast their net a bit wider these days. I'm not surprised with the amount of women that lot have been through...'

Cally nodded, her head spinning as she tried to reconcile the new information with the Logan she thought she knew. The hot air balloon, the show, all the picnics, the nice things. Had it all been a lie? A façade before he got bored and moved on to his next conquest? The thought made her feel sick to her stomach, made her want to run and hide and never look back.

She took a deep breath and flicked the switch. 'Right, yes.'

'I had to let you know.' Cassia wrinkled her nose. 'Just be wary. You can never be too careful in life, right? Us girls have to stick together, too.'

Cally heard herself speaking before she'd thought about it. 'I'm actually here with Logan, not Alastair. I err. I guess I'll talk to him before I make any judgements.'

Cassia's eyebrows shot up in surprise. 'Logan? You're here with Logan? Oh my! Right, I see.'

Cally nodded, her heart pounding in her chest. 'Yes, I am.'

Cassia stared at her for a long moment, her expression unreadable. Then she let out a strange, rueful chuckle. 'Well, well, well, Logan Henry-Hicks, with a girl like *you*.' Cassia shook her head and made a strange upside-down grimacing shape with her lips. 'I never thought I'd see the day.'

Cally wasn't sure what to say. She narrowed her eyes. 'Sorry?'

'Pah! How is it? With him?'

'Good.'

'Good? Well, I hope you're right, darling. For your sake, I truly do. But just be careful. Keep your eyes open and your heart guarded, at least until you're sure you can trust him completely. Which you can't…'

Cally felt irritated by this beautiful woman. She wasn't going to say thanks. 'Sorry, I must go. Just on my way to the loo.'

Cassia smiled. 'Lovely to meet you, Cally. Truly.'

Cally nodded. She wasn't sure if it had been lovely from her side of the fence. 'Hmm.'

'I might bump into you again. See how you're getting on. If you're still around, that is.' Cassia turned and walked away, her head held high and her steps confident and sure as she disappeared in the direction of another marquee.

Cally stood still for a moment, her mind reeling as she tried to process everything that had just happened. The secret of Logan's previous marriage, the revelations from his ex-wife, the exhaustion from the day: all of it swirled around her. Squeezing her eyes together, she felt like heading for the nearest exit and not even going back to Logan. Part of her couldn't be bothered to confront him, to look at him even, but her mind raced with a thousand unanswered questions. However, right at that moment, exhausted from the full-on day, she was strangely too over it to even bother.

A million voices ranted in her head. The rational part of her brain trusted the Logan she knew and told her everything was okay and that there would be an explanation. The other part yelled doubts. Part of her wanted to just find Logan right there and talk about everything that had happened and everything that was still to come. She could just listen to his side of the story. Give him a chance to explain and defend himself. On the other hand, a sickening sense of betrayal churned in her gut.

After going to the loo, she weaved through a throng of guests and a maze of tables and chairs, made her way back through the crowd, out the exit, and headed in the direction of the main gate. As her eyes scanned the sea of faces for Logan, Cassia's words echoed in her mind. The accusations and insinuations about Logan's character and his past swirled through her thoughts. She felt as if a vile poisonous fog had swallowed her. The man she supposedly loved, the man who had swept her off her feet, was really nothing more than a player, a user. The thought made her feel sick to her stomach. She forced herself to take a deep breath and push through. Once she was home, she'd regroup and decide what to do.

As she got to the gate, Logan stood near the far side, his back turned from her as he chatted with an attendant. Even from a distance, Cally's stomach flipped—not so much this time with love but more with the fact that she wasn't quite sure *who* he was.

She quickened her pace, her mouth dry and tight with emotion. She flicked the switch at the back of her throat and popped her old fall-back smile on her face. As she got nearer to him, she blinked and started to hold up the sky. Things for our Cally were not good. She had been monumentally conned.

25

It was the day after the races. The evening before, after coming in for a cup of tea, Cally, unbelievably, mostly to her, had still not said anything. She'd been so furious and so tired it had made her mute. She'd somehow fobbed Logan off with the fact that she hadn't wanted to be woken by him getting up for the horses and so he'd headed off back to the manor without a clue about what was going on in Cally's very full head.

Once he'd gone, she'd run the bath, dissected the conversation with Cassia to within an inch of its life, and festered in her pyjamas. She'd opened carton after carton of blackcurrant, made herself almost sick with a sugar overload and in the end had collapsed into bed, not a happy bunny. She may have buried her face in her pillow and let the tears come pouring out in a long, drawn-out, cathartic flood.

It was the next morning and she was on her way to meet Eloise for coffee over at the harbour area of Lovely Bay. As she strolled along, she went over what the day before had revealed and decided she was going to give Logan the flick. Yeah, she loved him, sure she did, but he'd lied. The end. He'd wormed his way into her heart and let her down and she didn't like how that felt one iota. Not only that, the races had yet again made it clear that she didn't fit into his world. The revelation via Cassia only added fuel to Cally's already raging fire of self-doubt. She wasn't even going to go into it too much. She would just break up with him and that would be that. Move on and forget Henry-Hicks had ever set foot in her world. Treat him as the Henry-Hicks family did other people if Cassia was correct.

She walked into the coffee shop, ordered two coffees, and mindlessly scrolled through Instagram as she waited for Eloise to arrive. As she sipped her coffee, lost in thought, she barely noticed when Eloise slid into the seat across from her. As soon as Cally looked up, Eloise frowned and made a funny face.

'Crikey. You look like you've seen a ghost. What's happened to the glow?'

Cally blinked and shook her head in quick little movements. 'Sorry, I was miles away. I'm fine.'

Eloise leaned forward. 'You're not. You're doing that weird voice. What's going on? How did the races go?'

Cally sighed. 'Good and bad. I did enjoy it initially, but it got tiring having to keep up the pretence, if you know what I mean.'

'I'm coming next time.'

Cally raised her eyebrows. 'Trust me, there won't *be* a next time.'

'What? Oh, no, have you definitely decided to tell him to sling his hook because of the secret?'

Cally shook her head. 'Not just because of that. I found out something yesterday, something that's thrown everything into question even more than it already had. I'm over it.'

Eloise's eyes widened. 'What do you mean? What did you find out?'

'You're not quite going to believe this, but I actually met his ex-wife. And she told me things about Logan and his family that, well, that aren't at all nice. I should have picked up some red flags in the first place,' Cally stated glumly.

Eloise sat back in her chair. 'His ex-wife? Oh my goodness! You met her! Blimey, Cal, that's a lot to take in. *Awkward.* What did she say, exactly? Hang on. What, so he now knows you know about her?'

'No, not at all! I met her by accident. He knows *nothing*.'

'The plot thickens.'

Cally felt as if actual words were sticking in her throat. 'She said that the Henry-Hicks boys are all the same. That they use women, have lots of girlfriends at once, and then pay them off when they're done with them. That Logan's no different from the rest of them.'

Eloise let out a low whistle, her eyes wide with shock. She swore and then wrinkled her nose. 'Blimey. That's a lot to process all at once.'

'I know.'

'I'm so sorry you had to hear that, especially from his ex of all people.'

Cally felt a sting of tears prickling behind her eyes. 'I don't know what to think. Problem is bottom line: I love him, I really do. I can't even believe I'm saying this. I'm going to have to pull the plug on all this. I shouldn't have got myself mixed up with him in the first place. I did say that right at the beginning. Imagine if I hadn't found the certificate!'

'Hang on. What, so she just came out with this? You're standing there talking about your hats and she threw that into the ring. How did you end up talking to her if he thinks you don't know? Really?'

'No, no, it wasn't like that. I bumped into her when I was on my own. I'd gone off to have a cup of tea in peace and then it suddenly poured down with rain. The heavens opened. Long story short, we sheltered under a marquee together. She had no idea at that point that I knew who she was. She wasn't part of the family group area.'

'Right. I think I see what you mean.'

As Cally recounted the events of the day before more clearly, Eloise listened with her eyebrows raised in concern and her hands wrapped tightly around her coffee mug.

'So, there I was later, minding my own business and heading to the loo before we left, when suddenly Cassia tapped me on the shoulder. I nearly jumped out of my skin. I mean, what are the chances of bumping into your boyfriend's ex-wife not once but twice in the same day?'

Eloise's expression was sympathetic. 'It's like something out of a soap opera, Cal. I can't even imagine how weird that must have been, especially after your little run-in earlier in the day.'

Cally sighed. 'It was beyond awkward from my side. It was like the universe was trying to tell me something, you know? Like it was throwing all these red flags in my face and daring me to ignore them. You couldn't make it up.' Cally took a sip of her coffee. 'But the worst part was, Cassia had no idea who I was at first. She just assumed I was there with Alastair, Logan's cousin. And that's when she started spilling all these secrets, all these horrible things about the Henry-Hicks boys and their reputation with women.'

Eloise leaned forward with wide eyes. 'This is the gift that keeps on giving. She just told you all of that out of the blue? Without even knowing who you were or why you were there?'

'She said she felt like she had to warn me because she'd seen me with them. She had to let me know what I was getting myself into. Like she was doing me some kind of favour, looking out for a fellow woman or something.'

Eloise snorted. 'Right. Because I'm sure she had nothing but your best interests at heart, spilling all that dirt on her ex-husband and his family.'

Cally sighed. 'I don't know, Eloise. I mean, why would she

lie? What would she have to gain from making all of that up, especially to a complete stranger?'

Eloise raised a sceptical eyebrow. 'Oh, I don't know. Maybe a little thing called revenge? A chance to get back at the man who broke her heart, to make him and his family look bad in front of his new and very attractive girlfriend? Thinking about it, there's no way she didn't know who you were! No way. I reckon she clocked it and put two and two together. You know what those sorts are like. They all went to the same schools, mix in the same circles, they're all two degrees of separation. Then you turn up on the scene out of the blue. She knew who you were. Of course, she did.'

Cally sighed. 'I hadn't thought about that.'

'Totally. One hundred per cent. It's *way* too weird that she just happened to see you and then blurted all that out. Fair enough she didn't know you when you were sheltering, but the second time. Nup. I'm not buying it.'

'Okay, whatever. I have little to no interest in her, but what if she's right? What if Logan really is just using me, just biding his time until he gets bored and moves on to the next girl? I mean, he's already lied to me about his past, about his marriage. Who knows what else he's keeping from me?'

'I know you feel betrayed, but I don't like the sound of her. That's a different issue from the marriage secret, though. You need to think about the relationship you *do* have—what you've built. Just come clean and talk to him.'

Cally huffed. 'But that's just it. What have we built, really? A relationship based on lies, secrets, and things left unsaid? How can I trust anything he says or does, knowing that he's kept something this big from me?'

'You have to remember, people change. They grow and learn and become better versions of themselves. Maybe the Logan that Cassia knew, the Logan from her past, isn't the same Logan.'

Cally nodded. Maybe Eloise was right. But one thing she did know was that the hurt she felt was very raw and very fresh. Throw angry in there, too. 'I don't know. I think I need to end things before I get in too deep and end up getting hurt even worse than I already am. I should have called it off in the first place when I thought we were from two different backgrounds. He wooed me then and it seems as if it might be a pattern of his. I shouldn't have gone to the races, either.'

'Don't make any rash decisions. You should have got this all out in the open before the races. I don't know why you just didn't tell him right away. Give him a chance to explain properly and tell his side of the story.'

'Honestly, why should I? Why should I give him a chance to explain when he couldn't even be bothered to tell me the truth in the first place? When he let me fall in love with him, let me build a whole future in my head with him, without ever once mentioning that he had a whole marriage in his past? That's not nice.'

Eloise sighed. 'You have to give him the benefit of the doubt.'

'Maybe I don't want to.' Cally had had enough of giving people *anything*. She'd had years of caring for other people, always giving, giving, giving. Time for our Cally to not do anything for anyone but herself. She didn't care if she was being irrational, immature, or overly emotional. It was how she felt and she was, for once in her life, going to behave exactly as *she* wanted.

Eloise leaned forward. 'If he does turn out to be a lying, cheating scumbag, you'll let me have a go at him, yeah? I reckon I could do some serious damage.'

Cally let out a startled laugh. 'Deal, but it won't come to that. I can handle it. I just need to tell him that I'm done. We're done.'

'Well, at the end of the day, you've got to do what you've got to do.'

As they finished their coffees and Eloise went outside to take a phone call, Cally thought back to the moment in the marquee when Cassia had tapped her on the shoulder. Cassia had turned her world even more upside down with a few simple words. Perhaps Cassia's accusations and insinuations hadn't been quite as innocent as they'd seemed but really Cally didn't give a stuff about Cassia's intentions: the results had done their job.

She nodded to herself. She *would* give Logan a chance to explain and defend himself. But her gut feelings about what was right and what was true were telling her none of it boded well. She couldn't shake the nagging feeling of doubt or the persistent voice in the back of her mind that whispered that Cassia was correct. If Cally had not been blindsided, she would have known that all along. She wouldn't be in the mess in the first place.

26

The rest of the day had gone by. Logan had been busy at the manor and Cally had worked a short shift on the chatbot and then for Birdie on a late order, so she'd not seen Logan and it hadn't been an issue. Now, the next day, it was time for push to come to shove. Slipping her phone out of her pocket, her heart hammered in her chest. She made a determined tap on Logan's number and sighed as she waited for him to pick up,

Logan answered cheerily. 'Morning. I was just about to text you. How are you? I missed you.'

'Morning. I'm fine.' Cally's reply was short and clipped.

'You okay?'

'No, I'm not okay. Not at all. Everything's not alright. We need to talk. Can you come over, please? I think it's time we had a real, honest conversation about, well, about pretty much everything, really.'

There was a long pause. 'What? What do you want to talk to me about? You sound weird. What's happened?'

Cally felt tears at the corners of her eyes. 'Can you just come over? I'll tell you when you get here. It's important. Really important.'

'Alright, I'll be there soon,' Logan replied, his voice tinged with concern.

As she hung up, Cally felt a mixture of relief and dread at the same time. She'd kept silent long enough and had told herself once the races were over, she'd let Logan know exactly what she knew. She paced the room as she waited to hear his car at the back of the deli. About twenty minutes later, she listened to his footsteps on the stairs. Her heart skipped a beat as she heard his key to her flat go into the lock.

Logan stepped in, his expression a mix of concern and confusion. 'Hey. You sounded awful on the phone. What's going on?'

'I sounded awful because I *am* awful.'

'You're worrying me. What's happened? Let me make a cup of tea, and then you can tell me.'

'No need for tea. Tea is the last thing I want.'

'I'll make you a blackcurrant.'

'You're not making me anything.' Cally hissed.

'What is it? It can't be that bad. What's going on? What's wrong?'

Cally tutted. 'What's wrong? Why don't *you* tell *me*, Logan? Why don't you tell me about the little secret you've been keeping from me all this time?'

Logan narrowed his eyes. 'What?'

Without a word, Cally scrolled to the picture of Logan's marriage certificate on her phone and handed it to him. Logan's expression changed as he registered the picture and what it meant. All the colour drained from his face.

'Where did you find this?'

'Amongst a load of old documents when I was working for Nina.'

Logan looked up and closed his eyes for a second. 'I can explain.'

Cally shook her head. 'I don't see how you can explain that you didn't tell me about this. It's quite the detail that you forgot to tell me about.'

Logan's eyes darted between Cally and the marriage certificate. He ran a hand through his hair. 'This is not how I wanted you to find out. Not at all.'

'Find out what? That you're married? That you've been lying to me? Both of the above. What else don't I know about?'

'No, it's not like that. I *was* married. To Cassia. But it was a long time ago. We're not together anymore, obviously. Like it was *years* ago. It meant nothing. I was young and stupid. It was over right away after a few months and we split up. I did it on a whim. You can see that by the date on there. It was just us. No big celebration or anything.'

'Then why didn't you tell me? Why keep it a secret?'

Logan sighed, his shoulders slumping. 'It's complicated. It ended badly, and I just wanted to move on, to start fresh. When I met you, I didn't tell you and the longer I left it, the worse it got, so I did nothing.'

Cally stared at him and shook her head. 'You should have told me. I deserved to know.' Cally's voice was cold, unforgiving.

'I know. I was going to, but I kept putting it off. And then things got serious between us, and it just became harder to bring up. I'm so sorry. I never meant to hurt you.'

Cally took a step back, trying to process his words. 'Do you still have contact with her? With Cassia?'

'No! We haven't spoken in years. The divorce was finalised a long time ago. I've moved on, and so has she.'

Cally wasn't so sure about that. 'Why did you *never* mention her? Not even once! Like you were married, for heaven's sake. It's major!'

Logan shook his head. 'At first, it wasn't important because, well, you know, and then I thought you'd think less of me, that it would change how you felt about us. I know it was wrong to keep it from you, but I didn't know how to bring it up. Plus, it means nothing.'

'I need some time to think about this, Logan. This is a lot to take in. I don't know if I can do this.'

'What does that mean?'

'I'm just not sure I want to continue. I think you should go now. At least it's out in the open.'

'Please, let me talk about it.'

'I trusted you. I trusted you with, like, my whole life. And now I find out that you've been keeping this huge, secret from me all along. I stood at that stupid race event knowing that everyone knew, but they thought I didn't. How am I supposed to believe anything you say, anything you promise, ever again?'

'Don't be ridiculous! No one even remembers it. You're totally overreacting! It means nothing.' Logan took a step forward. He reached out to grasp her arm, but Cally jerked away, her whole body recoiling from his touch as if it burned. 'Don't touch me. Don't try to explain, justify or make excuses. I can't bear it, actually.'

'I don't know what to say.'

'I can't believe I actually trusted you. I feel like things are falling apart around me.'

Cally hated the weakness and *abhorred* feeling vulnerable. She'd spent so long, her whole life being strong, self-sufficient, and unbreakable. With Logan, she'd let her guard down. Now, it all felt like an illusion. She remembered how she'd felt as if being with Logan had clicked a missing piece of the puzzle, that was her heart, back into place. Now, she hated to admit that she felt as if, at least from her side, they would never fit together quite the same way as they had before.

'I need time and space to process all this and figure out what it means for us. No, not for us, for me. You know what, Logan Henry-Hicks?' Cally yelled, like *really* yelled. No doubt the whole of the third smallest town in the country heard her. 'I don't care about you! All I care about is me!'

'Well, that much is obvious.' With that Henry-Hicks turned on his heels and left.

27

Cally woke with a start, a heavy heart, and her mind working overtime before she'd even sat up. For a blissful moment, she couldn't remember why she felt so awful. Then it all came flooding back very quickly: the confrontation with Logan, his secret marriage, the anger and hurt. The fact that he'd said she'd overreacted. The fact that she acknowledged that perhaps she *had* overreacted. Him storming out. She groaned as it swirled around her and pulled the duvet over her head, wishing she could hide from the world. Here she was again, struggling and having to hold up that big old messy sky.

Morning light filtered through the gaps in the curtains, and she could hear the faint sounds of Lovely Bay coming to life outside her window: a very distant clanging of boats in the harbour, a few snippets here and there of early-morning risers from the street, the occasional squawk of a seagull. All an ordinary, very normal day in Lovely. The world had continued to turn and carry on as it usually did, even though she felt as if *it* and *she* had been shattered into a million pieces. Dramatic much? Totally.

She reached for her phone on the bedside table, wincing as

she saw several missed calls and messages from Logan. She couldn't bring herself to read them. Instead, she opened her messages from Eloise and tapped.

Cally: *You up? Need to talk.*

The response came almost immediately.

Eloise: *Course I am. Come over. xxx I'll put the kettle on.*

Cally: *Thx. I'll just have a quick shower x.*

Cally dragged herself out of bed, shuffled out to put the kettle on, walked into the bathroom and pulled the lever on the shower. As she stood under the hot water, she tried to sort through the jumble of emotions whirling inside her. She'd never quite experienced the feelings before. Sure, she'd felt angry and hurt at times. Betrayal, too. This was different, though, and she knew why: anger, hurt, betrayal, and confusion mixed with the fact that she loved the bones of Logan in the midst of it all. It really was as simple as that. She felt drained and overwhelmed by her emotions; the long day at the races and a rubbish night's sleep all merged to make her feel a million times worse.

Without even thinking about what she was putting on, she dressed quickly in her usual uniform, then paused in front of the mirror. The face that looked back at her did not look good. There was no glow. Older somehow than a few days before, more weary, and not a whole lot of fancy going on there at all. She shoved on a bit of mascara and a swipe of lip gloss so as not to frighten the locals, wiped the shower down, gave the loo a quick clean, washed her hands and went back out to the kitchen.

After making hot blackcurrant in a travel cup, she scooted down the steep stairs from her flat and caught a whiff of freshly baked bread from the deli below. Her stomach growled, reminding her that she hadn't eaten much since before the confrontation with Logan, at the same time as the thought of eating anything made her feel a bit sick.

Just as she was walking out of the back of the deli, Alice, with a huge bag in her arms, came the other way.

'Morning, our Cally!' Alice called out cheerfully. 'You're up early. Fancy a coffee?'

Cally held up her travel cup. 'Thanks, nope. I'm meeting Eloise. How are you?'

'Great, thanks. You?'

'Oh, yes, fine, thanks.' Cally lied, flicking the switch at the back of her throat which allowed her to sound perfectly okay when she was anything but. 'Just a bit tired.'

Alice frowned. 'You seem subdued. Not your usual self. Everything alright?'

'I'm fine.'

Alice didn't look entirely convinced but didn't push. She rummaged in the basket and held up a bag. 'Croissants and they're still warm. I've just been to collect them. Take these.' She winked. 'Looks like you could use a bit of cheering up.'

'Aww, that's so kind of you. Thank you.'

'See you later, then. All ready for the Chowder Festival?'

Cally nodded. 'Yes, can't wait.'

On the way to Eloise's, Cally found herself dawdling, lost in thought. She replayed the confrontation with Logan over and over in her mind, analysing every word. He'd not looked great when she'd shouted. Had she overreacted? She had. Should she have given him more of a chance to explain? Possibly. But then she remembered the look on his face when she'd shown him the marriage certificate – the guilt, the panic. She felt as if he had kept it from her deliberately, letting her fall in love with him while holding back a huge part of his past. She might be dramatic, but part of her absolutely *hated* him for that.

By the time she reached Eloise's house, she didn't know what to think. She pushed her finger in the bell and waited for Eloise to answer. Eloise opened the door, took one look at Cally's face, frowned and pulled Cally into a one-armed hug. 'Oh, what in the world? It obviously didn't go well. Go in the sitting room. I'll get you a tea.'

Cally slipped off her shoes and walked into the sitting room, sinking into the familiar, squashy sofa. She gratefully accepted the mug of tea and wrapped her hands around it.

Eloise sat in the armchair opposite. 'So, I take it you confronted Logan?'

Cally nodded. 'God, it was awful. What have I done? I really yelled at him!'

'Tell me everything. Start from the beginning.'

Cally recounted the whole confrontation. '...and then I just told him I needed space. I couldn't bear to hear anything else.'

Eloise gritted her teeth and made a swooshing sound. 'Blimey. That's a lot to process.'

'I know. I just don't know what to do now. It's so weird because, at the end of the day, I love him. I really do.'

Eloise shook her head. 'I know you're hurt. And you have every right to be. What Logan did was pretty bad, no two ways about it. But...' she hesitated, clearly choosing her words carefully. She narrowed her eyes. 'Are you sure you're not using this as an excuse?'

Cally blinked, taken aback. 'What? No! An excuse? For what?'

'You've always had one foot out the door since you decided your background wasn't good enough, haven't you? Always waiting for the other shoe to drop, for some reason why it wouldn't work out between you two.'

'That's not fair,' Cally protested, but even as she said it, she felt a flicker of doubt. Hadn't she always felt, deep down, that she and Logan were too different, from two different worlds?

Eloise held up her hands. 'I'm not saying what Logan did was right. It wasn't. He should have told you about his marriage. But people make mistakes, Cal. They have pasts. The question is, does this one mistake outweigh everything else? Everything good about your relationship?'

Cally slumped back into the sofa, feeling suddenly exhausted. 'I don't know,' she admitted. 'I just feel so betrayed. Like I can't trust anything he's ever said to me.'

'I get that. Think about it, Cal. Has Logan ever given you any other reason not to trust him? Has he ever lied to you about anything else?'

Cally thought about it. To be frank, Henry-Hicks had not put a foot wrong. He'd introduced her to his family, brought her into his world despite their different backgrounds, wined her and dined her, looked after her, treated her—done just about everything right every single time. 'No,' she said finally. 'He hasn't.'

'So maybe, and I'm just saying maybe, this was a one-off mess-up. A big one, granted, but still.'

Cally rubbed her temples. 'Even if it was, I don't know if I can get past it, El. I don't know if I want to. You know?'

Eloise was quiet for a moment. 'Don't bite my head off, but are you more upset about Logan's secret marriage or about the fact that he comes from a different world than you? And that, well...'

'What?'

'Sometimes I think you have a shield up because of everything that happened before. You like to keep people at arm's length.' Eloise pressed on. 'You've spent so long taking care of others, Cal. Your mum, your brother, your grandma. You've been strong for so long. But sometimes I think you're afraid to let anyone take care of you. To let anyone in. So, you get to dump Logan over this when really is it a dump-able reason? I know what my answer is...'

'That's precisely it. I let Logan in and now look. I shouldn't have done that.'

Eloise challenged. 'Thing is. You say you did, but have you been waiting for a reason to push him away all along?'

Cally opened her mouth to argue. Deep down, she knew Eloise was probably right. She had been waiting for a reason, hadn't she? Some proof that she and Logan would never truly work, that their worlds were too different, but maybe it was a way to actually protect herself.

She groaned, burying her face in her hands. 'I'm such a mess. I shouldn't be out in the real world.'

Eloise moved to sit beside her on the sofa and put an arm around her shoulders. 'You're not a mess and you've been through a lot.'

'That doesn't help me about what I do now. What's next?'

'First, you're going to finish your tea. Then you're going to have a proper cry if you need to. And then you need to think about what you really want. Not what you *think* you should want, or what you're afraid of wanting or what anyone else wants or needs you to do. But what you *truly* want.'

Cally wiped the corners of her eyes. 'And what if I don't know what that is?'

'There's no rush. The world won't end if you don't have all the answers right away.'

As if on cue, Cally's phone buzzed with another message from Logan. She glanced at it and her heart clenched at the sight of his name on the screen. 'He keeps trying to contact me.'

She turned her phone around and showed Eloise the string of missed calls and messages.

Eloise peered at Cally's phone. 'Well, at least he's persistent, I'll give him that. What does he say?'

Cally hesitated, then opened the most recent message.

Logan: *I know I've messed up. I know I hurt you. Give me a chance to explain properly. To make things right. I love you. I'm sorry I stormed out. Call me when you're ready to talk. I'll wait as long as it takes.*

Cally pursed her lips as she read the words. 'He wants to explain.'

Eloise nodded. 'Yup.'

Cally bit her lip, conflicted. Part of her wanted to delete the messages, to cut Logan out of her life completely. The other part of her loved him. 'I don't know. I'm still so angry, but…'

'But you love him,' Eloise finished for her.

Cally nodded miserably. 'I do. God help me, I do.'

'Maybe it's worth hearing him out.'

Cally turned her phone over in her hands. 'And if I'm not ready to talk to him yet?'

'Just do it on your terms.'

Cally nodded. 'Thanks, El. I don't know what I'd do without you.'

Eloise rolled her eyes. 'Probably make a right mess of things. It's a good job I'm here to keep you on the straight and narrow.'

Cally chuckled. 'What a nightmare.'

'I'll make another pot of tea.'

Cally pointed to the hallway. 'There are some croissants in my bag.'

'My kind of comfort food.'

As Eloise went out to the kitchen, Cally thought about what Eloise had said about using her background as a shield. Had she really been doing that? Keeping one foot out the door, always ready to run at the first sign of trouble? It was sobering. It was probably true. She had to get a grip or she was going to lose the best thing that had ever happened in her life.

28

Later that day, with a bit more musing on the situation, Cally became less than happy about what had happened with Logan. In fact, she was angrier than she'd been when she'd first found the marriage certificate. The more she'd dissected it, she just simply hadn't liked the way he'd seemed to think that he could say sorry and move right on. For her, it threw everything up in the air. There was one teeny-weeny little problem, though; she was still head over heels for him. She wished she could just flick him off and be done with it. There was no chance of that happening anytime soon. Since the showdown, she'd not seen him, but she'd been thinking about him night and day.

She mulled over what he'd said about the marriage to Cassia. How they had got married on a whim and a few months later, it had been over. That had been good news as far as Cally was concerned, but it still hadn't changed the fact that he'd lied by omission. Cally hated that. So much.

She walked into the kitchen at work, flicked on the kettle, got two mugs out for tea and waited for the kettle to boil. A few minutes later, with the Shipping Forecast playing from her left shoulder, Birdie, in her white pharmacist's coat, came into the kitchen, sat down and gossiped about a woman who had just been in to pick up a prescription. Cally chatted and listened, made the tea, passed over a mug, and sat down.

Birdie smiled. 'Everything good with you? How did it go at the races?'

'Really good.' Cally tapped her phone, opened her pictures, and slid the phone over the table.

'Wow! Alice said you looked fabulous; she wasn't wrong.'

Cally smiled. 'She did an amazing job with my hair. I felt like a different person.'

Birdie scrolled through the photos. 'I'll say! Look at you, hobnobbing with the toffs. You look like you stepped right out of a fashion magazine.'

Cally chuckled. 'I've never worn anything so posh in my life. The dress was like something else. Honestly, I felt fabulous.'

'What was it like? Did you see any celebrities? Did you win any bets?'

Cally cradled her mug. 'It was good. Everything was so grand and everyone looked perfect. I felt a bit like a fish out of water some of the time, but loved it, too.'

'But you look so confident in these photos,' Birdie observed, gesturing to the phone.

Cally nodded. 'I got more comfortable as the day went on. It came and went in waves.'

'That hat, though. How on earth did you keep it on your head?'

'A lot of hairpins and an entire can of hairspray. I think my hair is still crunchy from it all.'

Birdie laughed. 'Well, it looked fantastic. You could've been on the cover of Vogue.'

Cally scoffed. 'Hardly! It was nice to dress up, though. Just goes to show.'

'What about the food? I bet it was fancy stuff, not a bowl of chowder in sight.'

Cally laughed. 'You're not wrong there. It was all very fancy. Tiny little canapés that looked more like art than food. And the champagne! I've never seen so much champagne in my life. I think some people were pickled by the end of the day.'

'Ooh, look at you, living the high life. Don't go getting too used to it, now. We can't have you turning your nose up at Lovely.'

'Trust me. No fancy canapé could ever replace this place. I have to say, though, the people-watching was next level. Some of the outfits were incredible. Some though, let's just say not everyone has good taste, even with a lot of money involved.'

'Did you see any real fashion disasters? When I see it on the TV, I always think surely it's not real that people would wear those getups.'

'Well, there was one woman with a hat that looked like an entire flower shop had exploded on her head. I swear, it must have weighed a tonne. I don't know how she kept her neck up. Another one looked like a walking ball of green feathers.'

'Too funny. How was Logan?'

Cally's smile faltered slightly at the mention of Logan, but she quickly rallied. 'Yeah, fine.'

Birdie, ever perceptive, noticed the shift in her mood. 'Everything alright with him?'

Cally forced a smile. She didn't have the energy to go into it with Birdie. 'Yep. I'm just a bit tired, I think. It was a long day, and I'm not used to all that excitement.'

'Well, it sounds like you had a wonderful time. I'm so glad you got to experience it. You deserve a bit of glamour in your life, our Cally.'

For a moment, Cally was tempted to spill everything—her discovery of Logan's previous marriage, her conflicted feelings, her fears for the future—but she held back. She needed to sort through her own thoughts first.

Birdie got up and picked up her mug. 'Right, well, best get on. Those prescriptions won't dispense themselves.'

'Yep.' Cally rinsed the mugs and walked into the back room. As she settled back into the familiar routine of the chemist, she felt slightly calmer. One step at a time, she told herself. That's how she'd navigate the complex situation with Logan.

The rest of the afternoon passed in a blur of unloading drug cartons, missing prescriptions, and deliveries. Cally lost herself in it all and found comfort in the familiar rhythm of the chemist, such a contrast to the pomp and glamour she'd been right in the centre of at the races. She knew which one she preferred. As she sorted and worked, she felt an odd appreciation for her little job. It was certainly not glamorous, but it was very real and there was something oddly grounding about that. Just as she was pulling a cardboard carton out of the back room and heading toward the dispensary, Nancy came walking up to the counter on the other side of the shop. Nancy beamed.

'Our Cally, how was it? I've been thinking about you. That post on Facebook! You looked stunning!'

'Aww, thanks. Yes, it was good.'

'Good? It looked more than good. I'm so jealous!'

'Ha! Yep, it was a lovely day. How are you?'

'Can't complain, can't complain. Not gadding about with the upper crust, like you, and going to the races, no less!'

Cally laughed. 'News travels fast. It was quite an experience, I have to say.'

'I bet it was. Did you see the King? I hear he loves the races.'

'No King sightings, I'm afraid. Just plenty of fancy hats and even fancier people.'

'Well, I hope you didn't let them turn your head. We need you here with us Lovelies.'

'No fear of that.'

'Good to hear.'

'What are you up to?' Cally asked.

Nancy held up a planner. 'Up to my eyes in the Chowder Festival stuff.'

'I bet.'

'Are you up to date with what you're doing with Nina?'

'Yes, we're all set, I think. You know what Neens is like. She's all over it. There's a spreadsheet and Robby has assigned roles. I think even Faye might have a job to do.'

Nancy laughed. 'I know. She's one of the few the organising committee has nothing to worry about.'

'I'm going over there to do the preparation soon. We're going to discuss the setup and suchlike.'

Nancy lowered her voice. 'I can't wait to see what her speakeasy is like. Don't tell Birdie I said that.'

Cally giggled. 'I know. I've already been told I'm a turncoat for not helping at the deli one.'

'Too funny.'

'Right, well, I'll see you for the Chowder Festival, if not before.'

'Yeah, let me know if you need any help.'

'Will do.'

Cally went back to her cardboard cartons and continued to sort. At least she had the Chowder Festival to think about and a few things to take her mind off what was going to happen regarding the most important thing in her life.

29

It was the next day. Cally had not replied to Logan's attempts to contact her, but rather had stewed about him more and more. Not having bothered with a shower, with her hair stuck up on top of her head and in too-big trackie pants, our Cally was not looking or feeling her best. In her oldest, daggiest slippers, she shuffled over to her desk in the corner of the sitting room. As she flipped up the lid and plonked herself down, the glow of the laptop screen illuminated her face in dim early morning light. She'd woken before dawn to a shrill alarm for a chatbot shift, her mind full of tumultuous thoughts, and had not wanted to get out of bed. The chatbot work waited for no one, though, not even for a girl with a missing piece in her heart, so she'd dragged herself out of bed and settled in for an early morning full of entitled moaning from women up and down the country who had nothing better to do with their time. Deep joy. Or not.

Outside the balcony doors, the morning light around Lovely began to change as she navigated through customer queries, her fingers flying over the keys as she responded to complaint after complaint. She'd seen it all before, but sometimes, the mindless work, in a way, was both a blessing and a curse at the same time. A blessing because it gave her something to focus on. A curse because she'd done it so many times that it left enough space for her brain to wander, to replay what had happened with Logan, to question every decision she'd made.

After a good few hours of a constant barrage of messages and then a lull in real-time questions, she sat for a bit with her chin on her hand, thinking. As she looked at her laptop, she remembered when Logan had bought it for her and how over the moon she'd been. It was so far removed from the clunky old thing she'd been using before. A gift from Logan, given with thoughtfulness and care. She remembered the moment he'd handed her the bag.

'You can't keep working on that dinosaur, Blackcurrant,' he'd said.

Cally closed her eyes as she thought about how Logan called her Blackcurrant. The nickname had started as a joke, a reference to the stained blouse she'd worn on one of their first meetings. The name had stuck and she'd secretly loved it. It had never failed to make her smile. Until now. She turned the laptop over and traced the letters where Logan had had the laptop engraved. One word that had a lot of meaning as far as she was concerned. Now, it felt as if it was peppered by a big, fat, horrid lie.

Cally shook her head as she stared at the inscription, and her mind zoomed to Cassia and his marriage. She wondered how many chances Logan had had to tell her the truth, how many moments he could have come clean about his past but hadn't—agonised about why in the world he hadn't just told her.

She cast her mind back, remembering, and went through loads of times when he could have opened up. She shook her head, trying to dislodge the memories and turned the laptop back over. Cally sighed as the flashing light indicated a customer was waiting and rubbed her eyes tiredly. The chatbot work was going nowhere. After dealing with the customer who was moaning about the quality of a pair of cashmere socks and then another whose delivery had been eaten by the neighbour's dog, she glanced at the clock – still early, but late enough that she could justify another cup of tea. She pushed back from the desk, padding into the tiny kitchen to put the kettle on. As she waited for it to boil, she stared out the window at the quiet streets of Lovely Bay. The town was waking up with people on their way to work or out to grab a morning coffee. It all looked so normal, so unchanged, though, to her, everything felt different. The world had shifted on its axis the moment she'd discovered Logan's secret, and she was still struggling to find her footing. The first pull of the rug from under her had been when she'd found the certificate; then, the rug had been yanked right out when Cassia had imparted her wisdom about the Henry-Hicks boys.

The kettle clicked off, and she made her tea on autopilot, her mind still churning with memories and what-ifs. There had been so many moments and opportunities for Logan to have come clean, like a day at the manor when she'd been helping with the decluttering and had stumbled across an old photo album. She'd called Logan over, curious about the faded pictures of a much younger him. He'd groaned good-naturedly when he'd seen what she was looking at. 'I'd forgotten about those.' He'd said. 'Not my finest hour, fashion-wise.'

Cally had giggled, pointing to a picture of teenage Logan with wildly spiked hair. 'I think you pulled off the alternative look rather well.'

Logan had laughed, settling beside her on the dusty floor. 'I went through a bit of a rebellious phase,' he'd admitted. 'Drove my mum mad.'

They'd spent the next hour poring over the album, Logan sharing stories about each photo. He'd been fairly open, or so she'd thought, but he'd never once mentioned Cassia. Not even hinted at the fact that he'd been married.

Cally took her tea back to the desk, settling in front of the laptop. She traced the engraved 'Blackcurrant' with her finger and shook her head.

How many times had Logan called her that? How many times had he used that nickname? How many times had she loved it? All the while, he'd lied by omission. She felt as if him keeping his marriage from her wiped away all the good things he'd done. Cally shook her head, trying to dislodge the doubts. She knew she was being irrational, knew that Logan's past didn't necessarily negate everything they'd shared. Hurt, though, was raw. Nice and fresh.

Her laptop pinged three times and she turned back to the chatbot work. At least that would take her mind off Logan, but even though she was determined to lose herself in the mindless task of customer service, as she typed out responses to disgruntled shoppers, her mind kept drifting back to him. All she could think about was how she'd been taken in by him, how he'd princess-ed her, the moments they'd shared, all the opportunities he'd had to come clean. It made her wonder what else he'd not told her.

As she copied and pasted a predetermined response about a refund, her mind flitted here and there. There had been a weekend away in the countryside when they'd stayed in a quaint little bed and breakfast. They'd spent hours just walking, talking, sharing bits and bobs, discussing dreams, fears, all sorts. Logan had opened up about his family pressures, about his doubts, and insecurities. Cally had felt so close to him then, so connected. He'd said that when he was with her, he could just be himself with no pretences and no expectations. He'd told her that he was just Logan when he was with her. What a load of old hogwash that had been. Just Logan, who conveniently forgot that he'd been married. Now, looking back, she wondered if perhaps it might have been a line he used. Cassia's words about the Henry-Hicks boys echoed through her head.

As the little dots that told her another customer was waiting flashed, she sighed and got to it. A few hours went by with more of the same until the end of her shift when she logged off and closed her laptop. Pushing away from the desk, she had a really quick shower, got dressed, popped a jumper on and headed to the front door. She needed to clear her head, get out of the flat where everywhere she looked she could see Logan.

Stepping out of the gate at the back of the deli, she nodded a distracted greeting to Alice, who was just closing the boot on her car.

'You alright, our Cally?' Alice asked. 'How are you?'

Cally did a funny, tight smile. 'Fine, thanks. Just off out for a bit of fresh air. I'm heading over to the beach.'

Before having to get into small talk, she flicked her hand, waved and smiled. Setting off at a brisk pace, her feet pounded against the pavement. The familiar streets of Lovely Bay blurred past her, and she tried to focus on her breathing as if it would somehow cleanse her. It did nothing of the sort. Deep breath in, deep breath out. She thought about her grandma, about the courses she'd looked at doing, about how she'd managed to save up quite a bit of money for a deposit for a flat. Anything to keep her mind off Logan. But as she stomped along, all she could really think about was him. She could see him everywhere. A bench they'd sat on with a coffee, the ice cream kiosk where he had laughed at her for getting more ice cream on her nose than in her mouth. Even the seagulls reminded her of him and the time he'd tried to defend their chips from a persistent bird.

Cally pushed her legs and picked up the pace. She was hurrying along so quickly she was almost at jogging speed and didn't stop until she got to the beach. Standing looking over the sea, she caught her breath and her heartbeat slowly returned to normal as she watched the sun glinting off the waves and thought about how beautiful and peaceful it was. Inside, she felt anything but peaceful. Her mind trundled along with memories, doubts, anger, hurt and just to top it off, a whole lot of confusion too.

Part of her was trying to tell herself that she was being completely over the top and totally dramatising pretty much her whole existence. Was she being fair? Logan had lied, yes, he had kept a huge secret from her. But did that negate everything else? Was it that bad? All the good times, all the moments of connection? How much he'd said he loved her. How she loved him.

She remembered the way he had looked at her the day of the races, how proud he'd seemed before she'd told him what she'd found and it had all kicked off. She remembered the care he'd taken in helping her navigate his world. Cally sighed and shook her head. She was no closer to knowing what to do. One side of her wanted to forgive Logan and jump right back in. The other side wanted to guard her heart, to protect herself from further hurt. To never look in his direction or the stupid Henry-Hicks lot ever again.

Deciding that she'd give it a few more days of mulling it over and after sitting on a bench for a bit trying to take on as much fresh air as she could, she made her way back to the deli. As she walked past the front window, Alice was fiddling with the awning out the front. There was concern etched on Alice's face.

'Feeling better?' Alice asked as Cally approached.

Cally nodded. 'I think I am. Amazing what a bit of fresh air does for you.'

'You weren't the full ticket before.'

'I'd just done a shift and I got up before the birds, so I was feeling it.'

'Oh well. You need an early night.'

'I do. See you later.'

Cally trudged up the steep stairs to her flat, her legs heavy after her walk along the beach. As she pushed open the door, she sighed to herself; at least the flat was cosy and inviting *and* she felt safe. Feeling as if she'd been run over by a steam roller together with a bad night's sleep and the early morning, all she wanted now was to cocoon herself on the sofa. She needed blackcurrant, crisps, sour laces and any other junk food laden with chemicals she could find—time for chief comfort and distraction. She was going full-on wallow mode.

She padded into the kitchen, filled the kettle, and reached for a new bottle of blackcurrant cordial. As the kettle bubbled away, she rummaged through her cupboards and started to gather supplies; a packet of chocolate digestives, a bag of marshmallows, salt and vinegar crisps, the posh ones not home brand. Proper wallowing required proper bad full-on junk snacks.

With her steaming mug of hot blackcurrant in hand and her snacks tucked under her arm, she made her way back across the sitting room, set everything down on the coffee table, and went about creating the perfect cocoon for one. First, she drew the blinds, shutting out the late afternoon light, then she flicked on the fairy lights strung along the walls, grabbed the softest, fluffiest throw from the back of the sofa - a Christmas gift from Eloise - and wrapped it around herself like a protective shield.

As she sipped the steaming blackcurrant, she scrolled through her Netflix queue, searching for the perfect film to match her mood. Something that wouldn't require too much emotional investment. Her finger hovered over the button as she debated between a well-worn favourite and a new release. In the end, she opted for a classic romcom she'd seen a dozen times, and as the opening credits rolled, she snuggled deeper into her throw, cradling her mug of hot blackcurrant.

Stuffing crisps into her mouth one after the other, as the film progressed, she lost herself in the familiar plot. The misunderstandings, emotions, missed connections, grand romantic gestures seemed so simple on screen. If only real life were as easily resolved as a ninety-minute movie. In her case, not so much. She was just reaching for another biscuit when her phone buzzed on the coffee table. She froze, her hand hovering mid-air as she saw Logan's name flash up on the screen.

Her heart began to race. Should she answer? Was she ready to talk to him? She'd told herself she needed more time. Stuff that, though. The phone continued to buzz insistently. Before she could talk herself out of it, she snatched it up and hit the answer button.

'Hello?' she said, her voice coming out smaller than she'd intended.

'Hi, I wasn't sure you'd pick up.'

'I wasn't sure I would either.'

'Thanks. I really need to talk to you.'

Cally remained silent and waited for him to continue.

Logan cleared his throat. 'How are you?'

It was such a normal question at odds with what was going on in Cally's head that she almost laughed. 'I don't know, Logan. How do you think I am?'

'Sorry. That was a stupid question. I miss you, Cally. I miss being with you and it's only been a few days.'

'Same.'

'Can we talk? Really talk, I mean. I want to explain everything. I want to make this right.'

Cally hesitated.

'Please, Blackcurrant,' Logan urged. 'Just give me a chance. I know I messed up. I know I hurt you, but, well, honestly, it doesn't mean anything.'

Cally closed her eyes, remembering the reasons she'd fallen in love with him in the first place. 'I feel like I can't trust you now.'

Logan sounded regretful. 'I know and I'm so, so sorry. I never meant to hurt you. Honestly, I think I was chickening out.'

'What? Why?'

Logan was quiet for a moment, and Cally could almost picture him running a hand through his hair the way he did when he was trying to gather his thoughts. 'I just think that I thought if you knew about Cassia, you'd, I don't know, do this, I suppose.'

Cally felt a flicker of anger. 'So you thought lying was the better option?'

'No, I... God, I don't know what I thought,' Logan admitted. 'At first, it just didn't seem important. We were just getting to know each other, and I didn't want to burden you with my baggage. And then, as things got more serious between us, it just got harder and harder to bring it up. I kept telling myself I'd find the right moment, but...'

'But you never did,' Cally finished for him.

'No,' Logan agreed miserably. 'I didn't. You deserved the truth from the start.'

Cally couldn't believe how much she loved him but he was still making her feel so wildly angry. 'I just need a bit of space.'

'For what?'

'To think.'

'Right. You need space...'

'We all can't be as happy-go-lucky Henry-Hicks as you, you know. Things don't just get better when you decide, either.'

'What's that supposed to mean?'

'Nothing.'

'I don't understand.'

'You don't just get what you want because of your family and who you are.'

'I've never said that! That's so unfair.'

'So, is not telling me the truth.'

Logan's voice changed. He sounded angry. 'Look, I love you, but you know what? Come back to me when that is enough. I'm over this. It's like you're purposely trying to fight. I've said I'm sorry.'

Cally felt her heart clench at his words. 'You can't just decide that for me.'

'You're overthinking this.'

'You don't get to decide when I'm ready to talk. You don't get to push me into forgiving you just because you've decided you're ready to explain. You don't get to treat me any way you want because you are a super special entitled member of the Henry-Hicks clan. You can't buy people, Logan!'

There was a moment of stunned silence on the other end of the line. The air then went very blue from Logan's end. 'Right. I think you've made yourself well clear.'

Cally took a deep breath, trying to calm the anger that had flared up inside her. 'This isn't just about you explaining or apologising. This is about me processing what happened and figuring out how I feel about it all. And that takes time.'

'Yeah, right. Whatever. I just want to fix it.'

'You can't just fix it and buy yourself out of this.'

'What? Really! Buy myself out of this? Come on! Get over yourself. So, where does this leave us?'

'To be honest, I don't really know. You don't just get to say jump and I ask how high.'

'You are being *totally* unreasonable.'

'Whatever. I don't care.'

'Huh? Yeah, you said that before. Okay. Well, let me know when you've made up your mind. Come back to me when you *do* care. See you.'

Cally frowned. A bit stunned by Logan's change in tone. 'See you later.'

She watched as Logan ended the call, put her phone back on the coffee table, and slumped back onto the sofa, pulling the throw tighter around herself. On the TV screen, the rom-com still played, the characters dancing around each other in the final scene. Cally watched it with unseeing eyes, her mind too full of the conversation to focus.

She sighed, reaching to rewind the film to where she'd left off before Logan's call. As she settled back to watch, she replayed bits of their conversation. As the main characters on screen fumbled their way towards their inevitable happy ending, Cally envied and resented their fictional simplicity. If only real life were as easy, she thought ruefully.

She reached for another chocolate digestive, dunking it in her blackcurrant before taking a bite and remaining curled up on the sofa, alternating between watching the film and getting lost in her thoughts. She replayed her conversation with Logan over and over, analysing every word, every inflexion. His change of tone at the end. He'd been *furious*. Had that been what Cassia had been talking about?

By the time the film's credits rolled, Cally was no closer to answers. She stretched and began to tidy up, folded the throw and gathered up her empty mug and wrappers. As she moved around the flat, she kept being drawn to her phone. Did she call him back and forgive him? She wasn't sure. By the end of the call, he'd been just as angry as her. He'd turned on her when he hadn't got what he'd wanted. She wrinkled her nose. He'd told her to come back to him when she'd made up her mind. She nodded. She would not only call his bluff, but she would put herself first. She'd held up the sky for others for so long. She wouldn't be doing that again anytime soon. The Henry-Hicks of the world didn't get to call all the shots, not as far as she was concerned anyway. He could wait until she was ready.

30

A week or so later, there had been no further communication on either side. In a constant drizzle of rain, with her bag over her shoulder, a carton of blackcurrant in her hand, and without a smile on her face, Cally stomped through Lovely in the direction of the riverboat. She was on her way to Nina's on the harbour side of Lovely to start going through the decorations for Nina's Chowder Festival event. To be frank, discussing the ins and outs of the decor, lights, chairs, and whatnot of Nina's speakeasy was the last thing she wanted to do. Our Cally was not in a good mood but needs must if she wanted to be part of the Lovely community. To say that the Chowder Festival was a massive deal in Lovely was putting it lightly. A once-a-year extravaganza that was not only much loved but taken very seriously indeed. Woe betide you if you didn't go all in. You don't like chowder? Suck it up, buttercup.

As she stood under her umbrella, waiting at the jetty, she looked all the way down the river and watched as tiny little dots of rain punctured the top of a very still River Lovely. Since the phone call with Logan when he'd told her in no uncertain terms that she could come back to him when him loving her was enough, she'd been around in circles, but she'd certainly not gone back. She wasn't really sure where that left them. She supposed the Cally and Logan thing had come to an abrupt end. Bye bye, Henry-Hicks. Nice knowing you.

Not only that, it was as if the tables had turned a little bit. When she'd spoken to him, she'd sat there on the sofa thinking that she had all the cards, that she was oh-so high and just as mighty. That she had the upper hand because he'd lied. She'd been quite the superior one, or so she'd thought. Get out the violins that she'd always had to hold up the sky. Boo-hoo that she might be hurt. Poor Cally having to shield her heart all the time.

Logan had taken that on board but when she'd pushed him too far, he'd flipped it back on her. His take on it was that he loved her and that should be good enough.

Henry-Hicks had shown his own cards, thank you very much. Played a tough game.

Cally pondered the whole situation as she stood in the rain and watched as a young mum in one of the navy-blue Lovely coats with the hood up bumped a pram up onto the jetty. She'd not heard from Logan and she'd not contacted him either. To be quite frank, she had no idea what to do or think in the latest instalment in the scenario. Logan had more or less told her to take it or leave it. What was she supposed to think about that? She supposed she was leaving it. Cally de Pfeffer and Henry-Hicks were no longer a thing.

She assumed that by not contacting him, she was calling his bluff and wouldn't be coming back. Part of her wanted to run like the wind up to the manor and jump in his bed and stay there forever. Like, ever, ever. Instead, she did nothing but festered in a huge pool of self-pity and poor, poor, poor, old me. Eyeroll.

Somehow, though, our Cally *needed* the wallowing. Indeed, she'd spent the days since the call and Logan's harsh words in a cocoon of wallow; way, way, way too much blackcurrant cordial, ditto gin, and there had been a lot of partaking in Lovely Bay chocolate. There'd also been a lone walk past the lighthouse, along the beach, and back again as it had been approaching midnight. Even the stars and a clear, dark, Lovely night hadn't helped her. Melancholy was her new best friend. As she watched the boat chug along in the drizzly rain, she just about managed to smile as Colin waved. She wasn't in the mood for him, either. Shame that because he was his usual upbeat self.

'Afternoon, our Cally!'

'Hey, Colin. How are you?'

'I'd be better without the rain. We had sunshine this morning, and then it was windy, and now this.' Colin held his hand up to the sky just after he threw a rope.

'Yup.'

'I should be used to the four Lovely seasons in a day by now, right? Only lived here all my life.'

'Ha, yeah, you should.'

'What are you up to? All ready for the Chowder Festival?'

'I am. I'm just on my way over to Nina's now, actually. We're doing some prep.'

'Ahh, she'll have that all sorted.'

'I know. She doesn't really need me.'

Colin secured the rope to the jetty and glanced up at Cally, his weathered face creasing into a smile. 'So, you're off there now? She's a force of nature, that one.'

Cally nodded, adjusting her grip on her umbrella. 'That she is. I sometimes wonder why she even wants my input.'

Colin chuckled, his eyes crinkling at the corners. 'Ah, don't sell yourself short.'

The young mum with the pram approached the gangplank,

struggling to manage both the pram and her shopping bags. Cally stepped forward. 'Need a hand with that,' Cally offered, reaching for one of the bags.

The woman looked up gratefully, her hood slipping back slightly to reveal a harried face. 'Oh, thank you. That's very kind.'

Cally took the heaviest-looking bag and followed the woman onto the boat. She set the bag down next to the pram. 'There you go. All set?'

The woman nodded. 'Yes, thank you so much. It's not easy managing everything with a pram.'

Cally smiled, feeling a twinge of something she'd never felt before. Glancing at the sleeping baby in the pram, she smiled. 'I can imagine. Aww, so sweet.'

As she sat down under cover, the drizzle had eased slightly, but the air remained heavy with moisture. The river's surface was a mottled grey under a dense, overcast sky that stretched away. In the distance, on the opposite bank, the colours were a smudge of green and brown, creating a misty veil over the river. Once they were going, Colin came up the stairs, chatted with the woman with the pram, and then smiled as he passed Cally on his way back down.

Cally attempted to make conversation even though she most certainly was not in the mood for small talk. 'How are the Chowder Festival decorations coming along?'

'You thought you'd seen bunting? You ain't seen nothing. This year, we're going for the most we've ever had. You won't be able to move for it in Lovely. Blue and white bunting all along the harbour front and up the main street. Reams and reams of the stuff and not all that rubbish from overseas. Handmade right here in Lovely. We've been working on it since last year.'

'Sounds lovely,' Cally said, genuinely intrigued. 'What about the lighthouse?'

Colin's eyes twinkled. 'Ah, now that's where the real magic's happening. The whole thing is being covered in fairy lights as we speak. We have got millions of lights this year. Might even hit a billion.'

'You're joking! How on earth are you managing that? You'll need a lot of help, won't you?'

'Aye, that's Lovely for you. Everyone pitches in. It's what makes this place special.'

'Yep, it is.'

'It's all hands on deck, quite literally. We've got half the town working on it. Robby's blokes are doing the outside bit.'

Cally raised an eyebrow. 'That's right, Neens, did say. I guess he's well-qualified to throw himself down the side of the lighthouse to attach a few lights.'

'Too right. Rather him than me. There will be a turning on of the lights extravaganza just for Lovelies...'

'It does sound magical.'

Colin straightened up, puffing out his chest a bit. 'Well, it's a team effort, but I'd be lying if I said I wasn't proud. Now, tell me, what's Nina got you working on?'

Cally sighed. 'Oh, you know. Tablecloths, chair arrangements, napkins, that sort of thing. Nothing as exciting as your lights.'

'I know you're still finding your feet here in Lovely. But trust me, being part of this festival—even if it's just deciding on napkin colours—it's a big deal. You're weaving yourself into the fabric of the town.'

Cally looked up at him, surprised by the insight. 'I hadn't thought about it like that.'

'Course you hadn't. You've been too busy moping about a certain fella from up there at the manor.'

Cally's mouth fell open. 'How did you—?'

Colin tapped the side of his nose. 'Small town, love. Word gets around. But don't worry, we all have our dramas. It'll sort itself out.' Colin squinted up at the sky. 'Weather's turning again. There's a storm coming, if I'm not mistaken.'

'Yep, feels like it. Hope it doesn't rain for the festival.'

'Ahh, well, rain or shine, we do it anyway. It's about remembering where we came from, you know?'

'How do you mean?'

Colin's eyes were fixed on the river. 'Lovely wasn't always the quaint little town it is now. Back in my granddad's day, it was a proper fishing area and very isolated too. Harsh life it was. Men out on boats in all weathers, women keeping everything together back on shore. I'm not being sexist. That's how it was back then.'

Cally tried to imagine the Lovely of yesteryear. 'Must have been quite different in those days.'

'Oh yes,' Colin nodded, 'In actual fact, the Chowder Festival started as a way to use up the less popular fish, the ones that didn't sell so well at market. Waste not, want not – that was the motto. Over time, it became a celebration of the town's resilience, its ability to make something wonderful out of whatever life threw at it.'

'I love the history of it here.'

'Yup. Then there's the chowder competition. Will you be entering?'

'Me? No! I'm *so* not qualified.'

'You never know. Everyone's got a special recipe tucked away somewhere. Besides, it's not just about winning. It's about being part of it all.'

Cally laughed. 'Will you be entering?'

'Of course! We've got an old recipe book that's been in our family for generations.'

'Good luck with that.'

'You never know I might win. Right, I'd best get on.'

As the boat rounded a bend in the river, the harbour came into view. The misty rain created a dreamlike quality, softening the edges of the buildings and boats that lined the waterfront. At least Cally had Lovely to soften her landing. Right at that moment, she felt as if that was the only thing she had at all. Tended to occur when you were stubborn and dropped the best thing that had happened to you from a very high height just to see how far it would fall.

31

Cally smiled as she got to Nina's property on the harbour side of Lovely. Talk about house envy. A beautiful old place right on the harbour wall boasting tightly held views worth their weight in gold. Cally pursed her lips together as she went around the back and buzzed the gate. She could but dream about owning a property in Lovely and carry on tightening her purse strings. She wasn't going to let the vision go.

Having been in Nina's house a fair few times to do with Nina's business, A Lovely Organised Life, Cally was used to how nice it was, but as Nina ushered her in, Cally shook her head. One day, she said to herself. One day, I'll have something half as nice as this. Nina led her to a kitchen area where timber doors painted in a very pale duck egg blue were capped with brass pull handles. White subway tiles lined the wall up to a large picture window with sash panes that looked out over the harbour. The view was *phenomenal*. An old Butler sink with a goose-neck tap dropped into marble-style worktops under the window. Cally took in the gorgeous open shelving on either side of the window showcasing a collection of white crockery and china and a group of vintage chopping boards were stacked up in the corner.

Cally pulled out a chair from under a table with a butcher's block top and looked up at old pendant lights over the table and a huge white vase with a gigantic jumble of flowers. She shook her head at how nice it was and how she didn't know where to look first: pots of wooden utensils of all shapes and sizes, a very posh fridge, a double-width range oven where a vintage potbelly shaped pot with beautiful old-fashioned handles bubbled away to itself. Cally wanted to strip off her clothes, have a quick shower, steal Nina's dressing gown and possibly her husband, and move in.

'Make yourself comfortable,' Nina called over her shoulder as she busied herself at the kettle. 'I'll have the tea ready in a jiffy.'

Cally nodded and gazed out the picture window dominating the wall behind the sink, its sash panes divided the view of the harbour into lots of little picturesque vignettes. Boats bobbed on the water, masts swayed in the light breeze and little droplets of water ran down the panes.

'Sorry, I'm having a mental block. You're just milk, aren't you? Or milk and sugar?'

'Just milk, please.'

'I'm all out of blackcurrant.' Nina chuckled.

'I could do with a break from the sugar load, truth be told.'

'It's been that bad of a week, has it?'

'Ha! If only you knew.' Cally bantered, but inside, it was true.

Nina reached up to the open shelving and selected two mugs from her collection of white crockery as Cally fiddled with the leaves on a little row of potted herbs sitting on a tray in the centre of the table. Nina chatted away as she waited for the kettle to boil and stirred the pot on the stove. The aroma of chowder filled the air, homely and comforting. The vintage potbelly pan seemed perfectly at home on the double-width range oven, its old-fashioned handles adding a touch of nostalgia.

'That smells divine.' Cally noted.

'It's coming along nicely. It was originally Birdie's recipe, with a few tweaks of my own along the way until I ended up with my own version.'

The kettle clicked off, and Nina poured the water into a teapot that matched the mugs. She carried the pot to the table.

Cally nodded towards the huge white vase dominating the centre of the table. 'Love the flowers.'

'I picked them up from the market this morning. I thought they'd brighten the place up, what with all this rain we've been having.'

'Nice, I might treat myself to some, too.'

As Nina poured the tea, Cally gestured around the kitchen. 'I don't know where to look first. It's so homey in here, topped by that fantastic view. I love it.'

Nina chuckled. 'It's taken a while to get it right. But it's my happy place. I swear, half the reason I got into the chowder so much is because it's an excuse to potter around in here.'

Cally took a sip of her tea. 'Well, it shows. Everything looks so well put together.'

'Facebook Marketplace has been my friend.' Nina laughed.

'I love searching for stuff on there. Buried treasure.'

'Yup, especially here where people give stuff away. I do love being part of the Lovely community.

'I'm hearing you. This whole Chowder Festival thing is very serious, though.'

'I know. I'm a tad on the nervous side.' Nina got up to check on the chowder. 'Wait until you taste this. I think I've finally cracked the secret to my own recipe.'

Cally widened her eyes. 'Ooh, do I get in on your secret?'

Nina lifted the lid, and a cloud of fragrant steam billowed up. She stirred the pot. 'Nope.'

'Hilarious.'

'Joking. It's really about what you do before you even add the fish. The base is key. The bacon has to be good and then deglazed with white wine. Balances the cream.'

'Genius. You're killing me. It smells incredible.'

'You'll be sick of it by the time we're finished.'

'So, what's left to do?'

Nina slid a mini iPad across the table. 'All detailed down to the last fairy light.'

Cally read through. 'Looks like you've thought about everything. Today is setting everything up, then.'

'Yeah. The tables will take a while to put together. Pretty tablecloths and strings of fairy lights back and forth over the whole setting. I'm aiming to beat Colin.'

'Good luck.'

'The lights will take ages. I have thousands.' Nina got up and pulled a huge old tin from a cupboard. 'What do you think about using these as centrepieces?'

Cally pursed her lips. 'They're lovely. Where did you find them?'

'They were upstairs when I first moved in. I was going to chuck them, but something made me keep them because I loved the old patina.'

'Yeah, nice.'

'I want it to feel a little bit like you've stepped back in time in my speakeasy.'

'Love that idea. I'm starting to see that this festival is a big deal in Lovely. It's not just about the food, is it?'

'Nope, it's not. The chowder is important, of course. It's the heritage, connection to the sea and to the past of the place.'

Cally nodded. 'It's the belonging, for me.'

'Exactly. You're part of Lovely now, whether you realise it or not.' Nina joked. 'You have no choice in the matter. You get roped in for all sorts if you live here.'

Two hours or so into setting up the tables and chairs, Nina came down the stairs with a couple of mugs of tea. Passing one to Cally, she held up a couple of lengths of very thin rope tied into intricate nautical knots. 'What do you think about these for the napkin rings?'

'Love. Where did you find them?'

'Old Tom just down here made them for me. He's worked on the boats all his life, and so he knows a knot or two.'

The detail of the knots, so quintessentially Lovely, made Cally smile. 'Wow, so clever. It's simple but oh-so-Lovely.'

'I know. I love it, too.'

Cally gestured around the room. 'Well, that didn't take too long. It's really coming together.'

'Yep. It's exciting. Something's in the air. You can't put your finger on it.'

Cally nodded, understanding exactly what Nina meant. It was as if Lovely buzzed in anticipation about the upcoming festival. However, no matter how much she tried to look on the bright side or flick the switch, our Cally wasn't buzzing. Nor was she happy. Flat, more like. Very, very flat and down in the dumps. Her arms ached from being back to holding up that same old, same old sky. Not a good position to be in at all.

32

Cally had heard nothing from Logan. She'd considered messaging him but had decided against it. Instead, she stuck her head in the sand, buried herself in her laptop, and tried not to think about it. Eloise had told her in no uncertain words that she thought she was doing the wrong thing, but Cally's head had remained well and truly in the sand. Her grandma had always told her she was stubborn. It seemed she'd been right.

Part of her seethed about Logan and what she perceived to be his lies. Sitting at her laptop waiting for a customer to find their order number, she realised that while she thought about Logan and the situation, she was clenching her jaw so tightly it was almost as if her bones might crack. He'd riled her up and then some. And now he'd stuck to his word and not called or darkened the door. Poor devil couldn't do anything right. All of it would have been fine if she didn't care less. She did. The problem was that she still loved him and probably would until the cows came home.

Henry-Hicks might have stuffed up, but he was unknowingly still very much in the game.

She tutted as the customer gave the wrong order number and she had to instruct her that she needed an eight-digit number. The joys of working in customer service. Dealing with another three customers at the same time via different windows, she tried not to think about Logan. Easier said than done.

After making a cup of tea and working through an afternoon filled with complaint after complaint, by the end of the session, she'd had enough. She checked her watch and wondered whether she could bail out of the Chowder Festival progress meeting she was attending that was happening at a speakeasy at the back of the deli. She considered not going for all of about three seconds. Being part of the Lovely community was very important to her, and ducking out of the meeting would put a very black, very intense mark against her name. She wasn't in the mood for the meeting in the slightest, though. About the only thing she was in the mood for was comfort eating, a shed load of wallowing, and maybe a bit of a cry for good measure. Or perhaps getting into bed, putting the duvet over her head, and hibernating until the whole Logan mess was something she could forget. As she pulled the lever on the shower, listened to the water coming up through the building, and heard the pipes clang and bang, she cursed herself for the billionth time for falling in love with Logan. She rued the day she'd first set eyes on him when the bottom of her bag fell away on the riverboat. Rued his stupid surname. His manor house, no less. Shoulders, eyes, everything else.

After showering, putting on her usual short skirt uniform, and sticking her hair up in clips, she poured herself a hot blackcurrant and, with a bit of time to kill before the meeting, decided to have a little walk. She hoped the fresh air might do her some good. Walking out of the back entrance of the deli, she headed down the service road at the back, came out not far from the lighthouse, stood gazing at it for a few minutes, and then headed back in the direction of the shops.

As she made her way further along the street, she hoovered up the Lovely scene in front of her eyes. Even though she was not happy about what had happened concerning falling in love with one of Lovely's poshest inhabitants, she still adored the third smallest town in the country. The line of pretty boutique shops with paned windows looked back at her and oodles of bunting ready for the festival fluttered across the top of the street. A young couple sat in the window of the chocolate shop with steaming cups of coffee and truffles, and she smiled at the old bookshop with its striped awning and bench outside loaded with second-hand books. The old-fashioned hardware store, where timber trestle tables lined up against the shop window were stacked with old fishing baskets full of hardware items, was just closing up for the day. A little dog was tied up outside the charity shop and a couple of mums, one wearing one of the blue wax Lovely coats, pushed prams back and forth as they chatted outside the Co-op. Cally liked being part of Lovely. Quaint, old-fashioned, and from another time, it made her feel safe, as if she belonged and had somewhere to call home.

She smiled as she stopped at the pub, peered in the window, and looked along at the bow-fronted shop of the deli with bunting hanging across the top of the door. A chalkboard with bunting tied haphazardly around the top detailed Lovely Bay chowder was available and invited passers-by to pop in.

A few minutes later, she was standing in the deli. Alice frowned and smiled at the same time. 'Hey, our Cally. You're a bit early, aren't you?'

'I had to get out of the flat. I've been staring at my laptop for hours on end. Had enough of it.'

'Right, you are. Coffee?'

'Yes, please.'

Alice lowered her voice, 'You coming later?'

'Yes. Do you need any help?'

Alice looked over her shoulder in the direction of the back of the deli where the speakeasy chowder evening and meeting for the festival would be taking place. 'I think we're good. We set most of it up last night.'

'Shout if you need anything.'

'Will do. Take a pew. I'll bring it over in a minute.'

Cally sat down by the door and, as she settled herself in, inhaled the familiar scents: coffee, baking, and Lovely things. A few minutes later, Alice appeared, balancing a steaming mug of coffee and a plate with a large slice of carrot cake.

'Here you go,' Alice said, setting the items down in front of Cally. 'Thought you might fancy a bit of cake. You look like you could use a pick-me-up. On the house.'

'Thanks, Alice. You're a star.'

Alice pulled out the chair opposite and sat down, her own mug of coffee in hand. 'I'll join you for a sec. I've been on my feet all day. So, how are the festival preparations going on your end? Ready for Nina's big speakeasy debut?'

'She's been running around like a headless chicken, trying to get everything perfect. Actually not a headless chicken, an organised chicken. You know what she's like.'

Alice chuckled. 'I can imagine. It's exciting, isn't it? Her first proper event in that gorgeous house of hers.'

'I know. I have to say I am jealous, ha! It's like something out of a film. All those big windows looking out over the water. It's going to be quite the backdrop for the speakeasy.'

'I heard the tickets to her place went in minutes.'

Cally's eyebrows rose. 'Really? That's brilliant.'

'So, what's your role in it?' Alice asked, taking a sip of her coffee.

'Bit of everything, really. I'm helping with serving, of course. But I'm also on decoration duty. She's got everything planned. It's going to sparkle, that's for sure.'

Alice's eyes widened. 'Blimey. That sounds like quite the undertaking.'

'Yup, there are lots of fairy lights and more vintage glassware than I knew existed in all of Lovely.' Cally took a bite of her carrot cake. 'How are things shaping up here? I bet you're run off your feet.'

Alice slumped in her chair. 'You have no idea. Between the regular customers, the festival prep, and Colin's grand plans, I'm about ready to keel over. I love it, though. The Chowder Festival is in my blood.'

'Oh goodness, what's Colin up to now?' Cally asked.

Alice rolled her eyes. 'He's got it in his head that Lovely Bay needs to be the most festive-looking town in all of Britain. I swear, if he puts up any more bunting, we'll be visible from space.'

Cally chuckled. 'Yeah, I spoke to him on the river.'

'I think he's trying to break some sort of world record. Most bunting per capita or something ridiculous. I half expect to wake up one morning and find he's bunting-ed the entire coastline.'

'Bunting-ed?' Cally repeated, grinning. 'Is that even a word?'

Alice waved her hand. 'It is now. When it comes to Colin's obsessions, we need to invent new words just to keep up.'

Cally laughed. It was all part of why she adored Lovely: the funny little traditions and the sometimes quite odd characters. She'd fallen in love with them more or less from day one.

'I'm going to be absolutely cream-crackered by the end of it. I might need a holiday just to recover from the Chowder Festival.' Alice rolled her eyes.

'I know what you mean. It's exciting, but it's a lot of work. And it's not like we can just close up shop for a week to focus on it. We've still got our regular jobs to do. Birdie is beside herself.'

'Don't get me wrong, I love the festival. It's brilliant for the town, brings in loads of visitors, and it's a right laugh. But sometimes, I think we might be biting off more than we can chew. I say that every year, though and every year is better than the last.'

'It's what makes this place special. To be fair, I love it.'

Alice nodded. 'When it all comes together and we see everyone enjoying themselves, it'll be worth it. I just might need someone to prop me up by the end of it all.'

'I'll volunteer for that duty. As long as you return the favour when I inevitably collapse after Nina's speakeasy.'

'Deal,' Alice laughed.

'Right,' Alice said, glancing at her watch. 'I'd better get back to it. Those flapjacks for tomorrow won't bake themselves, more's the pity.'

Cally nodded, draining the last of her coffee. 'I might have another one if you don't mind.'

'Of course. Thanks for the chat. I needed a bit of a laugh.'

'Me too. More than you know.'

Alice frowned. 'Everything alright?'

For a moment, Cally was tempted to spill everything, but she held back. There was no way she wanted her personal drama going around Lovely, although she was fairly sure the Lovely grapevine was well aware of what was going on. 'Yep, fine. Everything's good with me.'

Alice nodded, though she didn't look entirely convinced. 'Alright. But my offer stands. Anytime you need to talk or just fancy a cuppa and a moan, you know where to find me.'

'Thanks.'

'Oh and later, if Colin comes at you with a clipboard, just run. Run far and run fast.'

Cally laughed. 'Noted.'

33

As she sat at the table daydreaming, Cally looked at her phone, hoping perhaps to see a message from Logan. Of course, there was nothing. She wondered where the situation was going to go. Would she ever see him again? Would they not have a story now? Was this the end? It made her heart hurt to think that because she couldn't deal with not knowing about Cassia, they were no longer together. A tiny part of her felt quite impressed that he had called her bluff. The other stubborn part of her wasn't going to have a bar of it.

Just after Alice put another coffee on the table, she answered a message from Nina about that evening's meeting, took a phone call, and started to doom scroll through her phone, shaking her head at what was going on in a couple of other parts of the country. Seeing not-very-nice scenes in the streets reminded her how nice it was in Lovely Bay. Almost as if the little town was exempt from stuff that was happening elsewhere. As if Lovely existed in its own little bubble. Eventually, putting her phone down, she people-watched out the window for a bit and watched Nancy from the station walk past, chatting away to Penny, the woman she'd met at the lighthouse.

Then she waved as Clive from the riverboat, with a shopping bag from the Co-op over his arm, strolled past with his dog.

She sat staring for ages and stayed where she was as Alice shut up the deli for the day. As Alice pottered around setting up for the next day, she asked Cally if she wouldn't mind going to the Co-op to grab an extra pint of milk. Cally gladly went, happy to take her mind off thinking about Logan. She stopped on the way to chat with Colin, who was heading in the direction of the deli for the meeting. Lost in a world of her own as she walked into the Co-op, she found herself in the biscuit aisle, shook her head, and made her way to the end, where the milk fridges stood all along the back in a row. Just as she was opening the middle fridge and wondering if Alice wanted skimmed or not she smelt Logan before she saw him. Instinctively, she turned around to see him standing at the end of the adjacent aisle in front of the cheese fridge, looking at blocks of cheddar.

Her mind raced as it toggled between running as fast as she could out the door without a backward glance or waiting until he turned so that he bumped straight into her. Deciding she couldn't deal with it and very much wanting to make a hasty retreat, she grabbed a pint of milk. She then turned to leave with the door still open right at the same time as Logan glanced up. Their eyes met and Cally's heart leapt. She stood there with the fridge door ajar. Unsure of what to do, she half-smiled. It was not reciprocated. 'Hi.'

'Cally.'

'How are you?'

'Yep, fine.' Logan's tone was clipped and not happy.

'I, err.'

Logan put his hand up to stop Cally from speaking. 'Sorry, I've got to run.'

Cally was a bit flabbergasted. 'The least you could do is talk to me.'

'I could say the same.' Logan's face tightened and his expression was *very* guarded.

Cally shifted uncomfortably, clutching the pint of milk to her chest like a shield and slamming the fridge door shut. She gestured to the bottle. 'I was just getting some milk for Alice. For the deli.'

Logan nodded curtly, turning back to the cheese display. 'Right.'

Cally felt a flare of irritation at Logan's dismissive attitude. She raised her voice a little bit. 'As I said, the least you could do is speak to me properly, Logan. We're both adults, aren't we?'

Logan's shoulders stiffened, and he turned back to face her fully, his expression now tinged with anger. 'Pah! Speak to you properly? That's a bit rich, coming from you. You've been avoiding me and you knew about the certificate for ages and didn't let on. What a joke.'

'I haven't been avoiding you.'

Logan scoffed, shaking his head. 'Don't give me that.'

'I've needed time, as I said, and I've been busy...'

'We both know that's not the real reason. You made up your mind about something that happened years before I even met you and you don't like it. You're punishing me for that. End of.'

Cally's cheeks flushed. 'Punishing you? Is that what you think this is?'

'What else am I supposed to think?' Logan retorted. 'You find out about a marriage that ended long before we met, and suddenly you can't even look at me, and there's been no communication. You know you really need to grow up. How is that fair?'

Cally glanced around, acutely aware that they were having the conversation in the middle of the Co-op. 'I, err...'

Logan cut her off. 'Do you have any idea what it's like to be on the other side of this? You suddenly shut me out completely. Yeah, whatever. Not impressed. Not at all.'

Cally felt irrationally angry. She couldn't quite compute that he'd turned the tables and was blaming her for everything. 'Oh, I'm sorry. Am I not reacting the way you'd like? *You're* not impressed! I've heard it all now!'

Logan's eyes flashed. 'I didn't lie to you. I simply didn't tell you about something that happened years ago and has no bearing on our relationship whatsoever. Honestly, get over yourself.'

'No bearing? You were *married*, Logan. That's not exactly a minor detail! How do you work out that that's not important?'

'It was a mistake,' Logan hissed, clearly trying to keep his voice down. 'A brief, stupid mistake that I'd rather forget. Why can't you understand that? So infuriating.'

Cally also hissed. 'Because you didn't trust me enough to tell me. Because I had to find out by accident. Do *you* have any idea how that feels?'

Logan grimaced in frustration. 'I've apologised. I've explained. What more do you want from me?'

Cally, actually, wasn't entirely sure *what* she wanted. 'I wanted to be able to trust you. To know that you're not keeping other secrets from me.'

'I'm not! You're blowing this completely out of proportion. It was one mistake years ago. It doesn't change anything about us, about our relationship or what's left of it.'

'How can I trust that you're not hiding other things from me?'

Logan's expression hardened. He also rolled his eyes. 'It's just ridiculous, and as I said, come back to me when you can deal with it or, you know, don't. Your choice.'

Cally felt as though the ground was trembling beneath her feet. There was a small earthquake happening in the Co-op in Lovely Bay. 'You're making yourself very clear.'

'Same to you. I think we both need some time to think about things.'

Cally nodded and before she could speak, Logan grabbed a block of cheese, turned and walked away, disappearing down an aisle without a backward glance. Cally stood there for a moment, clutching the forgotten milk bottle, feeling as though her world had just tilted on its axis again. What in the world? To be frank, she didn't know what to think. One thing was for sure: Logan was no walkover. He took no prisoners. So handsome when angry. Phew.

Mechanically, she made her way to the checkouts, paid for the milk, and stepped out into the warm Lovely Bay evening. As she walked back towards the deli, her mind whirred like crazy. Part of her wanted to run after Logan to try and fix things. But another part, the stubborn part that had been nursing her hurt, held her back. She replayed their conversation in her head, getting angrier and more upset by the second. As she approached the deli, she took a deep breath, trying to compose herself. There was no way she was going to take her personal drama into the festival meeting. She pushed open the door, the cheerful jingle of the shop bell ringing in her ears. Alice looked up from behind the counter and made a funny face. 'Are you okay?'

Cally flicked the switch and forced a smile. 'Yep, all good. Here's the milk. I couldn't remember if you wanted skimmed or not.'

'Doesn't matter. Thanks.'

'I'm going to pop upstairs for a second. I just need to check my emails quickly.'

'Okie-dokie. See you shortly.'

After popping to the loo, Cally looked in the mirror as she washed her hands. She spoke to her reflection. 'Why couldn't he just have told me in the first place? Grrr.'

She shook her head, tutted, and wrinkled her nose and face. A little voice whispered that she was being an idiot, that she was pushing Logan away because of her pride and stubborn streak. The voice was one hundred per cent right. She'd lost the game.

34

Cally kicked off her shoes and peeled away her socks, leaving them in a jumbled heap on the beach. As she stood for a second looking out to sea, little grains of cool and damp sand shifted beneath her feet. She wiggled her toes, dug them further under the sand, and stood there for a minute, waiting to see if being by the sea would do its thing. With a heavy sigh, she began to walk along the shoreline, peering in front of her at the endless expanse of water all the way to the horizon. Waves lapped on the shore and she crossed her fingers that they might actually do something to alleviate the chaotic thoughts swirling in her mind. They didn't really, but it was worth a go. Seagulls wheeled and screeched overhead as she pounded along, taking in huge lungfuls of fresh sea air and tried to do something about her discombobulated mind.

The further she walked, though, the more Cally's mind tumbled here, there, and everywhere. It drifted from Logan to her little flat, to the races, and then back over the previous few years before she'd even known about the existence of a family named Henry-Hicks. She thought about her own pathetic excuse for a family and the familiar low-frequency dull sort of sadness about all that it had ended up being. A lot of heartache every which way she'd turned and no one ever being there to help hold up her sky. Her brain flicked back to the latter years of her caring role and how her grandma, in her increasing frailty, had required near-constant care. How utterly exhausting and draining that had been. How sometimes the constant, never let up of it had made her so tightly wound she'd wondered if she'd ever be able to let go. As the sea washed over her feet and she pummelled along the sand, she was suddenly back in the room with the bed hoist, the smell of talcum powder and lavender soap in her nose, the sound of laboured breathing in the night, soft papery skin, watery pale blue eyes, the shrill of the alarm when something went wrong. Worry. So much dread.

Cally shook her head and tried to remember the good times, but her mind instead went to her mum. Her mum had battled all sorts of demons, and somehow, it had often been Cally's fault at the end of the day. The ins and outs of her mother's mental health had given her mum a very good excuse not to have to bother with the intricacies of the parental role. Indeed, since Cally had been able to do things for herself, she'd been the parent in the situation. Ever the adult as far as Cally was concerned. And adolescence, the teenage years, and navigating through them? That hadn't been an option in our Cally's world. No option to have her own life. Sucking it up for everyone else all the time.

With the waves not doing much to help, she thought about her half-brother too. The tantrums, the moods, and the doctor's appointments swirled around in front of her face. Patience, understanding, care, all of the things. Just a shame the same hadn't ever been extended to her. She paused on the sand for a bit, letting the cold water wash over her feet and took a few steps forward. The water was so chilly it sent a shiver up her spine. In a way, she quite liked the cold rush of icy water. Maybe it would be good for her. Enough people raved on about the benefits of getting out in the sea. Open water swimming or something, wasn't it called? Worth a go? As another wave fell onto the sand and splashed up and over her ankles, she shivered. Maybe not.

Her mind moved from caring to her fight with Logan. Something about the two were somehow linked in her brain. She just couldn't quite work out what, how, or why. Perhaps because with Logan, she'd, for the first time ever in her life, let herself go and he'd then gone and let her down. She'd dared to believe that she could have something for herself that was really good, really special, that she could really be loved. Something not tainted by duty or obligation or the thoughts and needs of anyone else. She shook her head and gritted her teeth. She'd gone in feet first. Look where that had got her. It felt as if she'd ended up right at the end of a creek without a paddle.

She kicked at the water, sending up a spray that glittered in the light. At least she was sad in a beautiful place. There was that, she supposed. She loved the smell of the sea, the curve of the bay, the distant silhouette of the magnificence of the lighthouse standing sentinel over it all. Despite her mood, Lovely Bay still worked its magic. The lighthouse stood right there in front of her, tall, strong, towering, doing its thing. At least she had that in her life.

Resuming her walk, her feet left a trail of footprints in the damp sand as she pondered what she was going to do with her life. Her intention when she'd first settled into Birdie's flat had been to save up as much money as she could, eventually buy her own place, and do a course in something that would mean she'd be set up for life. There hadn't been many big fancy pants dreams, really. No harbouring ideas of travel to foreign lands, no big plans for adventure, no real thoughts about a career that would set the world on fire. She felt almost as if she'd missed the boat on any and all of that. What Cally de Pfeffer really wanted was to simply feel safe. Coming in second, a good old dose of stability and a little place to call her own wouldn't go amiss. In third place, a relationship with someone she trusted and who loved her. Someone who didn't need her to care. And, with Henry-Hicks she'd thought she'd found just that. But it had all come crashing down around her ears.

No matter what she told herself or what Eloise said, the secret of Logan's previous marriage had made her feel as if he'd whipped a very nice rug right out from under her feet. Even though the rational part of her brain tried to argue that she was ultra-sensitive, another part was so hurt and downright raw that she just *couldn't* let it go. She'd abhorred the feeling of being lied to so much that it messed with her head. Made her quite unable to listen to reason. Made her forget all the good stuff and see red.

The wind picked up, whipping her hair around her face. She tried to let it get into her head and take away the hurt. It smelt of the Lovely smell and her favourite things: salt and seaweed, the coast, and fresh air. She let it wash over her and nodded. At least being by the sea was nice and constant. It didn't care about her troubles or give a hoot about what was going on in her jumbled mind.

Bending down, she picked up a smooth pebble and turned it over and over again as her brain very slowly began to decompress. She remembered the look on Logan's face in the Co-op. As if he couldn't quite understand what was going on in her brain. He wasn't the only one. She turned the pebble and ran her finger along its top. Was pushing away Logan, the best thing that had ever happened to her, out of some upside-down, ridiculous sort of pride? She remembered the shock of finding out about his marriage, the feeling that the ground had dropped out from under her feet. Putting the pebble in her pocket, she reached the end of the beach and clambered up onto a cluster of rocks, wincing a little bit as their rough surface scraped her bare feet. Plonking herself down she stared out over the sweep of the bay and the third smallest town in the country laid out before her like a miniature model. Tears pricked her eyes as she thought about Logan and how he'd cared for her. She'd been so tired of being strong. Always being the one who held it together while everything fell apart around her, and he'd swooped right on in and loved her. She nodded to herself. What was she making such a fuss about? It really was as simple as that.

A few minutes later, she'd clambered back off the rocks and ambled back along the beach. The fresh air and waves had indeed done something to her. Clarity had, perhaps, arrived. Yep, her mind was still churning, but it was somehow calmer than before. By the time she reached her discarded shoes and socks, her mind felt a bit clearer. She had to stop wallowing in it and move on one way or the other. She gave herself a bit of a talking-to. She couldn't change the past. She was unable to undo the years she'd spent as a carer. She could not go back and erase the Logan thing, but she could *choose* how to move forward.

As she brushed the sand from her feet and pulled on her socks and shoes, she told herself to get a grip. She would make a decision about Logan and what would be would be. She would make a list of what she was grateful for and reiterate that. She would put plans in place for her future and look after herself. She wouldn't sit around moping. She had a sky that needed holding up.

35

Cally sat at her desk, the little banker's lamp beside her nudged next to a picture of her with her grandma. It was late, far later than she usually stayed up, but since she'd come to the realisation that she had, in fact, broken up with Logan, sleep had been elusive. As she sat and flicked between tabs on her laptop, her mind spun between Logan, the upcoming Chowder Festival, and the nagging feeling that there was something more she should be doing with her life. She'd still not found a course or, indeed, any calling for what she wanted to do. Before, she'd always been tied to caring so she hadn't had much choice in the matter. She'd told herself in those days that there was no rush. Now, she felt as if she'd missed the boat altogether.

She glanced at the pile of course brochures piled neatly on her desk that she'd collected from the library. Their glossy covers promised new beginnings and exciting career paths, but to be quite honest, the beaming faces on the front all looked a bit false as far as she was concerned. With a sigh, she pushed the pamphlets away and opened a new tab on her browser. The cursor blinked at her as she pondered what she even wanted.

She'd been asking herself the question for months and had not quite found an answer.

Ever since she'd started working at the chemist's, she'd told herself it was temporary and that her real path in life was on hold. She'd seen it as a fill-in job. Another part of the caring role as she'd waited for the inevitable with her grandma. But as time had marched on, everything, including the elusive other path, had begun to feel more and more out of reach. Not only that, part of her had become quite comfy in the chemist. It was a fairly boring way to earn a living, but the pay was good enough, she was well-liked and fitted in, and now the commute was very short, too. Plus, it was flexible and easy and left her with time to fit in other things.

She typed "career aptitude test" into the search bar and hit enter. A flood of results appeared. Oh-so-many things grappling for her attention and lots of promises to unlock her true potential and guide her to her dream job. Pah. Yeah right. Cally clicked on the first link, scanned down a load of checkboxes, and methodically answered question after question about her interests, skills, and values. What could or would this website tell her about this elusive new career she was after?

She found herself struggling a little bit as she made her way further down the page and the questions got more detailed. What did she like? What experience did she have? Did she prefer working with people or data? Was she more analytical or creative? The further she got into the test, the more she realised how little she knew about herself outside of her caring role. Her experience, at the end of the day, was, quite frankly, dead-end jobs going nowhere at all. There was only so much brain power you needed to sort out a carton of drugs. Ditto responding to customers in a retail service role. The same went for decluttering other people's stuff.

When she finally reached the end and clicked "Submit", she didn't have a lot of hope that the algorithm and analysis would come up with much. The screen whirred for a moment, then presented her with a list of suggested careers, including but not limited to social worker, teacher, nurse, counsellor, or human resources specialist.

Cally stared at the list, blinked a few times, wrinkled one side of her nose, and sighed. None of the suggestions tickled her fancy whatsoever. She couldn't believe she'd wasted the time for the system to have come up with nothing she liked the look of. Reading through the suggestions again she realised that they all shared a common thread – helping people. She swore aloud at her laptop. She certainly knew how to care for people. She was borderline a pro. She had enough experience, too – she'd been doing it her entire life. She shook her head and made an odd growling sound: one thing the survey had brought up was that she didn't want caring in her future. Not one little bit. Not in any shape or form. Not even a sniff of it. Even thinking about the giving of herself and pouring her energy into others' needs made her shudder. Not doing that again anytime soon.

She closed the laptop with a frustrated groan and sat for a bit staring out over the rooftops of Lovely. At least she *did* have options now. She had to remember that and keep open to things that might come her way. It was just that she had no idea what they were. She *did* know that she was determined, that she'd get on and make a success of her life somehow or another. She reiterated that it wouldn't be long before she would be able to buy a flat and that she did have a degree. That she was carving a place for herself in a wonderful community where people knew her name and had her back. That there were are a lot of people in the world a lot worse off.

With the time well past midnight, outside, Lovely Bay was quiet. The streetlights looked pretty with their little pools of light landing on the deserted pavements and big, thick clouds moved quickly over a dark sky. Cally shuffled a bit closer to the balcony door and pressed her forehead against the glass. In the distance, she could see the outline of the lighthouse, watching over the town as she pondered the conundrum of what she was going to do with the rest of her life. The Logan thing had put her in limbo for a while, but now she was more determined than ever to be independent and put plans and things in place so that she would always be okay. Her destiny was up to her and her only. She had to make it happen.

The problem was that Cally felt stuck. As if everyone else had it all figured out, and she was the only one still trying to decide what she wanted to be when she grew up. She repeatedly told herself that everyone else was also still trying to figure it out, but really, she didn't think that was true. Birdie had told her that no one knew what they were doing and that it was just because some people were better at faking it than others. Inside, Cally had tutted and scoffed. Birdie was a successful, qualified pharmacist with a strong business and no financial worries—a whole different kettle of fish altogether.

Cally mused about Birdie telling her that Birdie herself sometimes questioned her own decisions and that she had been pushed into the family business with no choice in the matter at all. Cally had been surprised, floored even, by Birdie's admission. It had never even crossed her mind that Birdie was anything other than totally sure in her own role. She'd always seemed so confident, so certain about her path. Cally knew, though, that she'd rather be questioning a decision to be a pharmacist than stuck working as a customer service assistant and having part-time roles with no real purpose at all.

She turned away from the window and stared at the framed photo of her grandma. Twinkly but tired eyes looked back at her. Cally picked up the frame and ran her thumb over the edge. What would her grandma have said? She could almost hear her grandmother's voice telling her to knuckle down and get on with it, and if she wanted to follow her heart, then she should follow her heart. That in itself irritated Cally, precisely because she'd never been able to follow her heart or anything else in the first place. Shackled by responsibility from day dot; she'd had to care before anything else.

But what did her heart want? That was the question Cally couldn't seem to answer. She put the photo back down and moved to her wardrobe, pulling out a worn cardboard box from the back. It was one of the few things she'd kept when she'd decluttered most of her life. Inside were mementoes from her past—old school reports, a couple of art projects, and certificates from various school things. She hadn't looked through them in years, but something made her start rifling through the box. As she sifted through the papers, an old notebook caught her eye. The cover was faded, the spiral binding slightly bent, but Cally recognised it immediately. A sparkly pink journal stuffed full of all sorts. She'd kept it during her last year of school before everything had changed and her regular caring role had become even bigger. The first page opened at a pile of faded fluoro pink Post-it note squares. Lists of things to do in now-blurred blue pen. Her day slotted neatly into hours down the left hand side. Detail of her mum's care, shopping, study, cleaning, doctor's appointments, schedules. The fact that there was nothing in the book or notes for Cally's dreams and downtime jumped off the page.

She opened the book further and started flipping through more pages. Loads of little doodles of flowers and hearts around a list of her grandma's medicines. Her own loopy handwriting with lots of lists here and there. She flipped through for ages, swallowed, and shook her head. It was as if the person who'd jotted things down in the book had spent all of her time doing things for other people. As if that person had been buried so deep under the weight of responsibility and duty that they'd almost disappeared entirely. Perhaps, even that they'd never been there in the first place at all.

She closed the journal and just sat for a while with it on her lap. It hadn't really told her anything she didn't know. It had not informed her about anything new. It had, though, reiterated what went around in her head. She'd spent so long defined by her role as a carer that it had put a halt to almost everything else. Now, who even was she without that? Time for our Cally to get on with it and work that out. She could at long last put herself first.

36

Cally was out for a walk over by the marshes and had just stopped for a breather on a bench when her phone buzzed in her hand. Trust Eloise to call just when she needed a friendly voice.

'Impeccable timing, as always.'

The response that came through wasn't the usual cheerful Eloise greeting, though. Instead, Eloise's voice sounded shaky, breathless. 'Cal? Thank goodness you picked up. I've had a bit of an accident. It's not good.'

Cally's heart dropped. 'What? An accident? Are you okay? What happened?'

'I'm fine, I'm fine,' Eloise rushed to reassure her. 'It was just a car accident. Nothing *too* serious, but, well, the car's a bit of a mess. I'm a lot of a mess.'

Cally was already on her feet. 'Where are you? Do you need me to come and get you?'

'No, no. I'm okay, really. Just a bit shaken up. I'm at home now. The police brought me back after they took my statement.'

'The police! It must have been serious. Are you sure you're alright?' There was a pause. 'I'm coming over.'

'Ahh, would you mind? I'm shaking like a leaf. I need a glass of wine. Or three.'

'Of course,' Cally said without hesitation. 'I'll be there as soon as I can. Just stay put, okay? Don't move a muscle.'

'Thanks, see you soon.'

As Cally ended the call, she set off at a brisk pace, tracing her steps automatically back through the streets of Lovely Bay. As she rushed, she nodded to a few Lovelies as she passed, but her mind whirled about Eloise. Eloise was not a drama queen. A car accident, even a minor one, was no small thing as far as she was concerned and if the police had been involved, it couldn't have been nice.

Cally reached her flat in record time and fumbled with her keys in her haste to get inside. She barely paused to kick off her shoes before heading to the kitchen. Opening the fridge, she grabbed a bottle of white wine, snatched a bar of chocolate from her emergency snack drawer, chucked in two bags of crisps, had a quick wee, washed her hands and face, and went back in the direction that she'd come.

As she left her flat, Cally felt more than a pang of guilt. When Eloise had called, she'd been wallowing. She'd totally wanted to offload on Eloise and hadn't expected Eloise to need help. Eloise *never* needed help. She always had all her balls nicely in the air.

Thinking the whole way through her journey how selfish she was, Cally quickened her pace as Eloise's road loomed before her. Cally bounded up the steps to Eloise's door. She rapped softly, then stood back, shifting from foot to foot as she waited for a response. After what felt like an age, but was probably only a few seconds, Cally heard movement from inside. The door swung open to reveal Eloise, looking pale, a bit dishevelled but in one piece. Without thinking, she stepped forward and enveloped Eloise in a tight hug. 'You look absolutely dreadful!'

Eloise stiffened. 'I'm okay. Really, I am.'

Cally pulled back and frowned. 'Are you sure? You're not hurt anywhere?'

'I'm fine. My bank balance won't be good when I see what this does to my insurance premiums.'

Cally chuckled as she slipped off her shoes and followed Eloise in. 'Well, as long as you're in one piece, that's what matters. You go and sit down. I'll open the wine and bring it in. Sounds like you are in need of it.'

Cally busied herself in the kitchen, finding glasses and opening the wine. She went through to the sitting room and asked Eloise to recount the details of the accident.

'It was so stupid. I was just coming round that bend by the old corner shop along the way; you know the one?'

Cally nodded, handing Eloise a glass. 'The one with the nasty blind spot? Yeah, I know where you mean.'

'That's the one. Well, I was coming around it, and suddenly, there was this cat in the road. I swerved to avoid it, and well, the next thing I knew, I was up close and personal with a garden wall, and a van was in the back of me.'

Cally winced in sympathy. 'Thank goodness you're okay.'

'I was lucky. The airbag went off and everything.'

'Ouch. How's the car?'

Eloise grimaced. 'Let's just say it's seen better days. The front's all crumpled. The airbag probably saved me from a nasty bump on the head.'

'It must have been terrifying.'

'It was. One minute, everything was normal, and the next... I keep thinking about what could have happened if I'd been going faster, or if the airbag hadn't worked properly, or…'

Cally sighed. 'I know. Gosh, you just don't want to think about it, really, do you? It sounds like it could have been a lot worse, though.'

'It's a bit of a wake-up call, you know? Makes you realise how fragile everything is. It all happened so fast.'

Cally nodded. 'I know what you mean. Life has a way of throwing these curveballs at us, doesn't it?'

'That it does,' Eloise agreed, taking another sip of her wine. 'Some things come to try us.'

Cally swigged a large gulp of her wine. All she could think about was how relieved she was that Eloise was okay. Just behind that, she felt sick to her core about how the accident might have had a different outcome. Then she kept thinking that, as Eloise had said, life was very fragile. You didn't know what was around the corner at any given time. You didn't know who might not be there for you to miss.

37

In a blue and white striped, limited edition, highly sought after Chowder Festival t-shirt, Cally walked along the main street of Lovely which had been cordoned off from cars and traffic. According to Birdie, and backed up in no uncertain words by Colin and the organising committee, it was a right palaver to get permission to close the road every year, but it was crucial to the success of the event. Cally walked along the street and smiled at thousands of little bunting flags fluttering back and forth in the wind. Lovely Bay had never been short of bunting, but this took it to whole new levels. Colin's plans were in full swing and blowing about in the breeze above Cally's head.

The entire street had been working for weeks to whip the place into a picture of prettiness, and it had very much worked. Lovelies, it seemed, knew how to host a festival. Gorgeous white lantern decorations hung off each of the old-fashioned lampposts, bunting swayed in the wind between the shops and all along Lovely Bay's main street, little stalls were getting ready for the next day; a coffee stall had been set up outside the deli, the hardware store was set up with trestle tables piled high with

Lovely flags to give away, and the co-op had a tombola outside ready to raise some money for the lighthouse building fund.

Lovely Chocolate Shop, though, was something else. As Cally approached the front of the shop a stall in front of it had been covered in long white linen tablecloths, a striped canopy was loaded down with bunting and trays were ready for truffles to be given away the next day. Cally smiled as she spied Nancy coming the other way with her friend Penny. Both women were dressed in the official uniform of the Chowder Festival helpers – navy blue and white striped tops and white chinos.

Cally smiled. 'Isn't it all looking fantastic? I've just been helping put the last few touches on the library.'

Nancy nodded enthusiastically. 'It's a picture, isn't it? I swear, every year, I think we can't possibly top the last, but somehow we manage it. And the weather?' Nancy held up crossed fingers. 'Let's hope it stays like this all weekend.'

Penny smiled. 'Well, we have more bunting this year than ever before, I can tell you that much.'

'Things aren't done by halves here if Colin's involved.'

Cally looked up at the masses of bunting criss-crossed over the street. 'It's going to be a job to get it down.'

'Speaking of not doing things by halves. Where are you working tonight? Nina's, isn't it? I had a blank for a bit earlier. I've forgotten who's doing what.' Nancy asked with a frown.

Cally nodded. 'Yep. She's gone all out with the decorations, you should see it.'

Penny joked. 'I've heard that's the hot ticket this year. Don't tell our Birdie I said that, though.'

As they chatted, a gust of wind sent the bunting into a frenzy of fluttering. Colourful little triangles danced above their heads, and the white lanterns on the lampposts swayed back and forth in the wind.

'And what about you two?' Cally asked. 'Where are you stationed for the evening's clandestine chowder operations?'

Nancy chuckled. 'Well, I'm holding down the fort at the lighthouse and the turning on of the lights, as usual. Most of it is ready for us all later.'

Penny piped up, 'I'm over at the RNLI.'

'Sounds like we're all busy.'

Nancy gestured toward the lighthouse, 'Right, I'd better get on. See you later.'

'See you later, yep.'

Cally began to meander further down the street, taking in the sights and sounds of the final preparations for the festival in full swing. Outside the bookshop, a helper dressed in the same helper's uniform sat reading to a group of Lovely children, and next door, the florist was setting up a tea urn alongside beautiful posies of flowers. Birdie hurried down the street with an armful of bunting in her arms. Cally wrinkled her nose. 'What in the world? Where are you off to with that?' She looked overhead. 'Surely we can't need more.'

Birdie rolled her eyes. 'Colin wasn't happy with the chemist. He said there needed to be more on the awning even after that lot we put up.'

'You're kidding!'

'Nope. I am *not* kidding and he is hyper. I decided I best just take instruction and do what he said before he had a heart attack.'

'Where've you been then?'

'Down to the lighthouse to collect it.'

'Ahh, you should have messaged me. I would have popped down there for you. I've just come from that way.'

'No worries. I needed to stretch my legs, anyway.'

'Busy?'

'Yep. Drugs still need to be dispensed in Lovely even when the festival is on.'

'True.'

Birdie shifted the bunting in her arms. Her eyes crinkled with concern as she looked at Cally. 'So, how are you doing?'

Cally sighed. 'Keeping busy with the festival and, well, you know...'

Birdie wasn't fooled. Cally had ended up telling her all the ins and outs of the Logan situation. Birdie's advice had been along the same lines as Eloise's. 'And things with Logan? Any change there?'

Cally slumped her shoulders slightly. 'No, we're still not talking. I don't know if we can come back from this. I guess it's officially over.'

Birdie clucked sympathetically and shifted the bunting to one arm so she could pat Cally's shoulder. 'Festival time brings out all sorts of good things, you know. People coming back to Lovely, others making up, a rekindling of old flames, all sorts coming out of the woodwork.'

Cally raised an eyebrow. 'Not in this case, I don't think.'

'Maybe it's time to think about forgiving Logan. I know he hurt you, keeping that secret about his ex-wife, but...'

Cally's smile faded. 'I know. I think I might have left it too late, though.'

Birdie nodded thoughtfully. 'When you picture your future in Lovely, is Logan in it?'

Cally bit her lip as she realised with a pang that everything was inextricably linked with Logan. 'He is but I think I've cooked my goose.'

'Rubbish. He loves you. That's obvious to just about anyone. Just text him.'

Before Cally could respond, a commotion further down the street caught their attention. Colin's voice rose above the general hubbub, sounding slightly panicked.

'No, no, no! The bunting in that section goes in the centre, not off to the side! We want it to be the centrepiece, people!'

Birdie and Cally exchanged a look.

'I think I'd better go and rescue Colin from himself before people start fighting.'

Cally nodded. 'You'd better.'

'Think about what I said. Life's too short, our Cally. You just never know what's around the corner. Ask me how I know. Call him or send him a message. Make up with him. You're both as miserable as sin.' Birdie patted Cally's arm and then hurried off towards the sound of Colin's increasingly frantic instructions, leaving Cally to ponder her words. Maybe our Birdie was right. She'd think about messaging him.

38

That afternoon, Cally was on her way to check on Eloise. If Cally was truly honest, she'd been shaken by what had happened to Eloise. Despite everything that had occurred in her world, since the day Cally had met Eloise strawberry picking one summer, Eloise had just always been there for Cally. Eloise's accident, careering her car into a wall and a van going into the back of her, played on a loop in Cally's mind. Eloise, who was usually calm and composed, had not looked that way at all. In fact, she'd appeared *very* shaken, as if someone had really rattled her cage. In turn, Cally's own cage had been rattled, too. The accident had shaken her more than she cared to admit. Eloise was a constant in her world and something threatening that made her have a long hard look at herself.

As she rounded the corner onto Eloise's street, Cally slowed her pace as the sight of her friend's blue car, usually parked in the driveway, was conspicuously absent. The car not being there was a stark reminder to Cally of how quickly life could change. She got to the house and rapped softly on the door. There was a moment of silence, then the muffled sound of movement from inside.

'Coming!' Eloise's voice called out, sounding strained. Eloise opened the door, looking pale and drawn. Her impeccable appearance was not as it usually was. She was slightly dishevelled, with her hair pulled back in a messy ponytail, and she had dark circles shadowing her eyes. A large, angry bruise had bloomed on her left arm.

'Yikes. You said you felt like you were bruised. You weren't wrong. That looks really nasty.'

Eloise attempted a smile, but it didn't quite reach her eyes. 'It looks worse than it feels,' she said, stepping back to let Cally in. 'I was just about to make some tea.'

Cally noticed a stiffness in Eloise's gait. It was more than obvious that Eloise was attempting to hide aches and pains. Eloise used only her right arm to move the kettle to the sink, lift the lever on the tap, and then put the kettle back on its base.

'Let me help,' Cally offered, moving across the kitchen.

Eloise waved her off. 'I'm not an invalid, Cal. I can manage to make tea.'

A few minutes later, Cally carried two steaming mugs and a plate of biscuits into the sitting room. As she put them down on the coffee table, Eloise lowered herself gingerly onto the sofa with a wince.

'So, how are you doing? How was the night?'

Eloise's smile was tight. 'I'm fine, Cal. Really. You don't need to worry about me.'

'You don't have to pretend with me. That bruise looks painful.'

Eloise glanced down at her arm. 'It's nothing. Just a bit of colour to liven things up.' Eloise's attempt at humour fell flat.

'Doesn't look like nothing to me. You're black and blue on your arm there.'

'It could have been a lot worse.'

'Thank goodness it wasn't.'

'When I close my eyes, and I'm back in that moment, it's

quite scary. There was such a screech of tyres and then a crunch of metal. I can't shake it. I can't believe I swerved like that.' Eloise closed her eyes for a second.

'Sounds traumatic.'

'I'm mostly unharmed. I'm grateful.'

'Yeah, it'll take you a lot to get over it. A traumatic thing like that...'

Eloise wrinkled her nose. 'You think? I'll be right as rain tomorrow.'

'You won't. You just need to take it easy. Rest up and let your body heal.' Cally instructed.

'Sorry, are you now the wise one?' Eloise joked. 'I thought that was my role in this friendship.'

'Looks like I'm telling you what to do for once.'

Eloise smiled. 'When did you get so wise?'

'I learned from the best,' Cally bantered.

'It's weird. Last night, even though I'm okay overall, I felt so overwhelmed.'

'Yep. When I was caring for my grandma, there were days when I felt as if I couldn't breathe. Sort of anxious or something.'

'Yeah. This has really given me a bit of a reality check.'

'How do you mean?'

'Well, what if the van had been going faster? I might be telling a different story or not telling a story at all.'

'Gosh, don't say that.'

'I'm not being dramatic, but all it takes is one silly little thing for your whole world to change.'

Cally nodded. She'd been thinking about Eloise's accident a lot. It had made her reassess the situation with Logan. She'd thought about calling him and asking him if they could talk. The accident, even though, overall, it had been minor, had served as a wake-up call. 'It made me think that, too. It's funny, isn't it? How it takes something like this to make us realise what's really important.'

Eloise leaned forward, wincing slightly as she reached for her tea. 'What do you mean? Has my little mishap got you thinking about Logan?'

Cally nodded, her fingers tracing the rim of her mug. 'Yeah, it has. Something like this can put things into perspective, you know?'

'So, what are you thinking?'

Cally took a deep breath. 'Well, I've been wondering if I've been too harsh on him. I mean, yes, he should have told me about his previous marriage. But life's too short to hold onto grudges, isn't it?'

'It certainly is.'

'I've been thinking about it for the last few days. The accident just pushed it to the forefront, I guess.'

Eloise nodded, taking a sip of her tea. 'Okay, so talk me through it. What's changed?'

Cally leaned back. 'It's like... when you called, my first thought was, "I need to tell Logan". And then I remembered that I couldn't. And it just hit me, you know? How much I miss him, how much I want him to be part of my life.'

'I *did* try to tell you this. It's like you had a mental block about it.'

'I know. I mean, yes, he should have told me about his ex-wife. But it was in the past, long before he met me. And he's never given me any reason to doubt him otherwise.'

'Don't we all have things in our past that we're not proud of? Things we'd rather not talk about?'

Cally nodded. 'Yeah. I was angry that he didn't tell me. But now, I'm wondering if I overreacted. If I threw away something good because I was hurt and scared. Then, your accident, and when I got home last night, I realised how stupid it all is. Life's too short, isn't it?'

Eloise smiled and shook her head. 'Finally.'

'Do you think I should message him?'

'If you feel ready and if you genuinely want to try again, then yes.'

'I need to try. I love him, El. I'll think it through.'

'Run, my friend, don't walk.'

39

Cally walked around the lower floor of Nina's harbour property to check that everything was done. She stood by the door with Nina's checklist and surveyed what they had put together for the speakeasy for Nina's part in the Chowder Festival. The two of them, with Nina's husband Robby's help at times, had worked hard and it showed. Cascades of sparkles ran down the walls in a glowy twinkle of warm white lights. Various tables had been begged and borrowed from all over Lovely Bay, each one had been covered in beautiful white tablecloths. On top of the tables, thrifted vases and the vintage tins Nina had found were stuffed full of ginormous bunches of pink and blue hydrangeas stolen from various gardens around the third smallest town in the country. The hydrangeas had been Cally's idea. Their impact was *fabulous*.

She ran her eyes down the list, checked a few things off, made sure each place setting was correct, and then got on with the last job of laying out the napkins beside the plates. Just like the tablecloths, the napkins were all made of pretty white linen, and the sailor's knot rope napkin rings finished the whole thing off. As Cally went around placing the napkins on each of the tables, she was both quite pleased and surprised at how well the decorating had gone. What she and Nina had started with had been a fairly large, nondescript back area of Nina's office that hadn't lent itself to a speakeasy in any shape or form. Now, through their endeavours, it was an intimate little place ready to welcome Lovelies into its fold.

Cally was just putting the finishing touches on the table settings when she heard Colin's booming voice echoing through from the backyard area.

'Hello? Anyone about? It's only me, come to check everything's ship-shape! Hello! Ahoy there.'

Cally smiled at Colin's enthusiasm. He was so hyper about the festival he was almost fizzing with it all. 'In here, Colin!'

A moment later, Colin's beaming face appeared around the doorframe. 'Ah, our Cally! Should've known you'd be here, making sure everything's perfect. Where's Nina?'

'She's popped over to pick up Faye.'

'Ahh, right. How's it all coming along? Looks like you've got everything well under control.'

Cally replied, gesturing around at the tables. 'Pretty well, I think, compared to what we started with.'

Colin stepped fully into the room. His eyes widened as he took in the elaborate setup.

'Blimey. You two *have* done well. You've outdone yourselves. Best one I've seen yet, I think.'

'We've fussed over every little detail. No stone went unturned. Nina has lists of lists and then a list of those lists.'

Colin chuckled, shaking his head. 'Sounds about right. Our Nina doesn't do things by halves, does she? But that's what makes these events so special when everyone throws themselves into it.'

'True,' Cally agreed. 'All we need now is to make sure our Faye goes down easily this evening and we'll be laughing.'

'How about the chowder? That's the real star of the show. How's that going?'

Cally smiled. 'I'm no expert like you, but it's amazing.' She led him upstairs to the kitchen area, where several large pots were simmering on the hob. 'The traditional version served in the sourdough.'

Colin lifted the lid of a pot and inhaled deeply. 'Oh, that smells divine. I might have to sneak a bowl.'

'Don't you dare. She'll have a fit. How's your organisation going?'

'Excellent, my end. No problems yet, but we've not even started, so I'm sure we'll have a few. It's the most bunting we've ever had, that I know for a fact.'

'It's a sight to behold for sure.'

'I might just put a bit more over by the church there.' Colin chuckled.

Cally wrinkled her nose. 'More? We're drowning in it! I'm not sure Lovely Bay can handle any more bunting. We'll be visible from space at this rate.'

'Nonsense,' Colin replied, puffing out his chest. 'You can never have too much bunting. It's all part of the festival! All joking aside, I've a feeling it's going to be our best year yet. It's all come together so well, and let me tell you, some years, it doesn't happen like that.'

'Aww, that's good to hear.'

'Actually, there was something I wanted to mention to you. We're having a bit of a Lovelies gathering later. It's a tradition that we all go up to the lighthouse after the first night. Sort of an after-party, if you will. Did Birdie tell you?'

Cally nodded. 'Yes, yes she did.'

'Rightio, good. I just wanted to make sure she hadn't forgotten.'

'What time does that go on until?'

'Oh, whenever, really. It's normally not too late because

everyone is shattered. It's just a chance for all involved to have a few drinks and a debrief. Nothing too formal.'

'I'm there with bells on.'

Colin beamed. 'Right, you are. I'll leave you to it, seeing as everything is under control here. I probably won't see you again now, but I'll see you later at the lighthouse, yes?'

Cally nodded. 'I'll be there.'

As Colin left, Cally shook her head fondly. Living in Lovely Bay was never dull; that was for certain. Going back downstairs for one final check she smiled to herself. She'd actually quite enjoyed helping Nina and being part of the festival. The community thing was nice and there was a good feeling of optimism and celebration in the air. She might not have Logan, but something was telling Cally that things were okay and that it was going to be a very Lovely Bay kind of a night. That sounded good enough for her, even though there was a sorely missing puzzle piece right in the centre of her heart. She took out her phone and decided that she would message Logan. She tapped, hit send and her stomach lurched. As she watched the message indicate that it had been delivered, she sighed as there were no little flashing dots. Hopefully, at some point, Logan would respond.

40

It was later that evening, just after Nina's speakeasy had wrapped up. The event had gone swimmingly and Nina had been over the moon at how her chowder had gone down.

Cally, Nina, and Nina's husband, Robby, were on their way to the lighthouse. The view that greeted them as they walked along in the direction of Lovely didn't seem real. It wasn't just that everything that didn't move was draped in gorgeous handmade bunting or that every other building sparkled with little festival lights. It was something about the lighthouse towering above it all standing up into the dark night. It always appeared magnificent as far as Cally was concerned, but for some reason, it looked even better than it normally did. She smiled at how the turning on of the lighthouse lights was a big thing for Lovelies and how it happened late when the locals gathered to debrief after the first night of the festival.

As if reading her thoughts, Nina sighed, 'Wow, it looks so tall this evening. The sky is very clear, too, or am I imagining it? It always seems to me as if it's darker here in Lovely than anywhere else. Maybe it's because the lighthouse is so white or there's no pollution. I don't know…'

'I was just thinking the same,' Cally said with a shake of her head.

Nina pointed upwards. 'That whole thing is going to be lit up shortly.'

Robby nodded. 'It is, indeed. The team has done themselves proud this year.'

'Rather you than me dangling off the side of that.' Cally noted with a chuckle as she looked up to the top of the lighthouse.

'I know, right? I won't be ever finding out.' Nina agreed and joked. 'I'll leave that to my other half. He's good at some things.'

'Shame little Faye's not going to see it in all its glory and all her daddy's work.' Cally noted.

Nina shook her head. 'She's better off with June. No one wants an over-tired Faye in their life.'

Robby laughed. 'Certainly not me. Thank goodness June is babysitting.'

There was something about the air, too. Cally took a deep breath, savouring the smell. 'You know, I never get tired of that sea air. So nice.'

'You and me both.'

As they got closer to the lighthouse, the details of Colin's excessive decorating became clearer as bunting fluttered in the breeze as far as the eye could see. It criss-crossed the street, hung down from lampposts, and draped between buildings.

'I see Colin's artistic efforts made the cut,' Cally said, nodding towards the bunting. 'It's everywhere!'

Robby followed her gaze and chuckled. 'He's gone for his life this year.'

'Bless him,' Nina said, shaking her head fondly. 'He does try so hard.'

Cally looked up at the hundreds of delicate paper lanterns carefully hung from the old-fashioned street lights. 'Wow, those look magical. They're so effective.'

'Penny's idea. I don't think you were at that meeting when she proposed them. She got half the town involved in making them. She said it would add a touch of whimsy to the festival.'

'Well, she wasn't wrong,' Robby said as he reached up and tapped one of the lanterns making light and shadows appear to spin across the pavement.

As they rounded the corner, the full majesty of the lighthouse came into view. It stood tall and proud against the sky, its white paint gleaming, and even without its festival lights yet turned on, it was an impressive sight.

'I always forget how big it is,' Cally murmured, tilting her head back to take in the full height.

'Wait until you see it lit up.'

They paused for a moment at the base of the lighthouse, taking in the atmosphere.

'What's the go-to then?' Nina asked. 'Where did Colin say to go?'

Robby gestured into the distance. 'We go to the old hall to get a drink, and then once everyone has arrived, we stand out in the yard for the official turning on of the festival lights. Even though it happens again tomorrow night, this apparently is the real occasion for Lovelies only.'

Cally felt ridiculously pleased that she'd been invited as they made their way to the old hall behind the lighthouse. As they walked in, Birdie waved and smiled, and Nancy ushered them to a drinks table.

'All good, our Cally?' Nancy asked.

'Yes, thanks.'

'How did it go at Nina's?'

'So good. The chowder was outstanding and we raised a fortune with the raffle. A good night was had by all. Yeah, it really went well, thank goodness. It was a lot of work.'

'That's just what we like to hear. Grab a drink, and we'll head out soon for the light ceremony.'

Cally did exactly as told and inched her way between people until she arrived in front of Birdie and Clive from the riverboat who were standing chatting about their various events.

Birdie beamed and clinked a glass against Cally's. 'Here she is. How are you?'

'Really good.'

'Good night?'

'Yep, all the hard work was well worth it. You?'

'Same. Mind you, don't forget I'm bagging you next year. I want you in the deli.'

Cally chuckled. 'Righto.'

Birdie lowered her voice. 'How was Nina's attempt?

'Attempt?'

'The chowder. I need to know who my competition is for next year.'

Cally giggled. 'I have to say she outdid herself. It was delicious. People were raving about it.'

Birdie rolled her eyes. 'Wrong answer.'

'You've got a contender for the number one spot.'

Clive laughed. 'Nah, no one will ever knock our Birdie off her podium.'

Cally chuckled. 'Actually, I make you right. No one would dare.'

~

Clutching her drink, Cally stood with her head back, looking up at the lighthouse, and counted down along with all the other Lovelies. 'Five, four, three, two, one!'

There was a momentary pause, a flicker, and then boom, the huge white tower above her was transformed. Cally's breath caught in her throat as the lighthouse dazzled in an array of twinkling lights that spiralled from its base all the way up to the top. It looked as though someone had taken handful after handful of tiny brilliant stars and scattered them across the whole of the structure. The huge, tall, spherical white building shimmered and twinkled in the night air.

'Oh my,' Cally whispered. 'I've seen it all now. It's so pretty. I want to live in there.'

There was no doubt that Lovely Lighthouse was an impressive landmark, but lit up from head to foot, it was truly magical. The whole thing appeared to gently pulse into the inky dark sky.

Birdie's voice cut into Cally's thoughts. 'Isn't it amazing? I feel the same every year, but this year, it's spectacular. There are so many lights! It's like we're standing in the middle of a star.'

Cally nodded, still somewhat overwhelmed. 'It's incredible. I can't believe Colin pulled this off. This will definitely be seen from space, let alone the bunting.'

Birdie cackled. 'Between you and me, I think he's trying to let us believe it's all him, but Robby's lot have done a stellar job.'

'They have. It really is very well done. Who would have thought?'

'Speak of the devil.' Birdie laughed as Colin approached. 'It looks fantastic. 'We were just talking about you.'

Colin beamed, looking thoroughly pleased with himself. His chest puffed up. 'It's better than I hoped.'

Cally gestured upwards. 'How on earth did you manage all this?'

Colin grinned like a Cheshire cat. 'Oh, you know, just a bit of Lovely Bay magic. And a very understanding electrician. Not to mention a certain few climbers I know who are a lot fitter than me. They made it happen.'

Birdie chuckled. 'Well, you've done brilliantly as far as I'm concerned. Well done you.'

Colin basked in the praise. 'Thanks. Right, I'm just going to make a little announcement and then we'll head up for a cuppa or whatever anyone wants and then I think it will be time for me to call it a night. I've had a very long day.'

'See you later. See you up there, our Colin.'

Cally turned to Birdie. 'Sometimes I forget how lucky I am to live here now, but this brings it right back. All of this and the community. Thank God I found you all.'

'I know. It never gets old as far as I'm concerned and just you wait, you'll soon have a little slice of Lovely all to yourself.' Birdie smiled.

'I hope so.'

'I *know* so. Good things are coming your way, my girl.' Birdie raised her eyebrows. 'So, what happened? Did you message Logan?'

'I did.'

'And?'

'Nope, nothing. No response.'

Their conversation was interrupted by the sound of Colin, illuminated by the thousands of lights above him, tapping on a glass, calling for everyone's attention.

'Friends, Lovelies, countrymen. Thank you all for coming tonight. I hope you're enjoying this little display just before the big day we're all going to have tomorrow.'

There was a murmur of appreciation from the crowd. Colin beamed, clearly in his element.

'As you know, the Chowder Festival has begun. Now, I know that everyone has been working their socks off, but I wanted to just reiterate that if you see any spots without bunting, please plug the gaps.'

'Is he serious?' Cally whispered to Birdie.

Birdie shrugged, looking both amused and slightly alarmed. 'With Colin, you can never really tell, can you? He *must* be joking. We can't move for the stuff.'

As Colin launched into more about the rest of the festival, Cally looked up at the lighthouse and thought about how the whole town had rallied together for the event. When Colin had finally finished, people started to shuffle towards the lighthouse door and some filtered the other way to head off home.

'Coming up for a cup of tea or something a bit stronger? One for the road?' Birdie asked.

'I might give it a miss if you don't mind. I have a shift in the morning and then I'm at the stall all day and at Nina's again. I'm quite tired, actually. Might get myself off to bed.'

'Okie-dokie. Want someone to walk you home?'

'No, no. All good. I've got my phone and there are loads of people still around.'

'Right, you are. See you tomorrow, then.'

Cally stood for a bit longer, taking in the lighthouse. Just as she was about to make her way out of the yard and into the street, she closed her eyes as she realised she could smell the Logan smell. She knew he was behind her. Instinctively, she turned around.

Logan smiled. 'I thought you might be here.'

'Hey.'

'How are you?'

Cally wasn't sure whether to answer with the truth or not: that she'd been pretending that she was fine. That she wasn't fine without him. That she was dreadful. So bad. That she was no longer whole. That she missed him. Loved him. Wanted him back in her life. Wanted him to click the puzzle piece into place. Wanted to love him all the time. She flicked the switch. 'Yeah, fine, thanks.'

'See, I knew if you did the voice, I'd be okay.'

Cally wrinkled her nose. 'What?'

Logan slipped his hand into Cally's. 'The voice you do. I said to myself that if you pretended you were fine and you did that weird voice, that really you weren't and that meant that you missed *us*.'

Cally felt her heart skip a beat as Logan squeezed her hand. A tingle shot up her arm. 'I didn't miss us. Not at all.'

'Oh.'

Cally giggled. 'Joking.'

'Not my idea of a joke.'

Cally decided to chuck every single one of her emotions out the nearest window. All the hurt, the rug coming away under her feet, the sadness, her stubbornness, the anger, pride. Stuff all of it. 'I think I might need to apologise.'

'It's fine.'

'I just…'

'I know, Blackcurrant. I know.'

Cally nodded. She loved the fact that Henry-Hicks *thought* that he knew. But oh, how he did *not* know. Not at all. No one would ever know how much her arms had ached holding up that big old sky. She didn't say anything for a second but just looked at the lighthouse in all its glory as it twinkled above them.

'I was an idiot. I should have told you about Cassia from the start. I was afraid.'

'Of what?'

'That you'd think I wasn't good enough for you.'

Pah! Oh, the irony. Henry-Hicks didn't even know he was born.

'Not good enough for me? You know that I've spent most of my time since I met you convinced it was the other way around. Cally from the chemist's. Not quite the Cassia Allegra Brommington's of the world.'

'You couldn't be more wrong.'

'But Cassia…'

'Was a mistake.'

'Right.'

'How could you ever think you're not good enough?' Logan

narrowed his eyes. He looked bewildered. 'I just don't get it, Blackcurrant. I really, *really* don't.'

You wouldn't Henry-Hicks. You never really will. Cally felt a tear run down her cheek. 'No.'

'So, what's next then?'

'I've missed you so much.'

'Same. More than I can say.'

Cally breathed in the Logan smell and felt the pieces of her world slowly clicking back into place. 'I'm sorry I was so stubborn.'

'Don't even go there.'

Logan kissed her, and as she kissed him back, she felt the real world fall away. Nothing was around her except for Logan, a deep, dark, dense, gorgeous, inky black sky, and a very large white tower covered in twinkling lights.

Logan pulled away, held her at arm's length, and raised his eyebrows. 'Well, that's one way to start the Chowder Festival with a bang.'

As Cally felt the puzzle piece click, she smiled as every little fibre in her body sighed out. She raised a glass in a silent toast. To her, to Logan, to Lovely. And to being what felt like home. To watching that beautiful sky fall down as it shimmered and twinkled and glimmered in Lovely Bay lights. To being loved purely and simply for being her. It felt so, so, so nice. This time she wasn't going to let it get away.

Purchase the next part in Cally's story.

One Perfect Day in Lovely Bay.

ONE PERFECT DAY

One Perfect Day in Lovely Bay

Cally de Pfeffer has settled down quite beautifully, thank you very much. For once, someone is caring for her, and it's very nice indeed. She's so happy she doesn't quite know what to do with herself and finally begins to dream and plan and scheme. Everything is tickety-boo in her world as she starts to house hunt and is finally able to stop holding up that big old sky.

What Cally doesn't quite realise is that there are still a few Lovely surprises ready and waiting for her along the way...

READ MORE BY POLLY BABBINGTON

(Reading Order available at authorpollybabbington.com)

One Nice Day in Lovely Bay
    One Sweet Day in Lovely Bay
    One Perfect Day in Lovely Bay

The Summer Hotel Lovely Bay
    Wildflowers at The Summer Hotel Lovely Bay
    Seashells at The Summer Hotel Lovely Bay

The Old Ticket Office Darling Island
    Secrets at The Old Ticket Office Darling Island
    Surprises at The Old Ticket Office Darling Island

Spring in the Pretty Beach Hills
    Summer in the Pretty Beach Hills

The Pretty Beach Thing
    The Pretty Beach Way
    The Pretty Beach Life

READ MORE BY POLLY BABBINGTON

Something About Darling Island
    Just About Darling Island
    All About Christmas on Darling Island

The Coastguard's House Darling Island
    Summer on Darling Island
    Bliss on Darling Island

The Boat House Pretty Beach
    Summer Weddings at Pretty Beach
    Winter at Pretty Beach

A Pretty Beach Christmas
    A Pretty Beach Dream
    A Pretty Beach Wish

Secret Evenings in Pretty Beach
    Secret Places in Pretty Beach
    Secret Days in Pretty Beach

Lovely Little Things in Pretty Beach
    Beautiful Little Things in Pretty Beach
    Darling Little Things

The Old Sugar Wharf Pretty Beach
    Love at the Old Sugar Wharf Pretty Beach
    Snow Days at the Old Sugar Wharf Pretty Beach

Pretty Beach Posies
    Pretty Beach Blooms
    Pretty Beach Petals

OH SO POLLY

Words, quilts, tea and old houses…

My words began many moons ago in a corner of England, in a tiny bedroom in an even tinier little house. There was a very distinct lack of scribbling, but rather beautifully formed writing and many, many lists recorded in pretty fabric-covered notebooks stacked up under a bed.

A few years went by, babies were born, university joined, white dresses worn, a lovely fluffy little dog, tears rolled down cheeks, house moves were made, big fat smiles up to ears, a trillion cups of tea, a decanter or six full of pink gin, many a long walk. All those little things called life neatly logged in those beautiful little books tucked up neatly under the bed.

And then, as the babies toddled off to school, as if by magic, along came an opportunity and the little stories flew out of the books, found themselves a home online, where they've been growing sweetly ever since.

I write all my books from start to finish tucked up in our lovely old Edwardian house by the sea. Surrounded by pretty bits and bobs, whimsical fabrics, umpteen stacks of books, a plethora of lovely old things, gingham linen, great big fat white sofas, and a big old helping of nostalgia. There I spend my days spinning stories and drinking rather a lot of tea.

From the days of the floral notebooks, and an old cottage locked away from my small children in a minuscule study logging onto the world wide web, I've now moved house and those stories have evolved and also found a new home.

There is now an itty-bitty team of gorgeous gals who help me with my graphics and editing. They scheme and plan from their laptops, in far-flung corners of the land, to get those words from those notebooks onto the page, creating the magic of a Polly Bee book.

I really hope you enjoy getting lost in my world.

Love

Polly x

AUTHOR

Polly Babbington

In a little white Summer House at the back of the garden, under the shade of a huge old tree, Polly Babbington creates romantic feel-good stories, including The PRETTY BEACH series.

Polly went to college in the Garden of England and her writing career began by creating articles for magazines and publishing books online.

Polly loves to read in the cool of lazing in a hammock under an old fruit tree on a summertime morning or cosying up in the winter under a quilt by the fire.

She lives in delightful countryside near the sea, in a sweet little village complete with a gorgeous old cricket pitch, village green with a few lovely old pubs and writes cosy romance books about women whose life you sometimes wished was yours.

Follow Polly on Instagram, Facebook and TikTok
@PollyBabbingtonWrites

AUTHOR

PollyBabbington.com

Want more on Polly's world? Subscribe to Babbington Letters

Printed in Great Britain
by Amazon